# Return to The Void

## KC Fetch

# Return to
# The Void

Of all the books out there, you picked up this one, or maybe *Drawing from the Void*. That's incredible! I appreciate all of my readers, all the people who take a chance on my work. I am so happy to share it with you.

To Nicole. Thank you for all the last-minute calls and brainstorming.

# Dragon

July 2019

Around the wooden kitchen table of Azalea Way, Pamela Keller-Wagner, the Dastardly Dragon of Massachusetts, sat beside her magicless daughter, Kimberly Becker, who nervously rubbed the rim of her coffee mug. The other chairs around the table were empty. Louie's booster pillow had been tossed in the trash two months ago, the day Ellie walked out.

With tears in her eyes, Kimberly recounted everything Elijah had told her. "She was sleeping in a park when some creeps jumped her. Then a monster showed up, and—and Louie..." Her voice broke. "Louie sacrificed himself."

Kimberly crumpled, sobbing.

"Pathetic," Pamela muttered. She cast a long, withering gaze at her wide daughter, hunched over tea and cookies. Through thin lips, she hissed, "And what are you going to do about it?"

Kimberly's beady eyes peeked from beneath her napkin. She dabbed her glasses back into place. "Hm?"

"Are you going to sit here and cry over these—" Pamela picked up a garish pink macaron and flung it across the table "—these miserable little pastries?" It scuffed the wood and crumbled against Kimberly's elbow. "Or are you going to do what you're supposed to do?"

"What am I supposed to do?" Kimberly's voice trembled. "She's out there all alone, Mother."

"Send a Guide to get her," Pamela snapped. "Word about her abandonment will spread around Oren. You must preserve the family name! It's barely holding on by a thread."

"The things they'll do to her. She's—" Kimberly burst into tears once again.

"The things she's earned!" Pamela slammed her cane against the table. "The things you and that long-haired, number-loving hippy enabled in her!"

Kimberly wailed into her napkin.

"She's weak and stupid! Bring her back and let the der Führer correct her. The best she can hope for at this point is a tattoo and a low-ranking husband," Pamela sneered. "If you morons—"

Pamela emphasized the insult with another wooden strike.

"—had just accepted that proposal from Armitage, then we would all be riding high into Oren with our family's legacy secured for the next generation. But no, you all wanted to live with your heads in the clouds. Let her be the first generation that marries for 'love'." She spat the word like poison. "Love doesn't put food on the table. It doesn't put a roof over your head."

Kimberly cried harder.

"You think I loved your father?" Pamela barked a laugh. "He was a stepping stone; nothing more, nothing less."

She paused, savoring her daughter's misery. Then her voice softened to a deadly whisper.

"Will you do what's necessary to save your family, Kimberly?"

Kimberly's mouth opened, but nothing came out.

"Fine," Pamela said coolly, rising to her feet. "Then I'll do what must be done. As always." She turned toward the hallway.

"No—please!" Kimberly scrambled after her, tripping over a chair. She landed in a heap. "There has to be another way!"

"You brought this on yourself," Pamela looked down at the pitiful mess on the floor. "My youngest daughter," she murmured, almost tenderly.

Kimberly looked up with swollen eyes and cheeks streaked with tears.

"I always knew you'd fail me," Pamela said. "I just thought it would come much sooner than this."

"No," Kimberly whimpered.

"Now I must do what needs to be done to correct these decades of errors and moral failings." Pamela's eyes grew distant. "Perhaps a phone call would be more suitable for this…"

"Mother, please!" Kimberly grasped the hem of her dress like a child.

With the faithfulness of a mighty blade, Pamela swung her cane. The sound of bone against wood echoed through the house as she landed a blow into Kimberly's ribs.

*Of course the pig squeals.*

"You'll have the opportunity to work that *excess* weight off." Pamela walked toward the door without the support of her now broken cane. "You've spent long enough getting fat on wine and chocolate—and terrible bread."

Straightening her spine despite the ache in her back, Pamela stalked to the front door and stepped into the late afternoon light. She strode purposefully down the country road back to her poignant pistachio green cabin.

"Disgusting color," she spat as she walked up to the front door. Each step up was considerably more difficult without her extra support but she wouldn't let anyone, not even the birds or plants, see that.

With a huff, Pamela shut the door behind her and closed her eyes. A smile pulled across her lips as she took a moment to relax against.

"Finally… I could get out of this hell," she declared to the air, "away from this pathetic, nobody town and take my rightful place on the council."

She pounded the door with her fist. It felt good.

"All these years," she choked, her voice trembling. Her bottom lip quivered just once. Then, she wiped away a lone tear. "Enough of that," she scolded herself, as she had a thousand times before.

Moving into the living room, Pamela drew the shades and dropped into her worn armchair. She swept aside a pile of unopened letters and reached for the dusty black rotary phone.

With a deep breath, she dialed.

"Oren Farms," said the girl's voice, young and chipper. "This is Lindsey. How can I direct your call?"

"Conrad Hurst," she said sharply.

"And may I ask who's calling?"

Pamela clenched her jaw. *Moron.*

"Pamela Keller-Wagner."

"One moment, please." Lindsey spoke with a well-rehearsed voice, like Pamela's name had no impact on her.

*I'll correct that.*

Relaxing piano music played softly over the receiver.

"Hello?"

All her irritation melted at the sound of his voice—thin, aged, but still carrying that familiar curl of amusement.

"Hello, darling," Pamela purred.

"To what do I owe the pleasure?" Conrad asked warmly. It had been decades, but she could still remember the smell of his cologne and the way his eyes glistened in the candlelight. "You always did prefer letters to phone calls."

Her voice turned steely. "I'm afraid a letter wouldn't do. This is urgent."

She glanced around her dark cottage. *Soon.*

"I'm calling to inform you that my granddaughter, Ellie-Lynne Betty Becker, has abandoned her family."

"Is that the weakling with a Familiar?"

"Yes. But no concern for der Führer," Pamela reassured him. "Her mother informed me that Ellie ran away to Boston and the basset hound is dead." She tugged a thread loose from her armchair. It snapped with a satisfying pop. "I hope you don't think me cruel," she said, her voice silken. "I only want to preserve my family's name. Set the child right."

"She shall be," Conrad replied, with something hard clicking in the background. "May the Void bless you, and may you be well," he said.

"And with you," she replied.

The line went dead.

# 2
# Settled

June 2019

Ellie sat on her purple and chrome Honda, the one her dad had surprised her with less than a month ago. The sidecar beside her was empty. It had been weeks since Louie shot into the sky with the corrupted Familiar, but the wound he left behind still felt fresh.

She inhaled slowly, trying to soothe the ache in her chest. It flickered—for a second, almost gone—but the hollowness remained.

*Fake it till I make it.* She pulled off the matching helmet and tossed it into the sidecar.

*"Help," Louie's voice rang out. Ellie jerked her gaze back. He was in the sidecar, his paws scrabbling at his goggles, his back legs twisted awkwardly beneath him.*

She shut her eyes. *It's not real.*

When she opened them, only the helmet remained.

Squaring her shoulders, Ellie turned her focus to the yellow-and-white cottage in front of her. The Sugar Shack. Specials board out. Open sign lit. A few cars in the drive.

"This is not how I imagined my first day of work," she muttered, climbing the stairs.

A hanging flowerpot beside the door caught her eye—one Louie had once oohed over in that goofy way of his, while he mocked her mom. *"A witch is nothing without a good clump of sage,"* he said with that silly grin.

*And I'm nothing without you.* She bit her lip and pushed open the door.

"Well, there she is," Mary called from behind the counter. "Five minutes early. Your parents raised you right—I love punctuality." Ellie followed as Mary ushered her around the patio seating and through the employee entrance. "Come on in. We don't bite."

*Void help me,* Ellie thought, swallowing hard as she passed through the swinging door and into the kitchen.

Flour dusted nearly every surface, but beneath it all were clinical, shiny counters, an industrial dishwasher, a small flat-top stove, and a wall of metal racks. The air hung heavy with yeast and bacon.

"Alright, my dear. Wash your hands, grab an apron, and let's get to kneading."

The aprons were neatly tucked into a cubby shelf on the far wall, each labeled.

*Mom would love this place.*

Ellie picked a black apron and fiddled with the fit, finally knotting it into submission.

"I have to say," Mary said, eyeing her with amusement, "I didn't peg you for a Def Leppard fan."

Ellie glanced down at the worn black shirt with neon colors and a chaotic group of drawn band members. "Thanks. Jean loaned me some clothes for today."

"Ah, a good ol' hand-me-down." Mary rolled a deep iron bowl from the mixer to the flour-covered prep table. Inside, a pale elastic blob of dough glistened. "One batch should give us fifteen loaves," she said, struggling to wrestle it free.

"I got it." Ellie stepped in and lifted the dough onto the table with effort.

"Such a strong girl. Did you grow up on a farm?"

Ellie hesitated. "Not really. Well... kind of."

Her mind flashed to summers behind Mee-Maw's pistachio-colored house—endless rows of tomatoes, basil, and too many skunk-butts.

"I like your spunk. Giddy-up-and-go, that's how I was raised." The bell at the front rang. "Pardon me a moment," Mary said, hurrying off. She called over her shoulder, "Scale's on that table—900 grams each. Think you can handle it?"

"Sure," Ellie said, more to herself than to Mary.

The vague gesture Mary had thrown toward the wall left her squinting at a cluttered workbench. She saw a mesh organizer stuffed with loose recipes, pens, a gingham-covered cookbook, notebooks, and a dusty plastic pastry case.

"She knows where she pointed, right?"

Ellie poked through the mess and crouched to check underneath, where she found baking sheets and cling wrap galore. On her fifth pass, something caught her eye: a thin black slab wedged between cookbooks. She pulled it out. It had rubber feet on the bottom. A digital display blinked to life: *0.0 g.*

"Alright then."

Ellie set the scale on the prep table next to the dough and grabbed a long knife from the wall's magnetic strip. In her experience, bread was guesswork—split the dough in half, call it good.

"Best guess," she said under her breath, slicing off a chunk.

*758 g. Not bad.* She trimmed and reshaped until the scale read *900 g,* then started again.

"Thanks, you too," Mary's voice called from the front.

At the sound of her footsteps, Ellie glanced up—and froze. Mary's smile dropped.

*Oh no, I screwed it up.*

"Ellie," Mary said, crossing the room quickly, "try not to have little bits—we risk over-kneading and ending up with funny-looking loaves."

"I'm sorry." Ellie's cheeks burned. "I'm not used to weighing dough like this. We normally just wing it," Ellie quickly explained. "I'll get it right, I promise."

Mary closed her eyes, then let out a soft chuckle. "It's okay. You're learning." Ellie opened her mouth, but Mary gently cut her off. "Our first few loaves might look funny, but we'll get there."

She walked Ellie through the process again—this time, step by step—until Ellie was consistently pulling perfect 900 g balls.

"There you go. I knew you'd be a quick study." Mary jotted something in a notebook. "For your first day, I'm putting you on bread. By the end of it, you'll be a pro."

It was fascinating to watch Mary work. The older woman moved effortlessly from task to task—whipping up a batch of oversized cookies, cooking breakfast for a small family, bringing Ellie a fresh glass of lemonade, and prepping emergency dough for the freezer—all while smiling like she hadn't broken a sweat.

With her elbows dusted in flour, Ellie worked on her third batch of bread. "Do you normally work here all by yourself?"

"Luna didn't tell you?" Mary slid a tray of chocolate chunk cookies into the oven.

*"Mary, such a sweet woman, needs help at her bakery," Luna had said, offering tea in Jean's kitchen. "I can throw your hat in the ring, if you'd like?"*

*"That's a great idea," Jean had chimed in. The two of them had gone on dreaming up possibilities.*

Ellie shook her head. "She mentioned it, but I didn't realize it was just you."

"My husband, Ned, helps when he can, but he's in the middle of some treatments."

Ellie's hands stilled. "I'm so sorry."

"Age will do that to you," Mary said with a soft, lopsided smile. "Only his body slows him down, though. His mind's still sharp as ever. We still do crosswords together every Sunday."

That made Ellie smile. For a flickering second, she saw herself on her bedroom floor, drawing while Louie dozed beside her. Her mom would leave behind word searches, ones with secret messages embedded in the answers. She'd spend hours uncovering them.

*"Can you grab my colored pencils?" she'd asked back then, erasing a stubborn line. The lazy pup hadn't even lifted his head, just stretched out one long leg to hook the fabric pencil container and dragged it over.*

The bakery day was filled with sugar, flour, yeast, and heat. Endless, sticky heat. The one perk—aside from taste-testing their "oopsies"— was that Ellie could drink as much lemonade or coffee as she wanted. She must've downed a gallon of lemonade by noon. Still didn't compare to what Louie used to haul her in the garden.

"Quittin' time," Mary called out as the clock struck noon. "See you bright and early tomorrow?"

Ellie wiped her face with a cold, damp paper towel. "Four?"

"Yup. Come in through the back."

Ellie nodded. *Regretting this already.*

Outside, her purple and chrome Honda shimmered in the sun. Her sore muscles screamed as she hauled herself onto the hot leather seat. Groaning, she pulled on her leather jacket despite the heat.

*"Every time you ride, please wear this jacket and that helmet." Her dad's voice echoed from a memory in the garage, late-night grease still on his hands.*

"Yeah, yeah," she'd groaned, zipping up. "Boiling hot."

"Someone's looking fly." Ellie grinned down at the image of Louie, who sat nearby with his paws neatly planted and his chest puffed out, sporting his doggy helmet and goggles. The urge to kiss him silly almost overwhelmed her. She swallowed hard and fastened her helmet.

*Still not real. He's gone,* she told herself.

The short ride home dragged. By the time Ellie pulled into the gravel driveway, her limbs were jelly. The stairs to her apartment felt twice as long with her heavy limbs. She caught her reflection in the window, with white streaks across her forehead and her hair flat with sweat.

"Got the makings for an Ellie pancake."

She unlocked the door and peeled off her clothes as she bee-lined for the shower. The water warmed as the bathroom fan whirred overhead and a breeze drifted in from the cracked window. Ellie stepped in and let the heat wash over her. With her eyes closed, she rolled her head as the flour and grime vanished down the drain. But the heaviest thing—guilt—clung to her skin like a second layer.

*Jean was right. Working helped. But is it really that easy to forget him?*

Images flashed again: that night on the beach, Louie fighting the monster off her.

*I can't forget. I don't deserve to.*

"I hope you're okay," she whispered into the rising steam.

Clean and wrapped in a towel, Ellie gathered her dirty clothes and padded down the hall. The ceiling was unfinished, the paint half-done. It didn't matter. Kimberly's voice was sharp and ever-present in the back of her mind.

*"Don't throw your dirty clothes on the floor!"*

*"Dog! Make the bed!"*

*"Wash the dishes!"*

With performative defiance, she tossed her clothes to the floor and stuck her tongue out at the ghost in the room.

Ellie rifled through her sticker-covered dresser, dug out another of Jean's vintage band tees, and tugged on a pair of cut-off jean shorts.

"Should've packed more than two days of clothes," she muttered, fighting the stubborn button. "First thing after rent—real wardrobe."

But she couldn't ignore the conversation she'd overheard.

*"I'm happy she's here," Peter had said through the open window one evening. "But... we had plans to rent that apartment."*

*"I know," Jean had sighed. "Maybe we can tighten the budget..."*

*"I don't know where we could do that," he'd replied, worn and weary.*

Ellie hadn't stuck around for the rest. She'd buried her head beneath a pillow and let the guilt smother her. She'd already caused so much. When Louie disappeared, she hadn't left her bed for days. But after Luna's visit—and an impromptu interview with Mary—she'd promised herself something.

*I won't let them suffer because of me.*

In fresh clothes, Ellie wandered barefoot across the unfinished plywood into the front half of her apartment. The sunlight streamed in through the windows. A modest table sat with four mismatched chairs in the dining nook. The loveseat and coffee table faced a TV four times the size of the one back home. Crisp. Clear. Hundreds of channels. Cartoons. Music. Static-laced nonsense. She barely touched it.

Behind the couch was a wide-open patch of floor. When she looked at it, she saw Louie—belly-up, legs floppy, ghosting through her mind. *He would've loved this place.*

The sharp thump-thump-thump of little feet echoed up the stairs. Ellie snapped back to the present. She peeked through the window. A shaggy head of dark hair bobbed into view.

*Brody.*

The doorbell rang. She opened the first door to her mudroom, sidestepping the stacked washer and dryer. Then the second door.

"Hi, Ellie." Brody beamed, with his round cheeks and messy hair, like he'd just wrestled a bear.

"Hey, Brody."

"Um… Mom said you can come over for lunch. Since you finished your first day. We're having turkey sandwiches." He leaned in like it was classified info. "Sometimes she puts extra cheese on if you ask."

*You play dirty, Jean. Sending your most adorable minion to come get me.* Ellie arched a brow. "Extra cheese?"

In her mind, she heard Louie's paws clicking on hardwood. Her stomach tightened.

"Yeah. So… would you like to come over?"

# Classes

The smell of onions and slow-roasting pork met Ellie as she stepped into Jean's kitchen. A red crock pot steamed on the butcher block. Stone floors, olive-green walls, and cheerful white trim gave the room its usual warmth.

Gracey sat at the table, stuffing orange slices into her mouth while scrolling on her phone. She had Jean's sharp nose, her dad's skin tone, and wore enough bright makeup to belong on a billboard. Michael, the miniature version of Peter but with Jean's hair, fiddled with a magnetic plastic toy. At nine, he already threatened a growth spurt.

"No magnets at the table," Jean called as Ellie and Brody entered. She handed Brody a sandwich, kissed his head, sniffed him, and grimaced. "You need a bath."

"No!" Brody hollered and bolted to the table.

"We'll take a bath tomorrow," she muttered to herself. "Gracey." Jean passed a sandwich to her only daughter.

"Thanks," Gracey mumbled as she took her plate. Her eyes were locked on her phone as she shuffled toward the table. Jean tried to sneak in a forehead kiss, but Gracey snarled and pulled away. "Come on, I'm trying to do something."

"No phones at the table," Jean barked in a way that made even Ellie's muscles stiffen. A glance toward Ellie brought a smile to her matronly face. "Hey! Happy first day. How was it?"

"Sadie's breaking up with Travis," Gracey explained as she continued to text on her way back to the table.

"Mom," Brody interrupted. "Ellie wants extra cheese."

"Does she now?" Jean smiled and glanced up at Ellie, who shook her head from side to side and mouthed, 'No.'

Michael was already halfway through his sandwich and only offered Ellie a quick wave.

"Lettuce, tomato, and onion?" Jean asked as the slices of whole grain bread awaited their dressings.

"No onion, thank you." Ellie stood at the counter with her aunt, despite the ache in her feet. "I can make it if you—"

"You're my guest. I'll make you a sandwich," Jean said firmly. "How was your first day?"

"Good." Ellie leaned forward on the counter. The marble space supported her weight in a way her tired frame appreciated. She propped her head up with one hand. "Mary's nice."

"You look exhausted." Her aunt grabbed Ellie's chin and tilted her head up to get a better look at her face.

"I'm fine. Just tired. It turns out making baked goods in a hot kitchen all day will do that to you."

"Oh, I can imagine. The heat just drains me. That's part of the reason we settled in New England and didn't stay in the South. The racism was the other reason. Did she let you do anything fun?"

Ellie let out a pathetic groan. "Just lots of bread… tomorrow is rolls and scones."

"Oh, I love Ned's scones." Jean rolled her eyes, let out a groan, and passed Ellie the finished sandwich.

Thick slices of turkey and tomato, crisp lettuce, and fresh-cut provolone cheese made Ellie's mouth water. While they ate, the two women caught up on the happenings in the Brown household: Gracey's new attitude grew more and more by the day, the boys found a snake and tried to make it their new pet, and somehow in the few hours Uncle Peter was gone, the upstairs toilet stopped flushing.

"Thankfully, Peter comes back tonight. I don't think I could go another day like this." Jean chuckled and dabbed her mouth with a bit of paper towel. "We welcome him home with pulled pork, his favorite. You wanna join us for some barbecue?"

Jean had come up with a million excuses to get Ellie over to the house.

"I might take you up on that, if I'm awake." Ellie's plan was to be asleep by ten o'clock. "You have any valerian root?"

"Trying to knock yourself out?"

"Hoping to." Ellie yawned. "Starting at 4:30 tomorrow."

Jean pointed toward the pantry on the far side of the room. "Help yourself. I need to run to the co-op to get more soon anyway."

"Co-op?" Ellie asked as she headed to the pantry.

"I actually have my own little mixture that could help you, if you're interested." Jean joined her with a cheek full of a sandwich. "Pardon my reach." She stretched up and grabbed a glass jar. "It's not from the Keller-Wagner books but something my friend Ellen turned me on to. It's already infused. Eat one tablespoon, but make sure you take it with some crackers or something, or it will give you indigestion."

"Thank you." Ellie took the potion. From what she could tell, there were probably a couple of tablespoons left. This potion was different from others she had seen before. Back in Connecticut, whatever they made usually had that classic light-blue tinge to it. The last one she made with Louie was a deeper color than they ever managed. "You know, I never knew there were different potions out there."

"Doesn't surprise me." Jean returned to her lunch at the kitchen island. "Keller's aren't known for branching out much."

"Yeah." Ellie raised a curious eyebrow and snuck a chip from the bag on the counter. "Why's that?"

"I always thought it was because Pamela thought she was hot sh—" Jean caught herself and glanced at the table.

"Shit, mom," Gracey said. "Just say it. Hot shit."

"Watch your mouth!" Jean pointed to the two younger sets of ears at the table.

"They hear worse things on the bus," Gracey countered before she went back to her phone.

Jean continued to stare at her daughter like she was waiting for the other shoe to drop. When Gracey didn't look up from her phone or say anything more, Jean returned her attention to Ellie.

"The, uh, Wagners, you know, Pamela's maiden name, are a hot-shot bloodline in Oren. They're a bunch of elitist snobs." Jean picked up the second half of her sandwich. "So, they always assumed their way was best. Surprise, surprise. It's not."

"Mom, what's an elite-tist?" Brody asked.

"An elitist is someone who thinks they are better than everybody else because of money or bloodline, some sort of prestige they never had to work to achieve."

"Prestige," Ellie repeated softly with a smile and raised eyebrows. *Three... two... one...*

"Oh," Brody said as if he had connected the dots. "What's prestige?"

*Called it.*

"Should've known better," Jean muttered to Ellie before she began the second half of her vocabulary lesson for her youngest.

"It's when jerks take credit for things they didn't do and everyone loves them for it."

Gracey didn't break eye contact with her phone.

"Sometimes they do earn it," Jean added quickly.

Gracey just raised an eyebrow before she decided she was done with her lunch and stepped away from the table.

Ellie helped her aunt clean up the mess and wipe down the large wooden dining room table as the kids scattered.

"Oh, before I forget, I snagged you the summer class schedules." Jean pulled a stack of fliers from a wall organizer labeled BILLS, KIDS, and LOVE. "I grabbed these for you." From the kids' section, Jean handed her a stack of brightly colored fliers: red, yellow, and green. "I circled the ones the kids will be attending. Your schedule at Sugar Shack is Thursday through Sunday, right?"

"Yeah, except when there are New Moon celebrations."

"That's great! Gracey's day camp should keep her busy until 2:00. I appreciate you offering to help with pickups every now and again. I told you the sitter got an internship, right?"

"With UMass?"

"Yeah, I did." Jean shook her head at herself and mumbled something about her age. "Anyway, I don't really know where you are with your education, so I just grabbed everything."

The packets were made up of thick paper stapled together and folded down the center. They read:

**Eastham's Naturalist Educational Society: Naturalist Private Library**

<u>Summer Educational Programs</u>

The red one:

> Beginners Classes

Yellow:

> Intermediate Classes

And the green:

> Advanced Classes

Jean's eyes burrowed into Ellie as she opened the yellow booklet and looked through the offerings. Some classes were magic-related, others were arts, history, and culture, but there was at least one per day.

"It's kind of on a rotation," Jean hopped in and pointed to a Monday morning offering. "See?"

> *Introduction to The Void*
> *Presenter Mrs. J. Brown*
> *Mondays 7:30 a.m.-8:30 a.m.*

"It's offered again two weeks later, but in the evening." Jean flipped the pages harshly to show the example.

> *Introduction to The Void*
> *Presenter Mrs. J. Brown*
> *Mondays 4:30 p.m.-5:30 p.m.*

"J. Brown?" Ellie raised an eyebrow.

The accentuated movement took her back to the cabin amongst the chickadees and cardinals. *The handsome young man wiggled his eyebrows in the mirror with a laugh on his lips that could brighten up the room.*

A fresh needle stabbed at her heart.

"The one and only." Jean curtseyed. "Way to give back, you know?" She pointed to another offering.

*Meditation and Mindfulness: Staying Centered in Chaos*
*Presenter Ms. L. Nordin*
*9 a.m.-11 a.m.*

"One of Luna's classes." Jean shared.

*Brief History of Magic in America: Series 1 of 3*
*Presenter Mr. M. Becker*
*9 a.m.-12 p.m.*

"Becker?" Ellie pulled her head back skeptically. "Do you think?"

Jean shrugged. "Who knows? Did your dad ever mention any family members who… moved away?"

Ellie slowly shook her head. "He never really talked about his family much. My Pops died when I was little, and Gram-Gram moved to Maine to be with some relatives."

Jean scoffed.

"What?"

Her lips parted like she wanted to say something, but she stopped herself. "I don't know if it's my place."

"Tell me," Ellie pushed.

Jean shook her head gently. "I…"

A loud crash came from upstairs. Jean flinched and held her pose as if waiting for something.

"Mom," Brody shouted. "Michael broke your vase."

She exhaled, and her shoulders dropped with defeat. "Word of advice," Jean whispered. "If you have kids, hide everything valuable."

As Jean hurried out of the room with the broom and dustpan, Ellie called out to her, "I'm borrowing these fliers."

"Bring 'em back when you're done! I know where you live."

The threat made Ellie smile.

Back in her apartment, she flipped through the offerings.

*Creatures and Critters, Presenter L. Staton* stood out to her. It didn't elaborate on which creatures would be covered.

*What if they cover Familiars? I could get answers about Louie.*

At the end of the brochure was an invitation to the end-of-summer carnival in Sandwich. She choked back a tear as she thought of the promises she made to the basset hound to go to a carnival with him. "Don't worry, buddy. Never without you."

For the rest of the night, Ellie relaxed on her couch, let the music on the television play, and came up with a plan for which classes to take. Even though History was her most dreaded subject, Ellie took note of it. She wasn't certain if she would take the class or just peek in to see if M. Becker looked anything like any of the Beckers she knew.

She joined her aunt and uncle for dinner. Uncle Peter's shoulders sat low and relaxed. He no longer looked like his lips would peel back to snarl at the drop of a dime. Where his plump lips had formed a pencil-thin line, his smile returned. Cheerful laughter replaced his silence and deep sighs. The effects of the full moon were gone.

Unfortunately, Gracey's attitude didn't seem to improve. In fact, she seemed even more annoyed by her father's presence. Frustrated with Gracey's ever-increasing irritability, Ellie ate quickly, washed her dishes, and used the excuse of work in the morning to leave, but really, she took the time to watch the horizon for any sign of Louie as the sun set.

"Any luck?" Jean asked well after the sun had dipped below the horizon. Ellie could barely make her out at the bottom of the steps.

"No," she admitted with defeat.

The stairs creaked as Jean approached. A warm blanket wrapped around Ellie, and plastic Tupperware scratched against the wood between them. "I brought brownies." Jean cracked the lid open.

"Thanks."

"And hot chocolate."

"I already adore you. Stop trying to buy my love," Ellie teased and stole a brownie.

Jean chuckled. Silence sat between them as the two looked up to the heavens for any sign. "Thank you," Jean added quickly, "for taking the job."

"No problem." Ellie tried to play it off as she chewed. "'Bout time I did something besides mope around."

Jean let out a sigh through her nose, then gently nudged Ellie with her elbow.

"You know it's true," Ellie admitted. "I've been pretty pathetic."

"It's not unjustified," Jean added.

"Justified or not…" Ellie shrugged. "I know I can be a heck of a burden to be around, so… thank you? For the push?"

The only response Ellie received was a tight hug.

# Processing

Aunt Jean's sleeping serum did the trick—but it also trapped Ellie in a loop of nightmares. She woke rested in body, but her mind bore the residue of that horrific night.

*A creature of darkness.*

With Louie gone, there was no comforting shuffle of paws in the night, no soft grunt to ground her. She had to invest in a nightlight just to be sure that a pile of laundry wasn't hiding the oozing shape of the Corrupted Familiar.

At three in the morning—her first real, full day of work—Ellie got up, ate breakfast, drank coffee, tossed in a load of laundry, and rode off to the Sugar Shack. Per Mary's instructions, she circled around back, where the scent of fresh coffee floated on the air, and a soft current of country music played on the radio.

An older man with bony, hunched shoulders and a white mustache smiled at Mary across the prep tables. His T-shirt drooped off his frame like it belonged to someone larger.

"There's my helping hand," he called when he saw Ellie, his smile warm beneath his bristly mustache.

*Dad would approve.*

"Vanilla latte?" Mary called as she shuffled towards the front. "Great way to start the morning, if I do say so myself. We have other flavors, too, if you don't like vanilla."

The memory of Louie lapping up coffee from a paper cup on a city bench taunted her. Ellie shut her eyes and forced the thought away. "I'd love one," she said. Her muscles still ached from her first shift. Who knew there was a whole different kind of 'fit' for baking?

"Mary said you've got a good head for the basics," the older man said.

"That was kind of her," Ellie replied, tugging on a fresh apron and folding it with the method she'd figured out yesterday. "I'm sorry, but I didn't catch your name."

"Oh, I'm Ned, honey." He gave her a wink as his hands worked dough with surprising dexterity. "Glad we found you."

"Me too," Mary said, returning with a tray of hot lattes.

"Oh, thank you." Ellie took hers. The couple murmured between themselves about the day's schedule. Ned would only stay for a few hours—he'd been dubbed the "Scone Master."

"Alright, Ellie, I am going to let you in on a big secret," Ned said, lowering his voice like he was about to share classified intel. "Most of what keeps the Shack running is our side business. We supply sub rolls, sandwich buns, and hot dog rolls to businesses all over the Cape." He winked. "And I'm gonna teach you those recipes so you can make hundreds of rolls on Fridays."

"Bring it on," Ellie said, tying her dark hair into a ponytail. "Whatever you need, Ned."

He gave a satisfied smirk and turned to Mary. "I like this kid."

"Told you," Mary said, bouncing on her toes. "She's got a spring in her step."

With Ned guiding her, Ellie learned to operate the massive stand mixer with its iron bowl. Load it. Mix it. Transfer to the rising station. Repeat. By eight and nine, they had stacks of fresh rolls ready to go.

In the background, country music played as Ned regaled her with tales from his life. Born and raised in Chatham, he had no connection to the Void like the rest of his family—but it didn't sour him.

"It's about finding magic in the little moments," he explained while brushing buttermilk on raspberry scones. "One time, I took Mary to Sunken Meadow. Stars were sparkling in her eyes... I proposed that night."

He told stories of lobster fishing, watching his kids grow, and enjoying the magic his children had, even if he didn't share it.

Their baked goods began flying out the back door to the various local businesses. The first in line to pick up an ungodly amount of hot dog buns and some hamburger rolls was The Hut Putt. Ellie passed it every time she came to Eastham. It was hard to miss—the massive putt-putt course with large, funny statues inside of the wire fence, glow-in-the-dark nights, and a cartoon cod fish with a wooden sign which read *"Best Lobster Rolls- Cod Approved."*

Different restaurants, owned by magic folk and non-magic folk alike, came through. Ellie was like a celebrity amongst the magic folk.

"You're the girl who lost her Familiar. Oh, honey."

"Yeah," turned into "I guess," which eventually turned into silence. There were too many unwelcome hugs to count.

"The Cape is one, big, small town," Mary said, lugging a bus tote. "Good news travels fast. Bad news even faster."

Once the scones were finished, Ned perched on a stool and kept Ellie company until he left for a doctor's appointment around ten. Just like the day before, Ellie spent the last stretch cleaning while Mary ran the front.

By the time she got home, she crashed onto the couch and didn't stir until her phone buzzed after 2:00 p.m.

"Hey, lovely, just checking in," came Luna's cheerful voice.

"Hey," Ellie mumbled. "Just woke up from a nap."

"Oh, afternoon naps are the best."

"Agreed." Ellie sighed.

"But what's even better," Luna added, her voice lifting into song, "is soaking up some sunshine with your friend!"

"It's cloudy."

"It's clearing up! The weather app says seventy-five and sunny. Wanna meet at Nauset Beach in an hour? I've got an extra chair."

"I don't have a swimsuit."

"Just wear shorts and a tank."

Against all odds, Ellie agreed.

An hour later, she pulled her motorcycle into the same spot she and Louie had parked that day at the beach—right after Boston, right after his transformation from bumbling basset hound to the bearded flannel-wearing dreamboat she'd seen in her mom's hiking magazines.

*"Maybe this can remind you of how we came back together," he'd said when he handed her the seashell.*

Her hand twitched at the memory of the shell on her nightstand. She cursed herself for not carrying it.

"Hey," Luna called from the next parking spot. Her black Jeep had snuck in unnoticed. Mitsy, her cotton-ball Pomeranian, sat alert in the back seat, her eyes darting. "She's looking for Louie."

*Me too.* Ellie smiled, though it took effort. After securing her bike, she helped Luna carry chairs, blankets, and supplies down to the beach.

Luna wore a cheerful tankini and a colorful sarong. Ellie, by contrast, tugged self-consciously at her cut-off shorts and old tank top.

They set up their striped chairs side by side. Luna brought two ice-cold water bottles and a few paperback books. Mitsy had her own setup: a pink umbrella, a blanket, and a water bowl.

"She doesn't need a tan," Luna said, patting the dog.

Ellie nodded and smiled.

"You seemed so sleepy I didn't want to bother you too much with questions, so I grabbed a couple of my favorite fun reads. Figured we could read, talk, and just be. Whatever vibe you're feeling today."

*Just be.* That sounded perfect.

Luna handed her three books: one on herbalism, a romance novel with a swooning couple on the cover, and a YA book about a sassy young woman who moved around with her military family and had issues with a clock.

"Not your style?" Luna picked up the herbalism one.

"Oh, no, all my style. Just not up for reading right now." Ellie stretched her arms over her head. Following a few loud pops from her back, she melted into the beach chair. "I want to borrow this one." She leaned back, stretching until her spine popped. "This is so nice."

"Mhm."

"You know," Ellie said, shading her eyes, "my Mee-Maw would have a cow if she saw me right now." She deepened her voice in imitation. "Showing all that skin! Where did I go wrong, Ellie-Lynne?"

Luna laughed. "She the type to serve a heaping tablespoon of guilt with everything?"

"Oh yeah."

The sun warmed Ellie's skin. Waves rolled. Gulls cried. The peace held—until school let out, and laughter carried on the breeze.

"I haven't seen you since you moved into your apartment," Luna said, fiddling with a book.

"It's big." Ellie didn't know why that blatant honesty just rushed from her lips.

"Yeah, I thought it was a decent size. Jean told me about it when they renovated the garage."

"I mean," Ellie spread her fingers and held her hands wide open. "It feels big."

"You're lonely." Luna honed in on the true meaning behind those words. "That makes sense. When was the last time you were actually alone?"

Ellie looked away. "Maybe so. I've never been alone before."

"Oh." Luna winced. "Mourning, so much on top of the changes you were already processing. Girl, I feel for you."

"Yeah." Ellie grimaced and placed her arm over her eyes. *What am I supposed to say to that? I really don't want to get into it all right now.*

"We need to get you sunglasses," Luna said gently.

Relief lifted off her shoulders. "Yeah, that would be nice. Maybe some clothes, too."

"Oh! Terry's shop! Remember Terry from the New Moon Ceremony? The jacked guy with the cat Familiar?"

"Yeah."

"He's a genius. He could help you find your style."

"I have style," Ellie protested. "It's just... back in Connecticut."

"I'm sorry, but I am relieved to hear you say that right now, because your look is second-hand tomboy, and you can do better for yourself than that."

Ellie's eyebrows furrowed at the assessment. It was accurate, but she thought she was pulling it off. *I look cute in jeans and oversized flannel, thank you.*

"I don't think Louie would stand for this outfit, either," she admitted. "He'd go through my closet and grab dresses for me to wear during special dinners."

"That's sweet."

*"Violet! The violet one." Louie exclaimed.* His voice was so clear, as memories from their last Friday night dinner on Azalea Way came back to her.

*"Your mother will do anything to get into Oren," Elijah said calmly. "But I will not sacrifice our daughter for her greed and ego."*

*Wood groaned beneath the strength of Louie's jaws as he protected Ellie from Mee-Maw's cane.*

Ellie's heart beat too fast. She licked her lips and tried to steady her breathing.

*Think of something happy, something happy. Anything happy. Dandelion fluff on the wind.*

It didn't help.

*"Look." Louie stood before the mirror in the cabin. "I have eyebrows." He wiggled and bounced them joyously.*

Her heart still thumped in her chest, but it began to slow.

*The basset hound sat back on his haunches, pointing with his paw at a large frog at the pond. "It looks so stupid! How does it even function?"*

A smile pulled at her lips.

*"Come here." She opened the sleeping bag, and the handsome young man climbed in.*

*"Okay, we can cuddle." His eyes lit up as she spoke. "But I initiate it, okay?"*

*"I can do that."*

*Ellie leaned her head into his chest. Louie mimicked the action against the top of her head. She put an arm around him.*

*Hesitantly, he put his around her. "Sweet dreams, Ellie."*

"Sweet dreams," Ellie mumbled, lost in the tender memory.

"What's that?" Luna asked.

Ellie removed her arm from her eyes and was blinded by the sun. "Oh! That was stupid."

Luna chuckled. "Did you start to fall asleep?"

"Yeah," Ellie replied. "Yeah, totally."

"I won't keep you if that's what you want to do."

Ellie regained her vision and sat forward on the beach chair. The memory of Louie's arm around her, the warmth that came off his body, and the comfort of his chest all lingered just out of reach in her mind.

Ellie ran her hand over her forearm, where his hand once lay. *Why'd I make such a big deal out of it? Yeah, he was cute, but it wasn't like that... well, maybe it was a little. I was worried it was. Ugh, what am I talking about? He's my best friend. Obviously, it was never like that when he was a basset hound. We should never have gone to Boston. This never would have happened. But then I wouldn't have found Luna and Aunt Jean... or found out Louie's actually my soulmate...*

"You said that Familiars are soulmates, right?" Ellie blurted out.

"I did." Luna turned her attention toward Ellie. "I also said that soulmates mean something different to different people."

"Right, so how do you know which it is?"

Luna placed the bookmark in her book before she closed it. "That's really something I cannot answer for you, and I don't think there is an easy answer."

Ellie's head dropped.

"For what it's worth," Luna offered, "I think that, maybe, you should spend some time reflecting on what the term *soulmate* means to you?"

"I always thought of it as a romantic term," Ellie admitted. "I never thought of it outside of that."

"You have a starting point then, right? What does that..." Luna created a circular shape with her hands. "...entail and look like?"

"I-I don't know." Ellie began to pick at her nails.

"I know it can be uncomfortable to dive into those depths, but that kind of internal exploration is the only way you'll get your answers,"

Luna continued after a long moment filled with the sounds of children playing in the surf.

"There's different kinds of love out there," Ellie finally spoke. "Like the love you have for your friends, the kind for family members. And that kind of… romantic love."

"Right. Now, how does it differ?"

"And romantic love is, um." She really couldn't look at Luna now. Her mouth started to go dry. "Like, the physical stuff…"

"Well, yeah, physical attraction has something to do with it."

Perhaps it was the smell of Mitsy's treats or the way that Luna gestured with her hands, but in that moment, a seagull fluttered down and landed between the two.

"Oh, not again." Luna shooed it away boisterously. "Ugh, sorry about that. As I was saying, love isn't just physical attraction. It's so much more than that. You can find someone attractive but not be in love with them."

"Can you romantically love someone you don't find attractive?"

Luna's hand dropped, and her lips twisted with uncertainty. "Attractiveness is more than just physical attraction. It's adoring those other qualities someone has, right? Like the way they laugh."

The collection of metallic bracelets on her right hand jingled as she put up one finger.

"And how it just warms you. Their sense of humor."

A second finger.

"And how they put a smile on your face when it seems the hardest thing to do so. Or the way their eyes light up when they talk about something they are passionate about. It's that closeness you can't find anywhere else or is shared with very few people. You can stay up all night talking, and you feel safe enough to bare your heart and soul."

Luna was so lost in her own train of thought that she stopped counting, but the bracelets danced away.

"Even when they are just irritating as all hell and you want to scream or just shake them, but you know that even though they are pressing every single one of your buttons, driving you up the wall, and putting you on edge, you still want them. You choose them every day.

Some days are harder than others, but you only want them pressing your buttons."

Ellie bit her bottom lip. *I've never felt that way about anybody… is it me? Shouldn't this be easy if he's my soulmate? Why isn't this an immediate 'yes'? Shouldn't this be screaming at me in the face?*

"This isn't going to be easy," Ellie admitted.

"Never is." Luna crossed one ankle over the other and opened the book once again.

# 5
## Cats

Three hundred and eighty-four dollars." Ellie smirked and shoved her first week's pay into her pocket.

"Big plans?" Mary asked as she checked off 'Pay Ellie' from her to-do list.

"Oh yeah. I'm outta here. Flying to the Caribbean." Ellie's hand danced into the air.

Mary chuckled.

"Maybe I'll open a Swiss bank account or whatever rich people do with their money," she added as the dishwasher beeped. Ellie turned around, grabbed the handles, and lifted the metal doors so steam barreled out everywhere.

"Invest in stocks," Mary suggested.

"Oh no, not risky enough for me." She shoved another load of dirty dishes into the machine. "I'm going to live it up. Tell you what I'm really going to do; I'm going to buy a pack of water balloons from the dollar store and bombard the boys from my stairs."

"Oh, my boys loved water balloons and squirt guns." Her eyes grew distant with memories.

"Yeah. I figure it's the best way to usher in summer vacation." Ellie held her hands out, with her palms face up. Then, she shut the door to the dishwasher, and it roared to life. "What can I say? I'm a giver." She shook drops of water off the freshly cleaned cookie sheets.

"Just make sure they don't have a stash of their own, or you're in for it," Mary warned as she shuffled through the beige order slips. "This week is going to be a lot. Hope you're ready."

"Wha'do we got?" Ellie unloaded the cookie sheets and brought them back to their rightful place.

"Every putt-putt is open now, so we have dozens of orders to fill, and Tuesday is the New Moon Celebration."

Ellie's abdomen tightened like she had been punched.

"And Miss Keswick always orders a ton of food." Mary tilted her head better to see through her bifocal glasses. "Oh, great, she wants strawberry shortcakes. Going to need to pick up buttercream from the store."

Ellie turned her back to Mary, and a thick, sludge-like weight filled her mind.

*A mouth full of gnarly teeth.*

*"Ellie, get down!"*

Ellie slowly exhaled. *It's not real. I'm here. I'm at work. Work. The Sugar Shack.*

Ellie grabbed the silver mixing bowl striped with deposits of softened butter. "This is a bowl," she whispered to herself before she grabbed the high-powered sprayer dangling overhead. "I am cleaning the bowl."

"What do you think, Ellie?" Mary called out.

"About what?" Ellie turned back to her.

*A chair. The prep table. Mary's notepad. The phone. The griddle.*

Mary picked up her list once again. "If we offer a limited menu tomorrow, take-out only, then we won't get bogged down with tourists." With a tilt of her glasses, she looked at Ellie. "Oh, honey, are you feeling okay?"

"Yeah, the steam just got to me." Ellie chuckled.

*I smell… dirty dish water. Syrup. Bacon.*

"Come, come," Mary ushered Ellie over with a frantic hand. "Sit! No need to pass out over some dishes. They can wait." Mary pulled out the other stool for Ellie, who took a seat.

*Mary's perfume.*

"I'll get you some water."

Mary hurried from the room, and Ellie muttered to herself. "I thought this was over with."

"So stubborn, just like Ned." Mary returned and placed a tall glass of ice-cold water in front of Ellie. "Willing to put yourself at risk rather than give up on a task." With a swat to Ellie's arm with her notebook, Mary added, "It's not healthy! Stop it."

"I stopped!" Ellie cowered away from the notebook as it came back at her bicep for a second time around. "I'm sitting." Ellie laughed and took a big sip from her glass. "I'm drinking."

Mary pointed the notebook at Ellie with threatening eyes, and Ellie took a larger gulp, taunting herself with possible brain freeze.

"That's right." Mary shook her head and dropped the notebook onto the table. "Worry me like you're my own grandkid." She directed her focus back on the list. "Alright, back to business. Ned's on Caprese salad skewers. You'll be on meatballs. I am on prep. If we—"

"Wait." Ellie tapped the table above the notepad. "I'm on meatballs?"

"Yes." Mary nodded.

"Like, the meatballs that were there last time?"

"Yes." Mary chuckled with a second nod.

"Oh," Ellie exclaimed. "Score! Best meatballs I've ever had, and I get to learn the recipe."

"Old family recipe, so don't blab," Mary warned her. "It'll be worse than a notebook beating."

Ellie mimicked locking up her mouth and throwing away the key.

"Good." Mary ran Ellie through the plan as she sipped her water. It was ambitious, to say the least, but Ellie was happy to help. She couldn't imagine leaving the older couple by themselves to tackle such a tall task. "Are you planning on staying for the celebration?"

Ellie raised a questioning eyebrow. Her water was almost done, and a pool of condensation formed on the metallic surface beneath it.

"I wouldn't blame you if you didn't want to, after everything that happened last time."

Her stomach tightened once again.

"If you ask me, you should give your Seer a gift and ask if Louie's still alive."

Tightening turned to sudden freezing. Ellie's mouth dropped open. "Come again?"

"You missed it last time. That's right." Mary connected the dots. "The Summoning Circle, it's to do a Giving. It's so we can give our 'thanks' to the Void and our Seers. Our Seer, my great-uncle Thadius, loved cigars, so I bring him one every month. Not that he can smoke it. Well, we don't know if they can enjoy it or not. We assume they can't since it all goes 'poof.'" Mary tossed up her pen to emphasize the point. "Sometimes we ask questions to the Seer and they may answer, or they may not."

"A Giving," Ellie muttered. It sounded so familiar.

"Have you seen one before?"

"I think so... but it was at a funeral instead of, you know, this..." she gestured to the room. "My um, my great-aunt Dorothy, my Mee-Maw's sister, she passed. Family members dropped flowers and pictures and things into the Giving Circle as my Mee-Maw read off a recap of her life..."

The painting of great-aunt Dorothy, a thin, mean-looking woman with thick glasses and short gray hair, stood beside Mee-Maw. A bright white bouquet of lilies at her side, and the Giving Circle open as family members tossed in trinkets, mementos, and secrets written on paper.

From behind her, Mee-Maw picked up Boopsy, great-aunt Dorothy's pet cat of a decade, and tossed it into the circle; it was gone in an instant. "Together for eternity, the way Dorothy would have preferred it."

Then came Dorothy's casket.

"What are typical gifts given?" Ellie asked abruptly as she rubbed away at the goosebumps the memory brought.

"Like I said, I give a cigar. Some give food; others give flowers or spices that the Seer was known to love. Nothing really expensive."

"No pets?" Ellie had to double-check.

"Heavens, no." Mary looked at Ellie, terrified.

"Oh, thank the Void." Ellie put a relieved hand on her heart and let out an awkward laugh. Mary shook her head with a polite smile on her face. The country music filled the awkward silence before Ellie gathered the courage to continue. "What if you don't know what to get them?"

"I find that flowers are always a good starting point. Everyone loves them, and if it's a man, well, it may be the first time anybody has ever given him flowers."

A smile pulled at the corner of Ellie's lips.

*"I found them," Louie called. The plump basset hound hopped up out of the tall grass, only to disappear a split second later. Small bright white flowers, bunched together, poked out of his mouth. "I got the primrose."*

After Mary retrieved her pen, both of them got back to work. Ellie loaded and unloaded dishes while she made a mental list of possible things to give Betty Fisher.

"Come back refreshed tomorrow," Mary demanded as she ushered Ellie out the door at noon.

With a smirk, Ellie pulled on her leather jacket, brought the Honda to life, and took off for Truro. By the end of her first week, Ellie could drive back to her aunt's house with her eyes closed. After a brief stop at 'For A Buck,' Ellie took a quick shower and secured her first week's pay inside her underwear drawer.

A well-loved soup pot filled with small colorful water balloons sat in the mudroom. Ellie waited on the landing before her apartment for her aunt's car, prepared for her summer assault. In her hand, she gripped an old leather-bound journal.

"Help me out here, Betty." Ellie opened it and began to read through the pages.

> Today was washing duty. I spent the morning bent over the washboard with our servant, my second cousin, Melody. I'd rather do my chores alone so I can have space to think. It's getting harder to hide my gift.

Other entries aligned more with what Ellie had experienced previously.

Wendigos and wolves. Wendigos and wolves.
The milk is spoiled.
Play in the woods, wendigos and wolves.
Don't leave the boy in the potato fields.
Find a source amongst the yellow ducks.
Quack, quack.

Pages of back-to-back nonsense, followed by unhelpful updates on her chores, were painful for Ellie to try to make sense of. When the little black car rolled into the driveway, Ellie tried to seem as casual as she got up, placed the journal inside the doorway, and grabbed a couple of water balloons.

"Ellie," Brody shouted excitedly. "Ellie!"

"Yes?" She held the balloons behind her back. "I got second place for-for running." Brody held up his blue ribbon.

"Hey, that's awesome, buddy!" They all wore T-shirts from school. Jean was in bright orange, Michael in dark blue, and Brody in highlighter yellow.

"I didn't win anything," Michael announced with a sour face as he walked toward the sliding glass door.

Ellie's wicked grin distorted into a thoughtful grimace. *I can't bombard them when he feels so down.*

"How was work?" Jean asked as she lugged a cooler towards the kitchen.

"It was hot… I thought you all might be a bit hot too with the sun out and all… so I thought we could…?" She held up a water balloon.

"What's that?" Michael asked.

"Water balloons!" Jean dropped the cooler. "Boys, run! Get your water pistols. I'll distract her."

"Hey, water pistols?" Ellie watched as they scattered. She tried to hit Jean with a balloon as she ran around the side of the house.

Everybody was out of sight. Ellie suddenly felt that her singular spot on top of the stairs was the perfect place to get cornered. She grabbed her pot of balloons, shut the door, and hurried to the bottom of the stairs. As soon as she rounded the corner, she was blasted by a stream of cold water.

"Think this is our first rodeo, Becker?" Jean laughed wickedly as she held up the hose.

"Not fair!" Ellie shouted and ran around the side of the garage, out of range.

Brody and Michael came out of the sliding glass door with bulbous, brightly colored water guns. "Fill us up, Mom!"

Ellie peeked around the corner and saw that they all had sought cover behind the opposite end of the house. "Luckily, mine are mobile," she whispered.

Using her T-shirt like a basket, she loaded herself up with balloons and snuck up to where they were hiding.

"Sitting ducks." She stepped out from around the corner and bombarded them with balloons.

"Aha!" Jean turned the hose on Ellie before she could run away. Michael, who had some water in his squirt gun, chased her around the garage. Ellie took refuge behind the trash cans, and Michael ran past her.

"Where'd she go?" Michael shouted when he got back to the stairs. Ellie patiently tiptoed up behind him. "Did she run by here?" he asked.

"No, we haven't seen her," Jean called back. "Be on alert! She could be anywhere."

Laughter and water filled the air. By the time they were finished, everyone was soaked from head to toe. The backyard was filled with puddles and mud when Peter pulled into the driveway. Jean and Ellie picked up bits of balloons as the boys ran through the sprinkler.

"What happened here?" Peter asked.

"Water balloon fight." Jean dumped her balloon scraps into the trash can.

"I miss all the fun." Peter pouted.

"Don't worry. I have plenty more stored upstairs. I'll get you when you're least expecting it," Ellie threatened.

Over dinner of hot dogs and macaroni salad, Ellie recapped her conversation with Mary to her aunt and uncle. "I tried to go through Betty's journal to see if it could help, but nothing."

Jean looked at Peter. He shrugged. "Yeah, flowers sound like a good enough place to start."

"I don't really know anything about her, either," Jean admitted. "I don't even know how you'd go about finding her. There are dozens of them in the circles."

Ellie grimaced as she stabbed a loose noodle. "I didn't even think of that."

Jean and Peter exchanged a quick glance before Jean added, "I'm sure it will work out."

Ellie offered a small smile, but that thought plagued her the rest of the night. She ran through Louie's story again and again, hoping for any clue, anything that would help her identify her Seer.

"Do I just start yelling Betty?" she asked Luna that night.

Her whimsical chuckle filled the air. "Never hurts to be direct."

"I'll make that my backup plan." Ellie sighed and fell back on her bed. "Are we still on for potion making tomorrow?"

"Heck yeah! Is it okay if I flip through your recipes?" Ellie and Luna spoke until the sun went down, and Ellie had to go to bed. As she lay there in the unfinished room, she thought of the water balloon fight—the smiles on everyone's faces, the way her aunt went for the hose. As she drifted off to sleep, a hollow ache settled in her stomach at the memory of goofing off with Louie—bombarding her dad with snowballs and startling her mom while she baked.

# 6
# *Needle*

Ellie slapped on the labels for *The Hut Putt* and *Chatham's Yacht Club*. The filled boxes sat on racks by the back door of the Sugar Shack. "Done," she declared and melted into her seat in the middle of the room. Her secondhand faded T-shirt was damp with sweat down her back and armpits.

*It feels so good to sit.*

Mary held up one last sign in her hand—"Do not Take."

Ellie closed her eyes, took a deep breath in through her nostrils, grabbed the sign, and escorted it to their in-house rack. She slapped the label on it.

"Done now?" She looked over her shoulder.

Mary gave her a thumbs-up. "Done and free! Thanks for staying the extra half hour. We're ahead for the week and will have plenty of time to work on Keswick's order for Tuesday night."

With an exhausted salute, Ellie walked towards the back door. "See you bright and early."

"Bye," Mary called back. "Get some rest."

The Sugar Shack's small flower beds along the building were filled with small, lovely flowers. The sun shone brightly in the sky, and birds chirped happily in the surrounding forest. Ellie took a deep, refreshing breath in and felt her back pop.

"Oh, and I still have to make potions," she groaned as she remembered her plans with Luna. "And I'm already late."

With a flip of her old phone, Ellie called Luna and filled her in on her status.

"Take your time, but show up ready to work. I'll put some iced tea together for you and use my Study Blend."

"Sounds good, see you soon."

*What I wouldn't give for some focus on an apple slice.* Ellie hung up the phone and pulled on her leather jacket. *It always tasted best when Mom made it. She knew the right amount of peanut butter to use.*

Following a shower and a change of clothes, Ellie shoved her backpack loaded with empty, old Tupperware containers into her sidecar and took off up the peninsula to the cozy town at the tip. As she passed the businesses and swerved past tourists, she noticed familiar faces. Jen, from 'Turn of the Page,' offered a wave as she installed window flower boxes in front of the store. Alphonse, the ice cream shop owner, smiled as she waddled on her bike down the slow-moving street. Ellie smiled and shrugged dramatically as she slowly wiggled through traffic.

*It's like being back in Connecticut.* She finally broke free of the crowd and made her way down the side street. *Can't go anywhere without running into someone you know.* The thought brought a smile to her face.

Luna's brick bungalow with the white picket fence overflowed with lush flowers. The pergola threatened to collapse under the weight of morning glories. Ellie shut off the engine and pulled off her helmet to hear the sound of a band in the distance and the buzzing of bees overhead.

"You be chill, and so will I, Mister Bee." As she pulled out her backpack and shoved her helmet into the sidecar, a bark announced Luna and Mitsy's presence.

"Go on. You can say 'hi,'" Luna instructed Misty.

The tiny dog with freshly groomed fur ran through the grass toward the driveway. All that remained of her grand coat was a puff ball at the end of her tail.

"Oh, poor baby! What happened to your fur?" Ellie laughed as she reached out to pet the dog.

"She was getting a little unruly, so I had her groomed. I think it will be more comfortable in the summer, too. Not as hot with a thick jacket of fur around her."

"I get that," Ellie said as she unzipped her leather jacket. The heat she had built up released all at once, like steam. In a well-mastered fashion, Ellie pulled her backpack out of the sidecar and dismounted the bike. The moment she had both feet on the ground, something gentle pressed against her leg.

Mitsy had one paw pressed against Ellie's leg. "You want up?"

Mitsy panted patiently.

"Alright then." Hesitantly, Ellie picked up the tiny dog. It weighed less than a bag of potatoes. Mitsy climbed over Ellie's shoulder and perched there like a bird. As she walked toward the front door, Mitsy gave her a few kisses.

"Oh, yeah? Look who is being a sweety." Luna approvingly scratched Mitsy's back and stepped aside so Ellie could enter the house.

Stacks of notebooks populated the counter in the kitchen just off to the left, accompanied by empty jars, Tupperware containers, and herbs. The mixture of fresh ingredients smelled heavenly. Ellie took a brief moment to bask in it.

"Sorry for the mess. I got kind of excited and just brought everything up from the basement," Luna admitted.

"I'm used to making potions in a pantry, so this is great." Ellie set Mitsy down as she took off her backpack. A small weight found its way onto the top of Ellie's foot the moment her boot came off.

"Mitsy, stop being needy."

Mitsy did not move.

"You're such a baby." Ellie picked up her small friend once again, who melted in her arms. She glanced around and saw that the open living room opposite the kitchen had every bit of furniture pushed against the walls, which created a wide-open space on the hardwood floors. "Are you cleaning?"

"You mentioned having trouble with meditating, so I thought we could do a guided meditation today to help you get right. No point in trying to make potions when your flow is skewed."

"Not a bad idea," Ellie admitted with raised eyebrows. "I don't want to waste your time with all that, though. I can give it a shot—"

"Oh, hush." The bracelets jingled their happy tune as Luna waved off the notion. "Helping a friend is never a waste of time. I enjoy it." Luna pulled the large glass pitcher of iced tea out of the fridge. "So, this is my own little concoction. I hope you like it; we have lemon balm and ginseng to help with focus, and an Earl gray blend I got from the co-op."

Ellie made a mental note before she set Mitsy down and stepped into the kitchen. Setting down the pup triggered a series of whimpers and paws against Ellie's leg.

"Go meditate, Mits." Luna ordered, and Mitsy let out a sneeze of disapproval before she retreated to her dog bed, a look of utter dejection on her face. Luna passed a tall glass of iced tea to Ellie and poured her own. "You said you did guided meditation before, right?"

"Yeah, my Dad did that with my mom and me when I was younger."

"Wonderful, so this will probably be a breeze for you." Luna took a big gulp of the tea. "You remember when we first met, I told you I could see our connections to The Void?"

"Yes." Ellie followed and took a sip.

"Well." Luna leaned over like she was revealing a big secret. "I can see more than that. I can see how it flows through your body, and well… with your permission, I'd like to fix your flow."

"Fix my flow?" Ellie's forehead wrinkled with uncertainty.

Luna turned to the countertops behind them, covered with their potion supplies. From the stack of books, she pulled out a leather-looking brown one. "You know how when you're stressed out, your shoulders become all tense and you get knots in your back?"

"Yeah."

"That can obstruct your flow." Excited, Luna scrunched up her hands like she was crumpling paper. "Of course, since what happened with Louie, your flow has been massively slowed." She took a pause and added, "I get that. It's completely understandable. You're emotionally dysregulated, so it's just going to go and be everywhere."

The heat rose in Ellie's cheeks as Luna brought up Louie. *I didn't realize it was so obvious.*

"Anybody would be," Luna reassured her. "That's why sitting with your feelings, processing, and talking about it all will help."

Ellie nodded, less enthusiastically this time.

"But there's more," Luna continued. "Since the day I met you, I could see this block."

Her hands came together like two doors slowly shutting.

"I think I know what it is. There's this thing at the base of your neck that's acting sort of like a choke point, a funnel."

Luna demonstrated this with two fingers drawn close together.

"It reminded me of this thing I read about once, so I had to find the book again."

Luna pushed the brown book towards the center of the counter space and turned it so Ellie could read the title. *Practice of the Old for the New.* Though it was a modern print, the cover was designed to make it look old with air-brushed edges. Luna opened to a page she marked with a yellow sticky note.

### *Channel Needle*

"Apparently," Luna pointed to the first line of underlined text, "they were used back around the time of the Salem Witch Trials to suppress someone's connection with the Void…"

"Why?" Ellie interrupted.

"For those who committed a heinous act, like murder, it was a form of punishment," Luna said tenderly. "It was also used to keep children from putting their powers on display and outing the true magical community."

"Wait, what?" Ellie snatched the book and pulled it close.

## Channel Needle

A Channel Needle, or Sliver, is placed under the first layer of skin for easy insertion and removal. It is advised to place the needle at a chakra point. If done properly, only a minor scar may form, and it can go unnoticed by the wearer for years. The needle may

stay under the skin indefinitely without fear of rotting
or infection. It may be used to limit the powers of a
witch or wizard by limiting the amount of Void
Essence that can be carried through the body.

Ellie's facial expression tightened as she continued.

This practice is common during times of crisis
within the magical world, such as the Witch Trials. It
has also been implemented on unruly children, or as
a form of punishment for witches and wizards who
have committed unforgivable acts, up to and
including murder. As the justice system has been
developed and the world of mental health has been
explored, the need to use the Channel Needle as a
form of punishment has been severely limited.
While this has been dubbed an archaic practice,
there can still be practical use and applications
today...

Ellie's lips parted to protest.

"Desperate times call for desperate measures," Luna added. "Not
that I am condoning it, especially today. But back then…"

Ellie observed a small drawing accompanying the text. It was the
shape of a grain of rice with sharpened edges. The text below said
'Drawing is larger than the actual object.'

Ellie's eyebrows pulled together as she reread the passage out loud.
"A Channel Needle, or Sliver, is placed under the first layer of skin for
easy insertion and removal. It is advised to place the needle at a chakra
point. If done properly, only a minor scar may form, and it can go
unnoticed by the wearer for years."

"Ellie?"

She looked up at Luna. "What?"

Luna studied Ellie's face, and her expression softened. "This was a
lot to throw at you. I'm sorry. This wasn't the right time."

"No, no. This… when is there a right time for this?" Ellie scoffed. "And the sooner it's out of me, the better. I just… *who* could have done this? *Why* would they do this?"

Ellie reached back to feel along the base of her neck. Carefully, tediously, she inspected the feel of her skin under her fingertips. Everything felt flat, even, defined. When her fingers did find a bump off-center, her eyes shot open.

"Oh crap!" She gasped and froze in place. "I think I found it."

Luna calmly walked around the counter and inspected where Ellie's finger was. "That's a mole."

A sigh of relief escaped Ellie's lips. "You said you saw it?"

"I said it looked like there was a choke point, yes."

"Well, can you take a look?"

Luna instructed Ellie to hold on to her mass of curly hair, then had her bend down to be at Luna's height. "Thank you." Luna's fingers gently poked around the base of Ellie's neck. During the inspection, Ellie busied herself with studying a fraying edge of the carpet.

*I hope she finds it. I hope she finds it…*

"There's a very small scar right here," Luna said and gently pressed above the bump where Ellie's spine met her neck. Ellie's free hand shot back to get a feel. "Wait." Luna pushed her hand away. "I said there's a scar, not that I found it. Do you mind if I poke around?"

"Be my guest." Ellie gritted her teeth and suppressed the urge to yell, 'Tear it out!'

A few pokes and clumsy rubs later, Luna announced, "I found it!"

Luna led Ellie's fingers back to the small patch of skin where, with just enough pressure, Ellie could feel a tiny foreign object under her skin.

"It's real." Her chest tightened as a list of suspects ran through her mind. At the front of the list, more prominent than anyone else, stood Mee-Maw.

*She wanted to control everything. Every relationship, Louie, my clothes, my family. Why wouldn't she want to control my powers as well?*

"I have a cousin," Luna said, breaking the silence. "She's a nurse down in Florida. If you can wait until Thanksgiving, she could…"

"No. Get it out of me." The words erupted from Ellie's lips.

"I've never done anything like this before," Luna admitted. "I've pierced some girlfriends' ears when we were kids, but nothing like this."

"I don't care, as long as you don't stab me in the neck and paralyze me. It's just a sliver, right?" Ellie tried to rationalize it. "Cut the end and squeeze it out."

Luna didn't say anything.

"If you don't do it, I'll end up doing it myself when I get home," Ellie informed her. "I just know you'll be more careful than me, so please. Before I lose my nerve."

Luna was still and silent for a few moments. "Fine. Let's go to the bathroom. The lighting's better in there."

"Yes!" Ellie hopped up and scurried off to the bathroom. A dedicated finger rested on the spot where the needle resided beneath her skin, while her other hand held her hair on top of her head.

Luna appeared with a First-Aid kit in hand.

"I really hope we won't need that." Ellie chuckled nervously.

"Well, we'll definitely need a band-aid," Luna said as she arranged her items on the edge of the sink——a band-aid, a pair of tweezers, some alcohol wipes, and an Exacto knife.

The small bathroom could barely fit both of them. A full-size bathtub ran along the far wall, with a toilet immediately beside it, and a wall-mounted sink beside that. Four bright, circular lightbulbs sat above the medicine cabinet.

Luna closed the drain of the sink and laid a towel over the top of it. "Just in case it falls off," she explained.

Ellie stole a hair tie from the medicine cabinet's knob and placed her hair on top of her head in a funny bun. Fly-away curls were pinned back with bobby pins.

"Before we begin," the pale-faced Luna began, "I am not a medical professional…"

"Don't worry about it," Ellie reassured her.

Ellie gathered up the edges of the towel on the sink and clenched them in her fists as Luna grabbed the alcohol swab and Exacto knife from the sink. With her head bent forward, Ellie felt the cool, wet swab over her skin.

She exhaled slowly.

Luna then pressed against one end of the silver. Ellie felt a sharp blade drag across her skin. It was short, quick, and burned horribly. She tried to suppress a whimper.

Luna swapped the blade for tweezers. Her fingers squeezed hard at the sensitive skin on the back of Ellie's neck. A warm trail of blood trickled down toward her spine.

*Don't think about it. Just head down, focus. Head down, focus. Dandelion. Dandelion. Dandelion!*

"Come on," Luna grumbled as her hands fidgeted with the object. After a long minute, she excitedly called out, "I got it!"

In the mirror, Ellie saw Luna's look of pride as she held the tweezers up towards the light. The bright lights of the bathroom didn't seem so bright, though, as a tingling sensation spread throughout her body. Suddenly, her head felt light, and her knees wobbled.

# 7
# *Echoes*

llie," Luna's curly-haired silhouette shouted. "Ellie. Damn, I almost called 911." Luna turned the cool cloth over on Ellie's forehead.

The world felt fuzzy, like the static on an old television. That sensation stretched from head to toe. Cautiously, Ellie sat up, and Luna directed her to lean against the bathroom wall. Ellie sucked air between her teeth and pulled her head away from the hard surface. A large bump had formed beneath the skin.

Luna winced apologetically. "Yeah, sorry, you were falling toward the mirror. I guess I panicked when I pulled you back."

"I'll take a wall over glass any day." Ellie inspected the lump on her head.

"How are you feeling?" Luna refreshed the cloth with cool water from the tap.

"Fuzzy. Fuzzy and tingly." The discomfort reverberated from the egg on her head through her sinuses and face.

"That makes a lot of sense. The moment we removed that sliver, it was like the levee broke. I saw the essence just rush through you."

"Levee broke." Ellie gently nodded. "Yeah, hits the nail on the head."

The influx of Void essence lingered on her nerve endings. The last time she felt anything similar to this was when Louie helped her with potions and they tiptoed along the peripherals of the Void.

*"The Void takes many things… including you."* His gruff voice echoed through her hazy mind.

After a careful inspection of her bewildering appendage, Ellie tried to relax and gain her bearings. Luna brought her a glass of water.

"I've spent a good few late nights on this floor with a friend and a glass of water," Luna mused. "Lots of tears and broken hearts."

"You're too nice to be a heartbreaker." Ellie took the wet washcloth and dabbed her cheeks. With each dab, it leached the overzealous Void essence. Eagerly, Ellie pulled at her collar and dabbed around the base of her neck.

"Nice or not, love is love. When it's not right, it's just not right." Luna leaned her head against the door frame. "I forget, you said you've never been in love, right?"

Ellie's lips parted, and she let out a sigh. "I don't know."

"When you know, it's just so…" Luna rolled her eyes and smiled whimsically. "I've been through it all: dating, marriage, divorce, rebounds, and hookups. Good love, bad love, and all in between."

"Are you in love now?"

"Oh yes, with a fisherman named Samuel. He comes back once every few weeks for maybe a few days before he's back out there. I miss him like crazy when he's gone, but when he's back…" A playful smile crossed her lips. "He is all mine."

Ellie held out the cool washcloth. "You need this?"

"Oh, stop." Luna giggled and covered her face with her hands.

"I think you need it more than I do."

"You're too much," Luna added with a chuckle. "Samuel may or may not be my soulmate, but I *can* say he's the love of my life."

Ellie closed her eyes and nodded as she continued to dab her neck. "I like that. I think my parents have used that term before."

"You miss them?"

The urge to say 'no' rushed forward, but she stopped it before it could leave her lips. "Yeah, sometimes." She chuckled and turned to look at Luna. "My Mom used to put a potion—it was really more like a paste—on a slice of apple for me... I really missed that earlier today."

Luna softly smiled.

Ellie shifted. "Even though she has... *they* have," she corrected herself, "betrayed me... I just can't stop this urge to want to talk to them, to have them be a part of my life. I want to... I genuinely want to be a good daughter, to be connected with them, but I just..." Ellie dropped her hands into her lap.

"You're hurt," Luna said softly. "It's okay to need space from some more than others. Take your time."

With a deep breath in, Ellie looked up to the wall across from her, where a metal sculpture perched above the toilet—sea grass waving in the wind on the surf. "You gonna marry him?"

"Oh, hell no," Luna brayed. "Don't get me wrong. Marriage is beautiful. I just don't think it's necessary in all cases. Each love is unique and different. Why do we need a legally binding contract to show it's valid in others' eyes?"

Though her head and body ached, those words hit Ellie differently. Dropping the wet towel into her lap, she mimicked an explosion with her hands.

"What?"

"Each love is unique and different," Ellie quoted Luna. "Then how can I sit here and compare it to yours and Sh-S-Sam. How can I compare it to my parents? Mary and Ned? Jean and Peter? I can't."

Luna gently shook her head. "That's why you need your own definitions."

Ellie's eyes wandered over the designs on the linoleum floor as she pulled at a loose string on the wet towel. *It all keeps coming back to my own definitions.*

"Before I forget." Luna pulled herself from the floor and exited the bathroom doorway. When she returned, she handed Ellie a shallow Tupperware container with a pink lid. Inside, the sliver rattled in its plastic container. "I wasn't sure if you'd want to keep it... burn it..."

Ellie took the container and scrutinized the pristine object. "Why doesn't it look waterlogged?"

"My best guess is the spell sort of preserved it." Luna took a seat on the edge of the tub. "Back in the day, they didn't have antibiotics or surgical steel. A wooden sliver would have caused an infection and could potentially kill the child."

"Lucky kid," Ellie grumbled. "I just don't understand why someone would have done this. I wasn't a bratty kid. I didn't go out and party with the locals. Nothing."

"In times of horrific tragedies, like massacres, terrorist attacks... survivors tend to look for rhyme or reason. For the senseless violence. The hope... maybe it will bring them some degree of peace, some sort of sense of control so they can hone in and predict it. I guess what I'm trying to say is, you may never get those answers. You may never be able to make sense of what, why, or who. At the end of the day, you need to process this betrayal and find your own peace, so it doesn't consume you."

With a twitching nose, Ellie shook the container violently.

"Or you could do that." Luna chuckled and helped Ellie to her feet. "Beat it with a hammer, burn it. Whatever you'd like."

Walking back out into the kitchen and living room area, Ellie shoved the container into the depths of her backpack.

"I understand if you don't have it in you, but would you like to give meditation a try? It could help all of..." Luna gestured to Ellie. "This calm down."

"Worth a shot." Ellie sauntered into the living room. "Don't let me forget to get a lock and key for that thing. Going to chuck it in the ocean attached to a brick."

With her legs pulled in, Ellie straightened her back and assumed her meditative seat. With a lick of her lips, she let out a sigh.

"I know you said you did this as a child, but be open-minded, as I may do things a bit differently than your dad." Luna stood near the kitchen.

"Alright," Ellie agreed.

"Mits, go meditate." Luna dismissed the non-fluffy pup once again. With her guidance, Ellie closed her eyes, relaxed her shoulders, and then her jaw. "I want you to loosen up, so first, some head rolls."

Ellie rolled her head to the right. The muscle from her shoulder to her ear was as tense as a tugboat's rope. "Alright, alright." She grunted. From left to right, back and forth, Ellie followed Luna's guidance.

"Your shoulders are already dropping," Luna commented before she added, "loosen your jaw and bring awareness to your forehead."

*What does that even mean?* Ellie tried wiggling her jaw.

"Good, but relax your forehead. You're all wrinkly."

Ellie chuckled. "Ah, I get it now." With a wiggle of her eyebrows, Ellie relaxed her facial muscles.

"Ready?" Luna's voice softened.

"Yes."

"A deep breath in… and out… and in… and out…" Luna guided, and Ellie followed. Soon, all she could focus on was Luna's voice and her own breath. "Good. Now, I want you to picture your happy place."

"My happy place?" Ellie countered.

*That's a laugh.*

"Focus," Luna reminded her.

"Sorry." After one more shoulder roll, she took a deep breath and tried to picture her happy place.

*What would it even have? Trees?*

Trees from the orchard swayed in her mind.

*No. Flowers?*

She couldn't even bring that image forth.

*Water?*

Waves crashed against the solid, wet sand before her. A magnificent, other-worldly, bright-red sunset fading into a deep purple welcomed her.

*I made it.*

This beach wasn't one she had visited. It was something new that warmed her soul.

"Do you see it?" Luna's voice whispered into Ellie's mind.

"Yes."

"Good. Now, I want you to immerse yourself in the moment." Long pauses persisted between each question. "Is there a breeze? Does it carry a scent on it?"

Ellie took a slow, deep breath in. The salty smell of the ocean filled her nostrils. She could almost feel the fine-grained, wet sand beneath her. Scattered around her, all along the beach, was an abundance of shells.

"What do you hear?" Luna's voice was distant now.

Ellie listened closely to the rhythm of the waves as they tumbled in and broke up against the ground. For a brief moment, the waves fell silent as they mingled with the wet sand and the shells, then retreated back into the ocean.

"*Sweet Ellie*," A familiar voice filled the air. Ellie looked around frantically.

"Louie?" she called out.

Over each shoulder, she saw nothing but dunes and grass, but when she turned back to face the waves, she spotted a paw print and one large, opposite handprint in the sand facing her.

Her lips parted, and Ellie let out a quivering breath. She reached out with both hands to scoop up the prints, but as soon as her hands hit the damp sand, the waves washed it away.

"No," she whimpered and dug at the ground.

"*I love you.*" The whisper came from over her shoulder.

She turned to look but stopped herself just before she could. In her peripheral vision, a tall fuzzy object stood above her.

"I miss you so much," she whispered.

"*I'm always here.*"

Ellie looked back to the sunset. It almost felt like he was there, just behind her.

After all the late nights adding to her mental list of things to tell him, she found herself without a single item coming to her lips. She wanted to sit in the silence with him and enjoy his presence.

"Come back to your breath." Luna's voice passed by like a whisper in the wind. "Focus."

*No, not yet.* Ellie's chest tightened.

"What do you feel?" Luna whispered.

*The wet sand.*

"What do you taste?"

*Taste? What a weirdo. Oh, wait… coffee breath.*

"Return to your breath."

With a deep breath in, Ellie's chest quivered.

"*Sweet Ellie.*" Heat rolled up her back. His voice was crisp and clear. "*Don't cry. I'm here.*"

High up overhead, in the portion of the sky still dark from the night, she saw one star that shimmered brighter than all the rest.

*It's me and you, and me with E, just the two of us, the world will see.*

"Hold on to your happy place and how you feel in this moment." Luna's voice barely broke through. "Wiggle your toes."

"*I'll love you forever,*" Ellie promised as her toes curled.

"Wiggle your fingers." The waves faded away as Ellie wiggled her fingers. "Now open your eyes."

She was back on the living room floor of the bungalow, but the feel of wet sand beneath her feet echoed on her nerves.

"I could hear him, Luna," Ellie whispered. "It was like he was here."

Luna took a seat in front of her friend. Her well-manicured hands took hold of Ellie's.

"I miss him so much," Ellie admitted softly.

"I know you do." Luna comfortingly stroked the back of Ellie's hand. "You will get through this, I promise."

As Ellie collected her things, Luna shoved some supplies from potion making into Ellie's backpack.

"When you're ready to get back to it, we can try again."

"Thanks," Ellie replied. When Luna offered her the book containing information on the Channel Needle, she dismissed it. "I think I need some time before I revisit that."

"Understandable." Luna stood in the doorway with Mitsy in her arms. They waved Ellie goodbye as she pulled out of the driveway and headed back to Truro.

*"Practical use and applications today,"* Ellie said sarcastically as she placed her backpack on her dining room table. "Load of crap."

She unloaded the contents of her hiking backpack onto the table. Stocks of dried lavender hit the table with enough force for the buds to spread out everywhere.

"Come on." She frowned and gathered up the bits. As she did, from the opening of the backpack, the Tupperware container rolled out. "This isn't about you," Ellie grumbled and shoved it back inside.

The hairs on the back of her neck stood on end. She gave it a quick rub to discharge the sensation and managed to rip off her band-aid.

"Ugh." She rolled it into a ball between her fingers.

Over the next hour, she took a shower, threw clothes into the washer, and turned on the television. Books, seashells, news articles, and television shows—nothing held her attention. Irritated, she dropped onto the floor behind the couch and stared at the ceiling. Outside, thunder rumbled in the distance.

*"Sweet Ellie, don't cry. I'm here."* Louie's voice echoed through her thoughts as she lay on the unfinished floor of her apartment. The trickle of rain on the window picked up quickly as the storm rolled in.

"How could it feel so real?" Ellie stared out into the darkening sky. With a dark chuckle, she turned the seashell over in her hand. "What I wouldn't give…"

The memory of Louie on the beach outside that Keswick woman's house plagued her mind. Against the starlit sky, he cheered on his brethren as it rushed off along the cosmos.

"He looked so handsome," she admitted as fury boiled up from within. "Of all the things!?" She shouted at herself and hit the floor with the side of her fist. "After years of loyalty, that's it? His looks? What's wrong with you?"

Disgusted with herself, she stood up and ran her hand through her hair. The dark sky lit up with the flash of lightning.

The red-lidded Tupperware container, which imprisoned the wooden needle, sat on the small dining room table, mocking her. As she walked back toward the kitchen, she knocked the Tupperware onto the floor and stuck her tongue out at it.

*"Practical use and applications today,"* she repeated. "You don't scare me."

Ellie walked toward the refrigerator and opened the door. The contents inside hadn't changed since the last time she checked not more than half an hour ago. A container of mac'n cheese sat close to the back.

*I'm not hungry. Why did I open the fridge?* She shut the door. The few condiments in glass jars clinked against the railings inside.

"I'm not scared. You're just a piece of wood!" Her eyes turned toward the dining room area. That needle was somewhere in there, probably hiding under the table like a coward. "And you have no control over me anymore."

Thunder rumbled.

*Every direction I turn, it's like someone else is making my choices for me!* She hurried off toward her room, where clothes lay out on the floor.

"I am choosing to pick these up," she shouted as she grabbed her flour-coated t-shirt and threw it toward the corner. "My choice! Not Mom's, not Mee-maw's. Mine!"

Ellie threw a dirty pair of pants in the same direction as she furiously cleaned.

"I could choose to go vegetarian." Lightning lit up the dining room as she threatened the world.

The well-made bed? She tore the blankets from it.

The top of her dresser, where she stacked library books, pens, and change? They were thrown to the floor.

Mess? Clean.

Clean? Mess.

Ellie left her apartment in absolute chaos by the time she tired herself out.

"Why?" She cried out on her knees in the living room. Hot tears streamed down her cheeks as she stared hideously at the small, red-lidded Tupperware container. It remained untouched in the apartment decorated by mayhem.

Speechless and powerless, Ellie settled for the one sound, which rushed like a bull to her open lips. The dark world outside lit up with a barrage of quick flashing lights as Ellie strained her vocal cords. Lights flickered, and the raw power of the storm reverberated through her being accompanied by the rush of the Void's essence. It poured into her like ice water.

The world and lightning danced like a puppet at her fingertips. Everyone on the island would feel the hurt that infected her heart.

When the air emptied from her lungs, the sudden rush of lightheadedness sent her face down into the floorboards.

# 8
# Robbins Pond

The smell of wood and dust welcomed Ellie from her sleep. Before her was the empty, unfinished wooden floor. "What the?"

The stove clock was dark.

"Great. Power's out."

Her flip-phone lit up—3:30 a.m. No texts. No missed calls. Nothing to say she shouldn't show up to work.

"Guess I'm going in."

After getting dressed and brushing her hair, Ellie hurried out the door. The road leading down to The Sugar Shack was speckled with dead branches, hunks of bark, and other debris. The sight of the untouched Sugar Shack in her headlights brought a smile to her face. *Thank the Void.* Pulling into her normal parking space, Ellie pulled the cover over the bike and walked around to the back. Mary's car was nowhere in sight. A large tree branch fell in the driveway directly where Mary would have parked.

"The storm was that powerful out here?" Echoes of her rage-filled screams and the lightning-filled sky ran through her mind. Cautiously, she reached back and touched the small scab on the back of her neck.

Luna's explanation of the channel needle came to her mind. *"It's like a choke point…"*

Ellie shivered. "Nope. Not thinking about that." She threw her weight into the branch and dragged it into the tree line.

When Mary's path up the driveway was clear, Ellie curled up on the porch, tucked her knees into her chest, and rested her head on her forearms. The skies were calm. Electricity dissipated from the air overnight and there was only the smell of the damp forest around her.

She rubbed the back of her forearm as she thought of the tingle of the Void mixed with the thrilling heat of the electricity. "Is it weird that I miss it?"

It wasn't long before the headlights of Mary's car rolled up the rocky driveway.

"One heck of a storm last night!" Mary called out as she opened her car door and killed the engine. "I don't think I've ever seen lightning like that. It was here in a moment, then bam! Gone all at once."

"Yeah, it was… intense," Ellie admitted.

The desire to share her experience and suspicions of her influence on the storm quickly retreated into the safety of her heart. "Hope you and Ned were safe."

"Oh yeah, takes more than some lightning to stop these old birds." She chuckled and walked up to the back door, keys jingling in her hand. Ellie stood up and opened her cellphone to provide Mary with some light. "Thanks. Want to get the generator started for us? It's in the shed."

"Yeah, I can do that." The shed was a disaster zone. The first thing in the way was the gas-powered push mower. It easily rolled out, and Ellie set it aside. Shovels, rakes, and an old leaf blower followed shortly after. Mary in the back of her head ranting and raving about her wonderful grandson mowing, shoveling, and landscaping the Sugar Shack.

"Where's that wonderful grandson of yours, today?" Ellie grunted as she pulled the ripcord. "Can't mow the lawn to save his life." It put up more of a fight than she anticipated. Ellie placed one foot on the metal bars surrounding it, grabbed the lever with both hands, and pulled with all her might. "Probably cozy in bed."

It roared to life.

"And not needed." She proudly wiped her hands off on one another before she neatly put back the unneeded equipment.

Back in the Sugar Shack, Mary handed Ellie her morning latte. "I was getting worried. What took you so long?"

"I reorganized the shed. It was like an old cartoon. I was expecting a bowling ball to fall on my head."

Mary chuckled. "Of course you did. How did I get along without you?"

Heat rose in her cheeks at the sweet compliment. She tried to play it off with business. "We have to prep for the ceremony, right?"

By nine, power was restored to the Cape. Ellie already had hundreds of hot dog buns baked and cooling. A few dozen hamburger buns were still baking, while the last large batch worked in the stand mixer, and Ellie caught up on dishes. Her head bobbed to the familiar country tune, even though her mind was elsewhere.

*"Sweet Ellie, don't cry. I'm here."*

For a moment, she closed her eyes and tried to feel the wet sand beneath her feet and the smell of the ocean air in her nose.

*"I'll love you forever."*

Louie's voice from her guided meditation felt so close, even in her memory.

*"Ellie… Ellie."*

"Ellie?"

*Crap!* Ellie jumped and turned to see Mary at her side, pulling the steamy, clean dishes toward her.

Mary brayed. Her hand reached for Ellie's arm and gave an apologetic squeeze. "I didn't mean to scare you."

On Mary's left hand sat her wedding rings. A beautiful, simple, pear-shaped diamond paired with a plain wedding band. Ellie must have seen them a dozen times before, but now the shimmering light caught them just so. A small smile pulled at her lips as a wonderful, creative idea crossed her mind.

"I pulled the buns out for you; they're cooling."

"Thanks," Ellie caught her breath and smiled at Mary. The plump old woman regained her composure and walked back to the table as Ellie muttered to herself, "Still got it."

By the end of the day, the normal aches and weariness following a busy day were replaced by inspiration. As soon as she got in the door of her apartment, she ran to her room and grabbed her oval shell from the nightstand. Eagerly, she ushered her uncle Peter to the garage.

"Just a little hole, that's all I need," she explained.

"I've never drilled a shell before." Peter inspected it awkwardly. "I'm worried I might break it."

"You?" Ellie pulled him by the hand to the garage. "Mr. Handyman? Come on."

"Okay, okay." He caved with a shy smile and took his place by the workbench. "Help me out. Grab a big Tupperware container and fill it three-quarters of the way with water."

Ellie raised a playful eyebrow. "And where might I find that?"

"Cupboard, right side of the oven, bottom shelf," Peter directed her as he started to set up his drill bit.

"You got it." She bounced away, singing, "Just me and you…" She slid open the door and hopped into the kitchen. "And me and E."

Brody stood at the fridge.

*Suspicious.*

"Hey, Brod. What are you up to?"

"Nuffin'." His wide eyes, which skipped from her to the inside of the fridge, said otherwise.

"Are you sneaking a snack?"

Brody's smile curled into a wicked grin as he pulled out a cheese stick.

*Called it.*

"You enjoy that cheese stick, buddy."

Brody giggled and ran off into the adjoining living room with his bounty. Ellie returned to her task. Just as Uncle Peter said, in the cabinet on the right-hand side of the oven, bottom shelf, there was a deep, square-shaped Tupperware container. Ellie filled it three-quarters of the way with water before she hurried back out to the garage.

By the time she returned, her aunt Jean's car was in the driveway, and Jean was standing with Peter. "What's going on?" she asked skeptically, "and why do you have my Tupperware?"

"Well, it's an experiment," Peter said, taking the Tupperware from Ellie's hands with a quick "Thank you. I've read about it but never tried it." He submerged Ellie's precious shell into the water and held it against the plastic bottom.

"You aren't going to drill a hole through my Tupperware, are you?" Jean interrupted.

"Absolutely not." Peter covertly gestured to a box filled with scrap pieces of wood.

Ellie picked up on the gesture and hurried over to grab a small piece.

"This." He held up the piece of wood Ellie snuck into his hand. "We will drill against it."

"Mhm." Jean crossed her arms, not convinced.

Peter leaned over the container and adjusted the drill. "The idea here is that the water keeps the shell from getting too warm, creating too much stress, and cracking."

As the drill whined, he said, "As an added benefit, the water will catch all the dirt."

Jean turned to Ellie. "And this was your idea?"

"Well, my request."

"Demand," Peter corrected her.

Ellie swayed from side to side as she told her aunt, "I was at Luna's house."

"She dragged me out here," Peter added in the background.

"We, uh-" she reached towards the back of her neck. Her fingertips touched the scab. "We did this guided meditation. She had me visit my 'happy place', which was kind of like the beach Louie and I hung out at on our first day. Well, in real life, he gave me this shell that day and I just—"

"Threatened my life," Peter chimed in.

"That's a lie," Ellie said, pointing at him. "I heard Louie during my meditation… I haven't felt that close to him in so long. So, I thought…"

The smile on her aunt's lips grew into a broad, proud expression. Jean looked toward her husband, who excitedly put down the drill and put his arms in the air.

"Did it! And not a single crack," Peter announced to the garage.

"I'm proud of you, babe. Best driller I've ever seen." Jean snuck a quick wink to Ellie.

"That's right, that's right." Peter pulled out the seashell and handed it to Ellie.

"And…" she said, taking it. "Best uncle."

Peter turned to Jean. "You hear that?"

"I did."

"Best uncle," he repeated with a grin.

"What are you going to do with it, Ellie?" Jean hid her face in her hands as she tried to hide her chuckles. Peter continued behind them about being the 'best uncle'.

"Make it into a necklace." Ellie tested it out at different lengths.

"Do you have a chain for it?" Jean asked.

"No."

"I have some fishing line," Peter called from the depths of the garage before he reappeared with the spool of thin line.

Ellie took it.

"Now, if you'll excuse me, I have a necklace and dinner to make," she informed her aunt and uncle as she began to walk out of the garage.

"We're having pork chops if you want to join," Jean called after her.

"No thanks," Ellie called from around the corner as she started to ascend her stairs. *Tonight is a Louie favorite; chicken parmesan.*

With the tomato sauce and cheese-covered chicken baking in the oven, Ellie chopped vegetables for a salad while she recounted her adventure to her father over the phone.

"It was just really nice to feel like he was close again. It was like I could actually hear him."

"That's fantastic, Ellie," Elijah muttered.

"What's wrong?"

"Worries for a parent to have, not a child." He brushed it off. "But I want to circle back. Did I hear you right? You said Luna pulled something out of your neck?"

"Oh, right. Can't believe I glossed over that." She chuckled. "So there was this thing in my neck, right? Some sort of Void blocker. Luna can see how the Void flows through us—"

"It doesn't *flow* through us, Ellie," Elijah corrected. "We channel the essence of it. If it flowed through us, the pure strength would destroy us. She sees the essence."

"Yes, the essence." Ellie rolled her eyes but continued. "Anyway, this blocker was under my skin, and it was limiting the flow of that essence."

There was not a peep from the other end of the phone.

"Hello?"

"Yes, sorry, I'm here. I-I'm just… speechless."

With a sigh of relief, she continued. "It was made of wood. I guess it was some sort of spell from the Salem Witch Trial days, before we had stainless steel. That's what Luna said, at least. They used it to punish murderers—or to keep gifted kids from showing off and getting killed. She had this book about it—*Practice of the Old for the New* Aunt Jean says there is an awesome library here. I'm gonna see if they have a copy of it." She barely paused for breath. "Oh! There's also a class I want to check out—Dispelling Myths. And another one taught by someone named M. Becker. Any chance we're related?"

"Becker?" Elijah cleared his throat. "Oh, um… perhaps? Any other information you can share?"

"No, not yet. I might sit in on the class. It's not for another week. I probably won't learn anything new—Mom covered all this stuff so thoroughly—"

In the background, Kimberly muttered something that sounded suspiciously like "ungrateful."

Elijah ignored her.

"Make me look like a bad parent." Kimberly ended her rant.

Ellie pursed her lips and shook her head. *Cares more about appearance than actually being a parent.*

"My apologies, Ellie—" A sharp knock hit against the door and pulled Ellie's attention.

"Hey Dad, someone is at the door. I gotta go."

"Oh, uh, yeah, yeah, honey. I love you, stay safe."

"Love you too." The line went dead, and Ellie headed around the false wall into the dining room. Through the double doors stood Jean. Ellie waved her in.

"Oh, yummy." Jean sniffed the air. "What are you cooking?"

"Chicken parm, one of Louie's favorites." Ellie returned to chopping the salad. Jean followed her in and stole a chunk of carrot.

"Do you wanna join me, carrot thief?" Ellie chuckled.

"Thanks, but I have dinner on the stove." Jean gestured back toward her house. "I won't be too long, just wanted to give you something."

From her side, Jean pulled out an old, matte-gray, thin cardboard box. "As you know, Peter and I ran off together when I was a teenager."

"Right." Ellie nodded.

Jean shifted her weight. "What you don't know is that a part of me genuinely considered staying and marrying that Canadian boy."

"Oh?" Ellie set down the paring knife.

Jean smirked, but her eyes were distant. "I was prepared to marry him so I could keep Kimmy in my life."

"Oh." Ellie looked away sheepishly.

Jean shook off the feeling. "What is important, that night I left, I met Peter by Robbins Pond and he proposed."

Ellie's smile returned, but it was now twice its usual size.

"He said, 'I can't promise or provide the same things he can. I guarantee your mother will never like me.'"

Ellie chuckled.

"'What I can promise you is love, devotion, and protection.' Back in those days, we didn't have much. I never asked how he got it, but—" Jean held out her hand to show Ellie her engagement ring.

The small diamond was held in place by exposed tongs. Out of the center, decorative bends in the metal gave it an artistic, delicate feel. Years of wear scuffed the sides.

Ellie admired it. "That's beautiful."

"Thank you. Originally, that diamond was on a long silver chain. We got it set into a ring when we got married." Jean took a moment to admire it on her hand. "I've held onto the chain for all these years. I never knew why, but now I do." Jean slid the box across the countertop to Ellie. "It would look a lot better than that cheap fishing line."

"I-I can't." Ellie fumbled with the box and pushed it back toward her aunt.

"You certainly can. It's been collecting dust on my shelf for years." Jean held out her palm face up to Ellie. "Now give me your shell; I won't hear another word about it."

Ellie passed the fishing line necklace over to her aunt just as the timer beeped. While Ellie pulled her dinner from the oven, Jean replaced the fishing line with the long silver chain.

"Perfect." Jean mused as she rubbed her thumb over the soft ridges of the shell. She held it up to Ellie. "May I?"

Ellie threw off her oven mitts and walked over to her aunt with her hair held on top of her head. Jean cautiously helped Ellie adorn the necklace. "Oh, what did you do to your neck?"

Ellie dropped her hair, ignoring the question.

"Oh wow." She chuckled as the shell dangled just above the bottom of her rib cage.

"He wanted to make sure I could hide it, if I wanted to." Jean rolled her eyes. "Thought I would be ashamed of him or something."

Ellie adjusted her hair so it wasn't caught by the chain. She opened her shirt and let the shell drop down into the depths. "There. Safe and sound."

Jean admired the bit of chain on Ellie's neck that she could see. Her eyes shimmered and threatened a tear.

"Are—" Before Ellie could get more than a syllable out, her aunt pulled her into a tight embrace. Jean shuddered in Ellie's arms, then quickly turned away and made for the door. "Don't forget, you're picking up Gracey tomorrow!"

Half dazed, Ellie returned, "Three, right?"

"Three!" Jean confirmed before she slipped out the door with a quick wipe to her face.

As soon as the door shut, Ellie chuckled to herself and returned to chopping vegetables. "And that's what happens when one cheeseball marries another."

Ellie ate her dinner out on the steps. The sun had set, and a blanket of stars, interrupted by the occasional cloud, kept her company. She studied the sky between bites like she did most nights.

*Dad was acting so weird,* she thought to herself as she spiraled spaghetti onto her fork. *He would normally ask a million questions. Someone cut me and shoved something under my skin! Shouldn't he be mad? I'm mad.*

Ellie grimaced and shoved spaghetti into her mouth.

*What if he knew?* The little gremlin in the back of her mind chimed in.

*He wouldn't.* Ellie's cheeks grew hot at the accusation.

"He did lie about… everything." The spaghetti in her mouth lost all flavor.

Ellie's hands sank toward the plate as her heart thumped in her chest. With her appetite lost, she set the plate aside and glanced up at the sky. The stars twinkled out of reach.

"You'd bite their head off," she said with a chuckle, but it quickly faded to a frown.

"Ugh, what am I even doing?" Her head sank once again with the weight of doubt. "Louie's probably not even out there."

# 9

# *Van Scones*

At the bakery the next morning, Ellie kept an eye on the clock as she worked tirelessly on the daily goods. Mary bounced back and forth between the front and the kitchen. Ned sat along the sidewall as he put together the more tedious appetizers for the New Moon celebration that night.

"She dares to call it a potluck when we make everything," Mary complained as she hurried into the back with a tub full of dirty dishes.

"As long as she pays, she can call it what she wants," Ned reminded her.

"But other people should be welcome to bring things, not have their family recipes hidden on the back porch with the hot dogs."

"I like hot dogs," Ellie added with a smirk. "Put them out there and I'll have a feast for myself."

"That a girl," Ned cheered her on. "Save me a seat?"

"I never said I'd share." Ellie cackled as she hauled a bun-loaded tray into the hot oven. She bounced back and forth between appetizer prep, buns, and dishes. Even with her extra hands, by noon, it looked like The Sugar Shack would struggle to make its deadline.

"You want me to stay late?" Ellie called out as she quickly stabbed a cherry tomato, a mozzarella ball, and a basil leaf onto a toothpick.

"I would love you forever if you did," Mary called back from the front. She bid adieu to a customer. "Yup, best scones on the Cape."

"I gotta get Gracey from the summer camp-soccer-league-thing at three," Ellie called back. "Boys have a dentist appointment."

"I'll take whatever I can get." Mary grunted as she lifted a tub of frosting.

"What do you—" Ellie rushed over and took the five-gallon tub from her. "I told you to stop lifting these things. I can get them."

As the afternoon went on, small treats were frosted, meatballs formed, and bread sliced. By three o'clock, Ellie had loaded finger sandwiches onto a large catering tray and secured the plastic lid.

"You're going to be late." Mary shooed Ellie out the door, untying Ellie's apron as she went.

Ellie snagged her helmet and jacket as she stepped outside.

"On the bike?" Mary exclaimed. "No, no, take the van, not that death trap."

"It's not a death trap," Ellie said defensively. Before she could argue, Mary shoved her inside the van with the keys.

"Well, I guess this is happening," she muttered to herself before putting the van into reverse. "I'll come back right after— crap! I forgot the flowers."

"Forget them, there's always next month. Or you can run out later, just go!" Mary waved her off.

The Sugar Shack van was loud, wide-set, and awkward to take around corners. The seats in the middle were replaced with shelves secured to the floor. By 3:05, the field and gravel parking lot were swarming with families. She managed to squeeze the van into a bare bit of grass by some pine trees. Even after angling her neck in every direction, she saw no sign of Gracey. Ellie pulled out her cellphone.

"Hello?" Even her greeting sounded annoyed.

"Miss Gracey's personal chauffeur service. We are awaiting you in the one, the only, Sugar Shack van." Ellie played it up, hoping to get a chuckle out of the moody teen.

"Ugh, you're kidding me. Right?" Ellie could feel the eye roll through the phone.

"No, I was running late and have to get back to work, so hurry up."

"There's no way I'm getting in there. What if someone sees me?" Gracey whined.

"Hurry up, or I'll make sure everyone sees. I have a horn, and I'm not afraid to use it."

"Don't you dare," Gracey warned.

"I have my hand right over it. Five, four—"

"Yeah, it's my cousin. She's being a dork." Gracey complained.

Ellie raised her voice. "Three, two— oh, look at that. My hand is on the center of the wheel—"

The passenger door opened. Gracey scrambled in and sank down in the seat. "You win. Let's get out of here."

"Not without a seatbelt, we're not." Ellie crossed her arms.

Gracey lifted her eyebrows and widened her eyes fiercely.

"Oh, I'm sorry. Did you want me to?" Ellie gestures to the horn. "It's really no problem, I could just—"

Gracey grabbed the seatbelt and made it a point to buckle it in as loud and as forcefully as she could.

"That's more like it." Ellie grabbed the shift stick. "Don't worry, if you are lucky, you'll find an old scone under the seat."

"Hey, Gran—"

"What the crap!" Ellie jumped in the driver's seat, smacked her thigh off the steering wheel, and prepared a right hook.

On the other side of the door stood a young man whose shoulders took up most of the window frame. A wide, welcoming smile overcame his lips as he pulled off his sunglasses and placed them on top of his head. Smoothly, he leaned against the door frame. "You're not my grandma."

"Er…" Ellie slowly shook her head from side to side. She lowered her fist sheepishly. "If I was, you would have given me a heart attack."

He brayed. The young man had dark brown hair that was neatly cut, green eyes like malachite, a bit of a five o'clock shadow, and a bright-orange shirt that read STAFF across the chest. A whistle sat around his neck.

"Hey, Coach Nick." Gracey's tune changed.

"Hey, Brown. Good job out there today."

"Thanks." She chuckled and played with her ponytail.

Coach Nick held on to the window and leaned back to double-check the writing on the side of the van. He looked back at Ellie, then at the sticker again.

"Yup, Sugar Shack." After a moment, he snapped his fingers and pointed to Ellie. "You're Ella!"

"Ellie," she corrected him.

"You're the new girl," he exclaimed. "I'm Nick, you work for my grandparents."

Ellie felt like such an idiot. "Of course, okay, the gran comment makes sense now."

"I've heard so much about you," he continued.

"Yeah? All good, I hope." Ellie returned to her comfortable position in the driver's seat and adjusted the rearview mirror. Gracey sneered at Ellie out of the corner of her eye.

"Oh, yeah. They love you." He continued on, and Ellie glanced at the clock. Her heart raced in her chest at the sight of 3:07 p.m.

"That's such a relief. They are such sweet people." The urge to pull out made her right foot bounce on the floor. "I gotta go. We're behind for the party tonight," Ellie explained and threw the van into reverse. "Nice meeting you."

"See ya there?" he called out as Ellie backed out into the busy lot and fought with other cars to get out.

No matter which radio station Ellie chose, there was something wrong with the music, according to Gracey.

"That's old."

"I hate country."

"Doesn't this piece of garbage get any of the good stations?"

When they pulled into the Brown's driveway, it took all of Ellie's self-control not to kick her cousin out of the van the moment she opened the door.

*You've got to be kidding me.* Peter's white SUV sat in the driveway beside her aunt's black Honda. Ellie swallowed her irritation at the sight.

"How was camp, honey?" Jean asked as she emerged from the sliding glass door.

"Great, except Ellie wouldn't stop flirting with Coach Nick." The passenger door to the van slammed shut.

"Don't slam the door! This isn't my vehicle. And I was not flirting," Ellie corrected her.

"Oh, Nick, you're so cool," Gracey mocked.

"That's not what I said—"

Jean stepped toward the van and cut Ellie off, motioning with a waving hand by her neck. When she was in the van's window, she informed Ellie in a hushed tone, "She's thirteen. She thinks the guy at Hamburger Land is flirting with her when he asks if she wants fries with her order."

Ellie's face relaxed. Jean stayed about a foot back as she looked the van up and down. "Gotta ask, why the van? I left my car for you, remember?"

"We've been swamped all day. I was running late—"

"You're still working?" Jean's eyes widened.

"I'm not abandoning a little old lady on her own with all that work." Ellie put her foot down. "Also, more money," she continued. "I would have made Gracey wait twenty minutes if I came here, grabbed the car, then doubled back. So, Mary let me take the van. Why are you back from the dentist already?"

"*They* canceled on us," Jean bit her cheek, and her fingers tapped against her forearm. "Does it have seatbelts?" She leaned her head in the window.

"Nah, I just figured I'd cover her in hot dog buns and wish her the best of luck."

Aunt Jean playfully shoved Ellie's upper arm through the open window. "Wise ass." With a quick glance over her shoulder, Jean added, "How was she?"

"Honestly?" Ellie leaned in like her cousin might emerge from the depths of the van. "I don't know what's going on with her, but she was kind of a jerk."

Jean sucked her upper teeth and looked off toward the road. "It's happening."

"What is?"

"Puberty." Her eyes were distant and filled with horror. "I'm losing my little girl… this is it; the difficult stage."

Ellie awkwardly smirked. With a glance at the clock, it was close to 3:20. Her foot began to tap again.

Jean chewed on her thumbnail, lost in thought. "She's going to Channel soon… or not…" Noticing what she was doing, Jean pulled her hand away and changed the subject. "Will we see you tonight?"

"Yeah, I gotta finish up the hors d'oeuvres, but I will be there!" Ellie put the old van into reverse before backing out of the driveway. It sounded about as happy as her lower back and feet felt. "Get the flowers, take a shower—somehow, I will be there!"

# 10
# *Sunflowers*

"What kind of bouquet would I even get?" Ellie complained into the air as the van puttered back to the Sugar Shack. "I don't know what's appropriate. Red roses are romantic, white lilies are for purity—"

"Don't overthink it," Luna's voice came over the flip phone positioned in the cup holder. "Just grab the one that speaks to you. It doesn't matter if it's red, yellow, peonies, or roses. It's the thought, the gesture."

"That's what Mary keeps saying, but I just—if this is my only link to find out what's going on with Louie, if she knows anything, I don't want to offend her."

Ellie came up to the corner that housed the Sugar Shack. The "Open" sign in the window was off, and the specials board was tucked away. Ellie sank into the driver's seat. *What a relief.*

Luna's voice came over the phone. "If anybody is ever offended about receiving flowers, you are associating with the wrong people."

Ellie chuckled.

In the back driveway of the Sugar Shack sat a small dark-green pickup truck. *Weird.* Ellie parked the van as far out of the way as she could. "Alright, I gotta get back to it, but I will see you later tonight."

"See you then."

The patio area didn't have one person in it, but it looked more alive this afternoon than ever before. Hundreds of tiny purple flowers created small bunches that trailed down like grapes on the vine. A faint buzzing came from the top of the ceiling, where hummingbirds zipped around.

Her hand trailed over the table where she and Louie once sat and admired a single hummingbird. "Soon, buddy," she whispered. "We'll know soon… I hope."

The back door opened, and an older woman with long, curly red hair accompanied by flecks of gray around her forehead emerged. She wore a long, flower-covered sundress and a deep-green apron that read "Miller's Greenhouse".

"Have a good one, Mary," she called back and held the door open for Ellie. Two circular loads of sourdough hung from her right hand.

"Thank you." Ellie took hold of the door and stepped inside, pulled on her flour-covered apron, and announced, "I'm back, let's get to—"

Against the side wall where all the bags of buns she made sat packaged, labeled, and ready for pickup, was a gorgeous bouquet loaded with sunflowers both big and small, purple bell-shaped flowers, tall ornamental grasses, bushy white flowers, and a couple of cattails. It was the most beautiful assortment Ellie had ever seen.

"You like it?" Mary asked as she set two large icy lemonades on the table.

"It's beautiful." Ellie gasped, "What's it for?"

"For you. For your Seer." Mary took a sip from her lemonade. "You've been such a big help today, I wanted to return the favor."

Ellie's mouth fell open, and her hand rested on her chest. She looked from Mary to the flowers in disbelief. "You?" Her eyes glistened with tears. "I—"

As tears boiled to the surface, Ellie turned away and pinched the bridge of her nose.

"Oh, sweety, I'm sorry. I knew this was a fragile—" Mary shuffled closer.

"No, this is great!" Ellie wiped the tears away and turned around to face her boss. "This is awesome. Amazing, even. Let's finish this up. We have a party to go to."

By 4:00 p.m., the trays were loaded into the back of the van. Both ladies looked worse for wear with their shirts drenched in sweat and exhaustion in their eyes.

"See you there in an hour?" Mary asked, her curly hair especially heavy and wild as she stepped inside the van.

"You betcha." Ellie gently pointed at Mary with the bouquet as she walked toward her motorcycle. Her shoulders were heavy, her feet ached, and her head filled with fog. *I can do this. I have to do this.*

In a race against time, Ellie sped home and took the fastest shower of her life. She wanted to lean into the hot water and let it caress her muscles and soothe the pain away, but she had to be strong. Mary needed her, Louie could be there, and sleep could wait until any other day.

Ellie put on the same outfit she wore the last time she saw Louie: a baggy purple sweater and jeans. Most importantly, a shell necklace was tucked beneath her sweater. Before her curls could get the best of her, she threw her hair up into a braid and secured down any flyaways with hairspray.

"Tonight," she announced to herself while looking in the mirror, "is the night I get answers." She exhaled slowly and took in the outfit once more. "Maybe."

*He could be alive. He could be dead. Don't get your hopes up.* The delicate chain twisted around her fingers as she pulled it up. With a kiss to the smooth backside, she whispered, "Let's go." Ellie gathered her things and headed back out to the house where she lost her best friend one month prior.

Ellie parked just outside of the driveway. A smiley face balloon floated above the mailbox. She pulled herself off the bike, grabbed the flowers, and gave the balloon a gentle punch while calling out, "Bop."

The sight before her, a barely empty long driveway, was loaded with memories. Louie crying out for her to stay down, her uncle rushing down the beach mid-transformation, the smell of the Corrupted Familiar. Ellie's chest tightened.

*Beep-beep.* The Sugar Shack van rumbled up the road. Ellie stood off to the side as Mary turned into the driveway.

"Perfect timing," Mary cheered as she rolled in. She looked as fresh as could be with all the energy she had first thing in the morning.

*How in the Void?*

Each step felt like she was walking on blisters forming on the bottoms of her feet.

"You look exhausted." Mary stood before the open van doors and slid the tray of cookies back on the rack.

"I am," Ellie halfheartedly chuckled. "How are you not?"

Mary grinned devilishly and pulled a small teal vial out of her loose, flowing green dress pocket. "Take a swig of this, you'll feel brand new." Mary handed it to Ellie. "Developed it in my mid-thirties. Raising two kids, cleaning a house, and running a business makes you wish you had more energy."

"How did you—this is amazing. What's in it?" Ellie opened the vial and sniffed it. "Oh, vanilla."

"Maca for endurance." Mary counted the ingredients on her fingers. "Ginseng for—"

"Focus?" Ellie guessed.

"Correct. Sharp little witch you are." Mary winked. "Reishi mushrooms and a sprig of rosemary."

"Why does it smell like vanilla?" Ellie shook the container a little, as if that would reveal its secrets.

"Tastes like it, too. Just a pleasant side effect."

With that vote of confidence, Ellie took a sip.

"Bigger swig," Mary instructed. "Or that will only help you for a little bit."

Ellie followed Mary's instructions and took a bigger gulp.

"More, more, more—and good." Mary took the bottle back. Ellie had gulped down half of it.

The sense of energy, of relief in her feet and lower back, swept over her like a wave in the surf. It was fantastic. Her joints didn't ache, and there was no fog in her brain. "I would love that recipe."

In the evening light, without the house bursting with people, the Keswick home seemed sterile and cold. It was like something from a magazine, untouched, perfect, and staged. The kitchen's open shelves were decorated with fancy oils and a chain of weaved garlic.

"On the island," Mary instructed Ellie. "We have to set it up all pretty and welcoming."

Mary reached beneath the island, opened a hidden door, and pulled out the three-tiered serving dishes. As Ellie unloaded the food from the van, Mary set up the plates and added serving utensils. The kitchen looked beautiful. There were no black serving trays in sight, only an eclectic assortment of porcelain bowls and trays. It did look like a potluck.

*What a phony.* Ellie and Mary carried all the empty trays back to the Sugar Shack van and stacked them. Mary climbed back into the driver's seat and reversed the massive van out of the driveway. As Ellie sat on the steps, waiting for Mary to return, a harsh voice from behind caught her attention: "Food girl."

*Food girl?* Ellie looked over her shoulder, glaring at the source. Naomi Keswick stood in the doorway. Her perfectly manicured, thin, wrinkled hand flipped through a wad of cash. "Give this to Mary, would you?"

Ellie stood up from her seat on the step and walked back to the doorway. "Sure." She snagged it from the imposter's fingertips.

Naomi pressed her lips together tightly as she eyeballed Ellie's appearance. With a judgmental chuckle, she stepped back into the house and picked up a glass of red wine from the banister to the second floor.

*Bet her and Mee-Maw would be best friends.* Ellie chewed on the inside of her cheek as she turned her attention back to the driveway. It took Mary a minute to come around the corner and join Ellie once again.

"A job well done," Mary announced as she climbed the steps.

Ellie handed her the wad of cash. "From Keswick."

Mary ran through the bills with the speed of a well-seasoned bank teller. "Perfect."

"Now what?"

"We wait for the other guests to arrive." Mary's eyes were still on the cash as she carefully counted out a few bills. "That should do it." She held out a good chunk of it to Ellie.

"What's this?"

"A bonus for tonight." Mary shoved the remaining cash into her pocket and waited for Ellie to take it.

"I can't." Ellie shook her head gently and stepped back.

"You most certainly can," Mary protested. "You are my employee, and you will take it." Mary forced the money into Ellie's hand and held her fingers around it.

Dumbfounded, Ellie stared at her hand with her mouth open.

"Good." Mary released Ellie's hand. "Now, go relax. You're officially off the clock. Get something to eat."

Flowers and a plate full of food in hand, Ellie found a cozy place on the beach by the fire she had sat by one month earlier, and settled in for a long night. Minutes felt like hours as she ate, watched people filter in throughout the night, and exchanged pleasantries with familiar faces.

"Those are gorgeous," Luna exclaimed as she joined Ellie by the fire.

"Thanks." Ellie turned them over in her hand for the fiftieth time. *I hope they're beautiful enough.* A kick to her leg made Ellie look down, and an overly excited Mitsy tried to climb up her. "Oh, hello."

Plate aside, she scooped up the small dog onto her lap. With the girls' company, time passed more generously. Jean and Peter didn't arrive until after the sun went down. The boys gave her a quick hello before they ran off to play with other kids.

"No Gracey?" Ellie asked as her aunt settled in beside her.

"No, she said she's not feeling well." Jean took a sip of her beer, that haunting twinkle glistening in her eye again. Peter gave his wife's hand a gentle squeeze, then a kiss on the back of it. The silent exchange between the two of them brought a small smile to Ellie's face.

Jean shook it off, then turned to Ellie with a forced smile. "Any sign of Tristan?"

Ellie shook her head sheepishly.

"He got called in," Peter informed her. "Hikers are missing out in Montague."

"Oh, our favorite," Jean leaned back in her chair and crossed one leg over the other.

Ellie looked at Peter with wide eyes. He smiled and shook his head. "We ran into some trouble out there when we were kids."

"Ah," Ellie nodded, her hand stroking the Pomeranian in her lap. Mitsy's fur was soft and wiry, nothing like a basset hound's. As she pet the beady-eyed puff ball, she couldn't help but remember Louie's rollie, clumsy antics. He'd lick her face in the morning, and they'd play fight until she was out of bed, or he was rolled up in a blanket. Now, her mornings were filled with alarms and dragging her feet to the bathroom.

Once again, that hollow, desperate ache in her chest ate at her. The sunflowers and cattails in her hand seemed unworthy of such an important task. Ellie licked her lips and looked at the orange and red flames. Bright, hot coals at the center drew her eyes as she remembered his molten core. With a shuddering breath, she turned to Luna. "How's your mindfulness class going?"

"Great." Luna began to fill Ellie in on the happenings of the last week.

By 10:00 p.m., Brody and Michael were tuckered out. They took up space on the beach blanket by their parents' feet.

By 11:00 p.m., the torches were placed in the Summoning Circle on the beach. Last month, Ellie had been so caught up in the conversations, she didn't notice the moving pieces of the party.

With minutes left before midnight, people began to migrate down to the Summoning Circle.

"I'll take her." Luna grabbed Mitsy from Ellie's lap and placed the pup in her own chair. "Stay."

Mitsy didn't put up a fuss.

"They'll be fine. We're going to be right down there," Peter reassured Jean.

The horizon was barely discernible except for a very thin line of gray where the sky met the water. Twinkling stars broke through the patches of clouds above, and one shooting star, with a bright-yellow tail, streaked across the sky.

*A shooting star who shot through your atmosphere at the right moment in time,* Louie's words played in her head again.

"And found my way to you," Ellie finished his sentence in a whisper. All those times she had playfully mocked him. Now she'd give anything to hear him say it again.

A hand took hold of her shoulder. Peter whispered, "We're right here, honey."

"We love you," Jean added from the opposite side.

Ellie bit at the edge of her lip and looked down at the bouquet.

"Just a few more minutes," Luna encouraged her softly.

Families gathered around the outside edge of the circle with the wall of tiki torches. While she couldn't see the markings in the sand between them, Ellie knew they existed.

"Three minutes," Naomi announced.

An aggressive, affectionate hand rubbed her upper back. "Don't be upset if we can't find her. There are so many of them, it could be difficult."

"Find who?" Ellie asked.

"Seer," Jean confirmed.

"Right," Ellie's shaky breath left her lips. "Betty, her name is Betty."

She tightened her grip on the bouquet of flowers and let out a slow, controlled exhale as she tried to convince herself. *She knows how important this is. She'll come.*

"Thank you all for joining," Naomi's tone demanded everyone's attention over the excited murmurs. "I am delighted to have you all here. Every month is a blessing; every new moon reminds us of how important the Void is to continue our way of life. I hope your generous offerings will please the Void and bless you all for years to come. If you are lucky enough to have a Seer, I wish you the best in locating it. To those of you who have lost," Ellie felt every eye on her, and her body stiffened. "I wish you the best."

*Yeah right.*

"Keep your eyes on the cosmos and may your month be fruitful," Naomi ended her speech. A brief, polite cheer from her audience filled the air, and they quickly dispersed.

The night air around Ellie was still, but butterflies erupted in her stomach. Her heart pounded in her ears as they entered the final minute.

"He's alive, I just know it," Peter whispered. "It takes more than that to take down a Familiar."

Ellie knew her uncle was only trying to help, but his kindness was never lost on her. She had to bite her tongue to fight back the tears that immediately threatened her tear ducts.

"Remember your happy place," Luna interjected from the right. "Open your connection."

*Open my connection.* The last time Ellie did that before a crowd, she was fourteen. Her free hand clung to the shell necklace, and she closed her eyes. She saw the beach, the sunshine when she woke up, and Louie when he gave her the shell.

*"This moment when we came back together, when everything was so tough."*

"Ten seconds," an unknown voice announced from the crowd. The rest joined in on the countdown.

"Six."

Hands rested on her shoulder.

"Five."

A collective hum filled the air.

"Four."

Her heart pounded harder in her chest.

"Three."

Tears threatened to rush up to the surface.

"Two."

She exhaled slowly to try to maintain her hum.

"One."

*Please.*

The lines in the sand flooded with shadows amongst the collective light of the tiki torches. Stillness followed—and then a sudden rush, the pure, life-sucking darkness of the Void shot down and connected with the earth. Grains of sand, leaves, and even small stones lifted into the air and slowly disintegrated. One by one, Seers dropped into the circle. Dozens of them. Shimmering, with oblong eyes, floating above ghost-like forms. With their wispy tails and undefined arms, each one was a mirror of the next.

*Be brave like Louie.*

Around the circle, families stepped forward. Offerings were made. Voices murmured in prayer and reverence.

"Betty?" Ellie called out.

The murmurs around them grew.

"Betty Fischer," Ellie called louder, demanding her presence.

"Do you think she'll remember her own name?" Jean asked. Peter shushed her.

"Mmmhmmmm," a familiar tune tickled the air and filled Ellie's ears. She returned the hum.

"Mmmhmm-hmm-hmmm." The tune continued.

"It's her." Ellie took off to her left. She knew that tune.

*It's my song.* "Mmhmmmm." It continued. Ellie pushed past person after person, Familiar after person. Curses and shouts followed in her wake.

"Mmmmhmmm, mmmhmmm." The tune was close.

Ellie came to a stop. Towering above her, the oblong eyes of a Seer locked on her. She swallowed hard, feeling dwarfed by the giant.

"Ellie?" Jean rushed up behind her.

"Wait." Luna held them back. "Give her a second."

"Please," Ellie held out the bouquet of flowers with one hand, towards her Seer. "I just need to know he's alive."

Her thumb ran over the lump under her shirt. The cool, smooth side of the shell pressed against her.

"I'd give anything—" The tiki torches and families around her disappeared. It was as if Ellie was transported to the peripheral of the Void. Her body tingled; thousands of whispers ran through the air.

"To become one..."

"The Void gives and the Void takes..."

"Scream Kimmy, scream..."

*What? Kimmy?*

"A creature of darkness..."

"A soulmate…"

"Stop," Ellie pleaded. "That one! Please. Just focus, Betty. Where's Louie? My soulmate."

The whispering stopped.

The presence of the Void dropped from around her, and Ellie's stomach felt weightless. She looked at her now empty hands, her stomach, her feet. Beyond her gaze, the sandy beach rushed toward her like she was falling.

Then it all stopped.

Waves rolled in from the ocean, crashing on the wet sand before her. The biting cold of the Massachusetts waters had no effect on her. *Weird.* A cool breeze rolled up the coastline, and there wasn't a cloud in the sky.

Standing before her was the bearded young man with shaggy blond hair, powerful legs, dressed in hiking gear and a plaid shirt.

"Louie." She lunged forward, but the excitement was short-lived when she noticed the young woman in a purple sweater and auburn hair standing on her tippy-toes and kissing him on the cheek.

*She kissed me!* His thoughts echoed through the air, like he was shouting from the sky. She looked around, only to see the sky and ocean around them. His excitement reverberated in her chest. Breathlessly, she clutched the shell under her shirt for dear life.

"You haven't given me a kiss since I changed." This voice left his mouth. It was more profound than the one that bounced around her.

*You deserve a thousand more.* Ellie thought to herself as she watched on.

The version of her from a month ago took his hand. "Told you I just need some time."

*Hold on to it tighter.*

*All the time you need, sweet Ellie.* The echoing voice made Ellie shudder.

"We should head back." Jean's face lit up by her watch face. Ellie could make out the knit cap she wore a month ago. "Don't want to miss your first Calling Circle… I hope the boys aren't giving Peter too much trouble."

"It would be pretty cool to meet this famous Seer."

As they turned back toward the party, Ellie snickered to herself. "I wasn't wrong."

*She's accepted me again. This is way better than being a basset hound.* The spark within him, housed in his core, grew like a bonfire beneath his surface.

"Every day," she reassured him. "I choose you every day."

A gentle, jazzy hum filled the sky, and Louie looked over his right shoulder, where the owl grabbed its dinner moments before. *Betty?*

Ellie swallowed hard.

"C'mon, they may have leftover meatballs." Past Ellie tugged on his hand.

*Betty… what are you trying—*

A horrific, painful screech, like something without an ounce of fluid left in its corpse, pierced the sky. Ellie dropped to her knees, covering her ears with her hands.

*No, not again.*

Louie looked up to the sky.

Pained, Ellie turned and followed his gaze.

A fireball rushed toward them from the heavens. A drooly, toothy-grinned slime ball behind it.

"Move," he shouted and pushed her out of the way.

*Such… a beautiful soul…*the Corrupted Familiar mused. *She must be for me. Y-yes, she—I watched her grow up.*

*You did not!* Louie's flame erupted inside of him. *Listen, brother, sister, friend.* He tried to center himself. *You're sick. You're not well. You're confused. She's not your witch—*

*My…*Its voice echoed through Ellie and sent shivers down her spine. *Witch.*

"Jean," Peter called out with a threatening growl.

*Betty, what do I do? Help me! I have to save her.*

*A creature of darkness.* Betty's soft voice echoed.

*I must…be close…* The Corrupted Familiar turned towards Ellie.

*One spring eve…*Louie thought to himself as the reality of the words sank in. *You'll never have her.*

"No," Ellie whimpered. "I won't let him die again."

Ellie dropped her left hand down to her side. Her connection pulled at the Void; the crown of her head, the base of her neck, her core, all began to tingle. It was so intense that it was almost painful, like when she woke up to her hand asleep.

The zip-zaps that formed felt much stronger than her normal zip-zaps.

Someone took hold of her wrist. Ellie looked to her left to see a young woman, only a few years older than her, with a layered yellow gingham dress. The neck was accentuated with a ruffled collar which stretched down to her abdomen, and the loose top was cinched in with a white belt. Her auburn hair was tucked into a large, brimmed hat. Her bright-blue eyes shimmered beneath fierce eyebrows.

*My mother's eyes…*

The woman's grasp burned against Ellie's skin.

"This is just a memory." Her voice was multi-layered, harsh on some levels, screaming on others, and melodic on the voice that sounded closest. "You're still on Earth. You'll hurt people you love, doll…"

When the young woman let go of Ellie's wrist, it was like she was torn between the Void and the present. Her hand calmed, and the surge of energy faltered.

The guttural, gurgling call of the Corrupted Familiar yanked Ellie's attention back to the memory. Peter grabbed her foot and pulled her back.

*Thank you, Peter. I owe you,* Louie thought to himself as peace took over him and he leaned into his decision. *I love you more than you will ever know, Ellie.*

*Mine…* it gargled out.

*I don't think so.* Peter, the wide, hairy man with darkened skin, braced himself as he embraced his curse.

*You deserve to know her.* The heat that Louie kept pent up, stored in the depths of his magically encapsulated core, ripped through once again. His amorphous form erupted from the center. Before this humanoid form could completely slip away, Louie lunged forward onto the Corrupted Familiar and wrapped him in a tight hug. *Please, don't make me do this.*

"Louie, no!" Ellie cried out.

His instinct to give her everything she wanted pulled at him.

*I must…be with…her…* The Familiar pulled toward Ellie.

*This is my choice,* Louie's voice rang out, and he kicked off, dragging the creature toward a tear in the Void.

As they struggled, the creature bit Louie over and over between words of corruption. *You held her back. She can't even look at you.*

"Yes, I can," Ellie yelled. "I love Louie."

*You're useless, pathetic,* the creature growled.

Ellie clenched her fist. "Stop talking to him like that! He's more than you will ever be."

The pain in his chest swelled, and he begged the poison to stop.

*I love you, Ellie.* He whimpered as another bite sank into him.

"Leave him alone," she cried desperately. Something wrapped around her arms and held her back. "Stop hurting him!"

"Betty," he cried out, desperate for help.

"Help him!" she echoed as Louie and the Corrupted Familiar fought in the Void. Like a stampede, the Seers rushed to his aid and eliminated the Corrupted Familiar.

Tired, hurt, and fading in Betty's arms, Louie lay. She fed him bits of herself, bits of other Familiars, whatever she could to keep his flame lit. Betty placed him by Ellie's puddle to watch over her once again.

*Ellie, I promise I will get strong enough to come back to you.* Images of the little ball of fire by the shimmering pool began to fade.

*The Void gives, and the Void takes,* Betty started, once again. *A soulmate… A creature of darkness… Save them, Ellie… Scream Kimmy, scream… To become one… Only in Oren…*

"Help him…" Ellie's voice echoed around and became lost in the repeating words. "Please, Betty. I'll do anything."

*Save them, Oren, soulmate, only in… scream.*

Ellie's flesh tingled and prickled. She gasped for air when Betty finally released her from the memory. When she opened her eyes, Ellie was looking up toward the sky. The darkness of the Calling Circle remained before her.

A burp rolled to her lips, which contained all the unease in her stomach.

"Hold her hair back," Luna's voice instructed, and a forceful set of hands rolled her over onto her side. It was like her entire body was waking up from falling asleep.

"The circle is closing," Jean's voice came from somewhere behind her.

"Thank you," Ellie managed to get out before a full body shudder and a gag.

The presence of the Void disappeared, and Ellie finally felt free from its sensation. As her senses returned and she could feel the sand beneath her, Ellie noticed the skin on her wrist was blotchy and the flowers were missing.

# 11

## Dispelling Myths

The ride home, changing, and climbing into bed was all a blur. When Ellie finally woke up that Wednesday morning, she lay on her back, tears of joy streamed down her face, and she laughed. For the first time in months, she laughed wholeheartedly.

"You're okay," she sobbed. "You're okay and you'll be coming home."

Ellie had to sit up in bed and hold her hands to her eyes to try to control the immense relief. "I didn't get my best friend killed. He didn't die for me. Oh, thank the Void."

Ellie wiped her tears, blew her nose, and took a deep breath.

"All the cuddles." She promised. "No more shy crap. I'm never letting you go after all of this. I miss you so much."

After that, she bounced out of bed and headed to the bathroom.

"Hey, Louie, I had that dream again—the one where the flowers were talking," Ellie said as she brushed her teeth. "I know it's just nonsense, but my brain keeps…"

Just then, Ellie saw the mark on her wrist in her reflection in the mirror.

*That's where Betty was holding my arm. Gah. Those splotches look bad. And my skin looks thin.*

"Why are my veins so prominent?" Ellie asked herself aloud.

After she rinsed her mouth, Ellie went to the cupboard and pulled down a Tupperware container of Luna's healing potion.

"You might think it's overkill, Louie, but she really did a number on me." Ellie slathered the goop over the affected site and made a cup of coffee. "Hey, Louie, today's that class taught by Mr. Keyes. Maybe I should skip it and just hang out with you."

Aunt Jean's voice rang in her mind. "You never know what you don't know."

With a crinkled nose, Ellie finished off her coffee. "Ugh. She's right. I need to go. I love you, Louie, but I can't spend the day talking to an invisible Familiar. No offense."

In a pair of jeans and a puff-sleeved green blouse, Ellie threw on her leather jacket, grabbed her keys, and hurried outside. Although it was just another June day on the Cape with a few clouds in the sky, the gentle breeze and the singing of birds made the world seem more alive.

"First day of classes, buddy," Ellie announced as she straddled her bike and slipped on her helmet. "Let's see what's so special."

The chatter didn't stop all the way from Truro down to Eastham. As she passed the Sugar Shack, she honked her horn.

"We'll have to go shopping when you get back. Get you some clothes so you have something more than that flannel to wear. With the money I've been making at work and what I've saved from Dad's money, we could get a car or an RV."

Off the beaten path, the library sat behind a dense tree line and was only identifiable by the large gray sign with thick black lettering,

*Eastham's Naturalist Educational Society.*

Mum was the word about magic out in the non-magical community. Businesses like the Sugar Shack kept it subtle, blending in to avoid attention. Still, part of Ellie had hoped the library would be different— some hidden gem that embraced the wonder of their world. She'd imagined pillars stretching to the sky, with gardens spilling out toward the sea. But standing here now, she couldn't hide her disappointment. Drab siding, plain white trim, and a handicapped parking sign were all that greeted her. A few bright-blue hydrangea bushes tried to liven it up, but even those were as common as sand on Cape Cod. Around back, the full parking lot looked just as ordinary.

"Guess we're off-roading," Ellie muttered as she pulled off into the grass.

The three-story building sat on a wide-open lot hidden amongst trees. It had light off-beige siding with white trim. Charcoal shudders accompanied every window. There was no porch to welcome guests, just a white ramp, and stairs which led up to a solid wooden door. A sign mounted on the right side of the door read:

*Private Library: No Entry Without Membership- No Exceptions*
*Monday-Sunday*
*Hours 8:30 a.m.-10:00 p.m.*

"Membership?" Ellie furrowed her brow with confusion. A little black box mounted below the sign had a button with a red light around it.

*Ring bell for service.*

Ellie pressed it.

"Welcome to the Eastham's Naturalist Educational Society, do you have a membership?" A man's voice with a Boston accent came over the intercom.

"Um, no? I'm here for the 9 a.m. class… A part of the Magical World Around You series? Dispelling Myths?"

A poorly hidden sigh came over the intercom followed by a buzzing noise. Something clicked. Ellie looked at the intercom, then the door.

"Open the door," he groaned.

Ellie glared at the intercom. *Yup, definitely from Boston.*

"Oh, thanks, er, sorry." Ellie tucked her helmet under her arm and gave the door a tug.

She entered a small mudroom with a thick black rubber mat on the floor. On the left-hand side, pamphlets lined the bottom half of the wall-mounted shelf which included the yellow, red, and green brochures.

*Calendars $10Proceeds benefit the youth summer program*

Above the brochures, a corkboard with different *Help Wanted-Babysitter* advertisements, a book club, a labeled card *Comfort in Chaos-* Ellie recognized the phone number on the card. *Oh, Luna.*

On the opposite side of the hallway was a bookshelf. Shells, decorative cross sections of wood with burnt words or pressed flowers beneath a clear, shiny coating, accompanied the titles for sale.

*Support Local Authors and Artists*, the sign read, *$5 per book, Wooden Medallions $10*
*"A Clairvoyant's Perspective"*
*"Flora, Fauna and You"*
*"The Unfamiliar: Interviews with Familiars"*

Ellie took note of the last title as she stepped inside.

The library was quieter than it had looked from the outside. Only a handful of people sat scattered in cozy chairs, sipping coffee, and reading.

The front desk, a beautiful, modern, tall desk made of different colored wood separated a man in a long sleeve, light-pink shirt from the rest of the people in the room. He waved her over. His hair was thinning, and he wore thick-rimmed glasses. His name tag read, 'Henry.'

"You said you're attending a class?" he spoke in a hushed tone, his accent still managing to come through.

"Yeah."

"Well, you do need a membership to attend the classes," he explained. "It takes two seconds and it's free."

"Okay. How do I get one?"

"First things first. Let me see your connection."

Ellie bowed her head and separated her hair to show the flat, mole-like black connection on the crest of her head.

"Perfect." He checked a box on a piece of paper on his side of the desk. "Address?"

"Why?" Ellie raised a cautious eyebrow as her father's warning of men with long sleeve shirts and windbreakers from Oren.

Henry didn't seem to notice. "It's for the late fee—twenty-five cents a day." He slid a small card and a pencil toward her. "Date of birth, too. And if you've got any non-magical folks who'll be borrowing under your name, jot them down. You'll be on the hook for their late fees."

The clock behind him read 8:55, so Ellie hurried to fill out the form. When she reached the space for non-magical users, she paused… then wrote, 'Kimberly Lynne Becker' and 'Louie.'

Writing his name made her smile. She could almost hear his voice teasing her again.

*"I can't read, Ellie," Louie had once whispered in her ear at the Sugar Shack.*

*We'll fix that*, she'd promised back then. She still meant it.

"That it?" she asked, sliding the card back.

Henry passed her a paper business card. "Membership card. Don't lose that. You'll need to show it at the door here and at any other participating business. Enjoy your class."

"Thanks." Ellie swung her backpack on and glanced around the bold lettering above the desk—*Keswick Memorial Circulation Desk*

*Emergency Exit->*

*<-Stairs*

*Ugh, Phony-Wick is more like it.* She snickered to herself.

As Ellie got her bearings, the librarian didn't have to look up to know where she was struggling to find. He pointed to Ellie's left-hand side of the room. "Take the stairs down, there are signs on the doors."

"Thanks."

Down the wide wooden stairs, Ellie came to a long hallway which stretched the length of the building. There were eight doors with frosted glass windows. Fluorescent lights lit up the warm wooden area. A sign greeted her at the bottom of the stairs.

*Bathrooms on the first floor*

"Good to know," she muttered before she proceeded down the hallway. Each wooden door had a small window above the door handle with glass and a brightly colored flier which hung from it.

On the first door, a bright-yellow flier read:

*Introduction to the Void*

Beyond the blurred glass, she knew Jean must have been inside setting up.

The door across from it on the right had a green flier:

*Overdoing it: Allergic Reactions, Dosage and Other Woops (Potions)*

Ellie's eyebrows rose with interest. "That'd be really cool."

After a few more doors, a bright-yellow flier read:

*Magical World Around You: Dispelling Myths*

She paused outside the last one, peeking through the glass to find a room full of kids about Gracey's age. Her stomach tightened like it was poked with a needle.

"Start small, right?" she whispered, glancing back toward Jean's door before swallowing her nerves and stepping inside.

***

## Connecticut 2012

Ever since middle school began, Ellie's life-long friends seemed more than just distant. It was like social walls formed over the summer. Her friendly smile was met with cold shoulders, disinterested expressions, and backs turned.

It was as if everyone got together and formed these subgroups of three to four members, and no one else was allowed in. Even Mindy didn't say "hi" to Ellie anymore. In the freezing, early morning air, people huddled together before the three sets of stairs which led up to Thompson Middle School.

"Morning Michelle, Sarah," Ellie greeted them, her homemade crochet hat pulled down snuggly on her head.

Sarah Herschbeck and Michelle Cyr were quiet girls who went to elementary school in the next town over. They kept to themselves, but more importantly, they welcomed Ellie when nobody else did. Though that didn't say much as she still felt like the odd man out.

"Did you finish the Home Ec project?" Sarah asked.

It was one of the few classes they had together.

Kimberly didn't put much stock in this mandatory class. Ellie had to admit, she didn't entirely understand the point of Home Economics when they made her write out the steps on how to make a peanut butter and jelly sandwich.

"Oh, no, I had a project to do for my mom," Ellie admitted.

"On what weird subject this time?" Michelle, who had frizzy dark hair, cherub cheeks, and an abundance of acne, teased.

Ellie wanted to make something up, but she wasn't creative enough to come up with a clever lie.

"Research on Skinwalkers and the gift of shapeshifting," She shared sheepishly.

The two snickered like there was some sort of inside joke. Ellie looked down toward the ground. The heat in her cheeks fought for dominance against the cold New England air.

When Michelle finally composed herself, she continued, "You mean, y-you mean, your mom is having you do research on an Indian legend?" She teased.

"Native American," Ellie corrected her quickly. "And shapeshifting isn't culture specific."

Sarah bit back her lip while Michelle snickered, "Oh, I am so sorry. I didn't mean to be insensitive."

Ellie's teeth clenched together so hard she thought they might break. "Ugh, whatever, you two are such jerks. I don't know why I even hang out with you."

The moment Ellie turned away, she lost traction and her foot slipped out from underneath her. With a hard thump, she fell on her back. The pile of textbooks and binders in her overloaded backpack forced her back to arch in an awkward way, but thankfully her head didn't hit the pavement. The aches, pains, and shock of the fall were not what caught Ellie's attention. Something uncomfortable happened that made her question if she just peed her pants.

Miss Englewood helped Ellie up. "Are you okay?"

Ellie's bottom lip puffed out. She wanted to cry. She was dismissed, humiliated, hurt, and probably peed her pants. She put her head in her hands to shield her face from onlookers.

"She's bleeding!" Someone gasped in the crowd.

"Oh no," Miss Englewood quickly hurried Ellie away from the crowd, up the stairs, and inside the doors.

***

## **Massachusetts 2019**

Ellie slid into the back row of the small classroom, trying not to make eye contact with anyone. Mr. Keyes was a wiry man with sharp features. With a well-practiced spin, he turned to face the board and wrote down quick notes. The board read:

*Mr. Keyes*
*Dispelling Myths*
*Folklore, Legends, and Current Media*

He looked up from his book to Ellie, and a look of confusion crossed his face.

It had been seven years since Ellie last sat in a classroom. Back then, she was about the age of her classmates around her. The world was cruel, friends were changing, and she had no idea she had just earned her mark. As soon as the clock hit 9:00 a.m., Mr. Keyes cleared his throat and began.

"Welcome to Dispelling Myths. Today we will be reviewing common myths you may encounter when speaking with the general public. Let's start with North American Folklore versus International Folklore. You will come across common tales like Little Red Riding Hood; does anybody know where this originates?"

Ellie looked around the quiet room of seven pre-teens and early teens. Nobody moved.

"Anybody?" he pushed. "We have a shy group today?"

Ellie took the bait and raised a lazy hand.

"Yes, you in the back." He gestured toward her.

"Charles Perault, France? 16, maybe 1700s?"

"Very good!" He cheered her on with a sway of his hand. "The purpose of folklore is to pass on information. Traditions, legends, and sometimes it can be warnings to children. It may seem obvious, 'don't talk to strangers', but that's just not how things were done back then. One common tale that has been spread across cultures is Cinderella. That narrative was not created in the 90s, it actually dates as far back as ancient Greece. That's wild, huh?" Mr. Keyes paused and looked around the room. He continued despite the lack of enthusiasm.

"Some folklore has become a part of everyday, common culture. We did not create stories of gnomes, fairies, and sea serpents." Mr. Keyes scribbled on the board as the marker squeaked in protest:

*North American Folklore.*

"We've got the Sasquatch." This was accompanied by his handwriting on the board. "Champy of Lake Champlain."

He continued to list mythical creatures and local folklore Ellie was very familiar with. The nights her mother spent at the dinner table sharing her findings was not lost on Ellie. According to Mr. Keyes, Sasquatch were extinct, and her mom's suspicions about a virus were right on the money.

Ellie smirked. *I'll have to tell her that… when she's talking to me.*

About fifteen minutes into the lecture, Ellie's thoughts drifted off to her real purpose of attending these classes- her Familiar.

She began to mindlessly doodle as she thought of the last night she saw him. How he ate the oyster whole and his use of Mitsy as a puppet. That was the same night she learned he was her soulmate.

*Soulmate, soulmate…what does it mean to me?* This morning, one answer became clear. Thinking of Louie- his presence and his smile- brought her joy. She knew she couldn't stop smiling. In her notebook, Ellie scribbled the word joy and slowly doodled around it. On the page it accompanied a puff ball with massive eyes and little flecks of hair that danced away from it.

"Glad my entry-level class could keep your attention… Miss?"

Ellie looked up from her notebook and realized that she was the only person left. Mouth agape, she closed her notebook and sat up. "I'm so sorry, I just-"

"It's okay," Mr. Keyes laughed and brushed it off. "I haven't seen you in the halls, are you new here?"

"Yeah, I just moved a month ago." Ellie shoved her notebook into the backpack. "I, um, I was homeschooled. My aunt, Jean Brown, thought it would be good for me to attend this class to figure out where my gaps are."

Mr. Keyes adjusted his glasses. "Not bad advice."

A soft knock at the door made them both turn. Jean stood in the doorway in a pencil skirt and a striped button-up.

"Speak of the devil."

Jean smirked. "How'd she do?"

"She survived," Mr. Keyes teased. "Though I caught her doodling more than taking notes."

Ellie's mouth dropped dramatically. "Well, I'd never."

"Gonna catch flies with your mouth open like that," Jean commented and turned back to her colleague. "How was day one?"

"The usual. We will see who sticks through 'til the end. I swear, kids these days lack the attention span or curiosity for deeper pursuits." Mr. Keyes sighed and lifted the palms of his hands up to his side.

"It's definitely a maturity thing, but we are kind of trapped by when we can share the information with them. Not everyone can see the value in their re-education like Ellie can." She nodded to her niece. Jean glanced at Ellie. "I was thinking she'd really benefit from a reintroduction into potions. I think her lessons may have been lacking."

"Absolutely," Mr. Keyes agreed. "It's so important to have a strong understanding of the basics. That's how you can make your own variations. What about foraging and identification?"

"Actually, Ellie's fantastic at identifying plants."

"Is that so?" Mr. Keyes shifted his feet towards Ellie. "Well, you know, Adam and Alice are looking for some help in that class, like a Teacher's Assistant, for the hike. Maybe?"

He pointed from Jean to Ellie, Ellie to Jean.

"That's a really cool idea." Jean looked at Ellie. "Would you want to?"

Ellie gently shrugged.

"You'd have to go through a few classes with them, make sure you all mesh well and what not, but you know?" Mr. Keyes offered. "Couldn't hurt?"

"That would be pretty cool, but could I think about it?" Ellie glanced towards the door. "I just started a job and am kind of figuring things out with my Familiar."

"Yeah, of course." Mr. Keyes nodded. "I will put a bug in their ears and if you decide, then you can talk to them. How does that sound?"

"That sounds great, Mr. Keyes."

Jean nudged the back of Ellie's elbow and the two walked out of the classroom after saying their goodbyes.

"I'm going to head home then off to work for a bit, alright?" Jean whispered as they entered the library.

"Gracey still faking sick?"

Jean sighed. "Yeah. Made her go to soccer, though."

Ellie raised a brow. "Kids and their phases."

Jean gave her a sideways look. "You're still a kid."

Ellie grinned. "I'll remind you of that next time you ask me to babysit."

Jean laughed under her breath and waved goodbye. Ellie watched her leave, then turned back toward the stacks. She had her own research she wanted to do before she bothered Luna.

# 12
## Sea Glass

Gracey's sour mood had outlasted the Ceremony, and Ellie had quickly learned to give her space, so the Eastham Naturalist Society had become Ellie's second home on her days off. The library had shelves full of books that caught Ellie's eye—*The Secret Lives of Shifters, Emotions and the Elements, Mushrooms, Madness, and Mayhem: A Family's Account of Hereditary Mycomancy*. She could have spent all day here, but the five-book limit and her slow reading speed forced her to be selective. She pulled out her phone and started snapping pictures of titles for later. That's when she noticed a small envelope blinking at the bottom of her screen.

> Hey, it's Nick. Grandma said you were going through a lot at the Ceremony, so I didn't want to bother you. Hope you're okay.

Ellie blinked. *Wait… what?*

She glanced around the library as if someone might pop out and yell, 'Gotcha!' But no one paid her any attention. She stared back down at the message, flipping the phone over in her hand like it might reveal some kind of answer.

*How did—Probably got my number from Mary*, she thought, dismissing it as nothing. She hit the back button and went back to scrolling through books.

The phone buzzed again.

*How's he doing this?* Ellie's thumb hovered over the keys, but she let out a quiet groan and backed out again. *Not today, Nick.*

It buzzed a third time. "Oh, come on," she muttered, only to see Luna's name flashing on the screen this time. Ellie answered quietly, "Hey, I'm in the library. Gotta be quiet."

Luna didn't waste time. "It's eighty-two degrees and sunny. We're heading to Race Point. Meet you there?"

Ellie smiled despite herself. "I'll be there soon."

After hanging up, she grabbed two books she couldn't leave behind—*The Unfamiliar: Interviews with Familiars* and *Ancient Magic: Forgotten Potions and Extinct Creatures.*

At the circulation desk, Henry scanned her books with a tablet, pushing his glasses up and down as he squinted at the screen. "You're Jean's niece, right?" he asked.

Ellie nodded cautiously. "Yeah."

He leaned in a little. "It's so tragic, what happened with your Familiar."

Ellie stiffened. *Here we go.*

"Oh… that." She tried to brush it off with a weak laugh. "He's fine. He'll be back soon."

Henry tilted his head, clearly surprised. "Really? You clairvoyant or something?"

"No," Ellie mumbled. "My Seer told me."

Henry snorted under his breath, like he wasn't sure if she was serious. "Well, aren't you something." He rang up her total. "Ten bucks."

Ellie handed him the cash, eager to get out of there. She tucked the books into her bag and headed for the door.

*What a weirdo,* she thought, already mentally clocking out of the conversation as she hit the sunshine.

The ride out to Race Point was nothing short of therapy. The farther she went, the fewer houses she saw—just sand, shrubby grass, and wide-open sky. Ellie parked near the weathered shack at the edge of the lot and kicked down her stand.

Out past the dunes, she spotted Luna already set up in the sand, with Mitsy curled up under a little shade tent.

"Hey," Ellie called as she made her way down with her backpack slung over her shoulder.

Luna waved her over and patted the empty chair next to her. "There she is! We were starting to think you'd gotten lost."

Ellie dropped into the chair with a grateful sigh.

Luna leaned over, nodding toward Ellie's wrist. "Looks like you're healing quickly."

Ellie turned her arm over and studied the faint blotches. "Yeah… better than last time, anyway."

"Last time?"

Ellie nodded, rubbing at the fading marks. "Back in Connecticut. Louie helped me with a potion, but I held on to the essence too long."

Luna raised her sunglasses. "Really?"

"Yeah. This time I didn't even hold on, but Betty's grip… it's like she pulled something straight out of me."

Luna gave a knowing nod. "The Void gives, and the Void takes. Probably extends to whatever lives in it, too."

Ellie shivered, then shrugged it off, and started peeling away her leather jacket. Beneath it, her lavender bikini top caught the sun.

Luna gave a dramatic gasp. "Ohhh, look at you!"

Ellie laughed, covering herself with her arm. "Stop. It was the only lavender one they had."

"Girl, I'm just saying—you look amazing." Luna's bracelets jingled as she leaned forward. "But I thought you were going for red?"

Ellie tossed her jacket onto the chair. "Lavender's Louie's favorite."

Luna wiggled her eyebrows. "So now you're dressing for him?"

"Why not? He always said I looked good in lavender." Ellie knelt by Mitsy's tent, pulling a carrot from her snack bag. "May I?"

"Go for it."

Ellie offered the carrot to Mitsy, who took it with her usual dramatic crunch. She watched the little dog settle back into her tent, a small smile tugging at her lips. *Louie would've gotten a kick out of this.*

Suddenly, Ellie froze, her heart doing an awkward flip, as a memory hit her—Louie's teasing and his stupid grin.

*"I swear, if you were a boy, you'd make me blush,"* she had said. The implication had all meant something completely different back then, when he was a plump basset hound. But the last time she had seen him, he had big, rounded shoulders, a full beard, a gorgeous smile, and a hug she could fall asleep in.

"I'm sorry, did I say something wrong?" Luna asked, breaking Ellie from her thoughts as her heart thudded in her ears.

Ellie swallowed and fanned her face. "No, I… it's just hot. I think I'm gonna take a dip."

Luna leaned back in her chair. "Go break in that bikini."

Ellie shot her a look but couldn't help laughing as she made her way toward the water.

*What the heck was that?* Ellie thought to herself as Mitsy barked at seagulls in the distance.

The icy Atlantic made Ellie suck in a sharp breath the second it hit her toes. She waded in slowly, letting the shock work its way up her legs as she scanned the shore for anything worth keeping. Bits of broken shells peppered the wet sand, but nothing felt right. *Not for Louie.*

*He deserves better than scraps,* she thought as she walked the length of the beach, all the way to the edge of the private property line. Nothing. Not a single shell felt good enough.

With a sigh, she turned back toward Luna, who waved from her chair.

"Find anything?" Luna called.

Ellie flopped into her chair with a groan. "Nope. Everything's cracked." She flexed her numb, bright-red feet.

"What about sea glass?"

Ellie perked up. "Sea glass?"

Luna reached for her wrist, holding up one of her many wire-wrapped bracelets. A tiny piece of frosted blue glass shimmered in the sunlight. "You've never gone hunting for it?" Luna asked, almost scandalized. "We'll have to go sometime. Early morning's best—right after low tide. Less tourists."

Ellie traced the little glass piece with her finger. "Louie's not really a bracelet guy."

"Make him a necklace, then. Or an anklet." Luna smirked. "I can totally see him in an anklet."

Ellie laughed, already picturing it. "Alright. Maybe I'll hit Skaket sometime before work."

"Take a flashlight," Luna added, settling back with her book again. "Any luck on that soulmate stuff?"

"You mean between class, work, and babysitting?" Ellie shot her a grin. "Let's just say I've learned… he brings me joy."

Luna peeked over her sunglasses and smiled softly. "Joy's an underrated and beautiful thing, you know."

Ellie let out a quiet hum of agreement and leaned back in her chair, closing her eyes. The waves, the sun, Mitsy barking at seagulls—it all lulled her into a peaceful haze.

The heat stayed on her skin even as the light dimmed. Ellie opened her eyes—or maybe she didn't, but she found herself standing under a sky streaked with greens and blues, like the northern lights had spilled over Cape Cod. Waves shimmered endlessly, meeting the sky in a perfect, glowing horizon.

There was no Luna, no Mitsy, no beach chairs, or parking lot behind her. The surf met the sky and amongst the waves, not a seal, but a young man with blond hair, a scruffy beard, and a kind smile.

"No sharks," he called out. "I checked."

Ellie didn't hesitate. She sprinted toward him, the surf parting effortlessly around her legs. She leapt into his arms, laughing as his grip tightened around her like she was something precious. His beard tickled her lip as he leaned in, brushing his nose against hers before their mouths finally met.

Warmth spread through her chest like a slow-burning fire, tingling all the way to her fingertips. The world, for once, felt quiet—calm. Like nothing else mattered.

Above them, streaks of silent lightning danced through the dark sky.

Ellie let herself melt into the moment… until a harsh buzzing started gnawing at the edges of the dream.

*No… not yet.*

The buzzing grew louder. She groaned as the sun seared through her eyelids. Blinking against the light, she fumbled for her phone in her jacket pocket. A small part of her expected Nick again—but no.

Dad

She rubbed her eyes, squinting at the time. Just past noon. He'd be at work.

*Weird.*

Ellie answered. "Hey, Dad? You alright?"

Elijah's voice lacked its usual edge. "Sorry, did I wake you?"

Ellie stretched, letting the warmth of the sand seep into her skin. "Nah, I'm just on the beach with Luna."

"Oh… I won't keep you, then. Just wanted to see how your first class went."

She smiled, remembering her easy win earlier. "It was fine. Kinda boring, honestly. But turns out Mom's theory about the Sasquatch extinction? Dead on."

She waited, hoping he'd comment. Nothing.

"That's nice," he finally muttered. "Learn anything else?"

Ellie sighed. "Not really. I'm thinking about checking out that M. Becker course tomorrow."

Elijah seemed distracted on the other end. "Mm-hm. Yes—? Hang on, I'm getting pulled into something."

Ellie chuckled. "Accounting emergency?"

He let out a tired breath, but she heard the smile this time. "Yeah. Call me tomorrow after class?"

"Promise."

# 13
# *Purists*

The classes offered this week were mostly the starters of a series, one-offs, or basics. According to Jean, that was typical for the beginning of summer break. That Thursday, she had to choose between *Entry Level Ceramics* and *Brief History of Magic in America: Series 1 of 3*. While she loved the idea of playing with clay, the curiosity to get eyes on this M. Becker pulled at her more.

"It will be offered again," Ellie told herself as she kept her sights set on the door with the red flier.

She stepped inside and, just like yesterday, found herself surrounded by kids not much older than Gracey. Sighing, she took a seat near the back and pulled out her notebook.

A girl in a blue-and-white striped tank top twisted around in her seat and grinned. "Hey—you're Gracey's cousin, right?"

*Oh no.*

The girl didn't wait for a response. She slid out of her chair and dropped to a squat beside Ellie, practically nose-to-nose. She had blonde hair with pink-dyed tips, hazel eyes, and way too much energy. Based on Jean's descriptions, Ellie knew who she was—Sadie, one of Gracey's soccer friends.

Ellie leaned back, but the cramped desk gave her nowhere to go.

Sadie dropped her voice. "Do you know what's going on with Gracey?"

Ellie shifted uncomfortably. "Not really. We don't… talk much."

"She's not really talking to anybody… I'm getting worried about her." Sadie's upturned eyebrows and small frown reminded Ellie of a child who dropped their ice cream in the sand.

"Have you talked to Jean or Peter about it?"

"No." Sadie glanced over her shoulder. "Gracey would kill me if she knew I told anyone."

At a loss, Ellie asked, "What are you expecting me to do with this? We aren't exactly close."

"She'll listen to you, trust me."

Ellie's shoulders slumped. She looked to the floor in hopes of any excuse to come to the surface, but nothing did. Looking back up into Sadie's pleading eyes, Ellie caved. "Alright."

"Oh, thank you," Sadie beamed and threw her arms around Ellie in an unexpected hug. Ellie froze, patting her awkwardly on the back.

The classroom door swung open. The sudden sound broke up the hug and Sadie returned to her seat. An older man with slicked back silver and brown hair strode toward the front of the room.

Although he carried the last name Becker, he didn't look like any Becker Ellie had ever met. There was no perfectly groomed facial hair, luxurious locks were missing, and his washed jeans and plain-grey t-shirt were far too casual.

*Dad would have a cow if he was caught in public without his button-ups and Oxfords.*

"I am Mr. Becker," he spoke with his back to the room. The squeaky black marker moved across the whiteboard quickly as he clumsily wrote his name. The only recognizable letter was the "B".

*Sloppy, very un-Becker-like.* Ellie began to take notes.

"And we will be starting our class at the best place to start - the beginning." A couple of polite chuckles resonated from around the room. "Welcome to Brief History of Magic in America."

He turned to face the class; a dimple accompanied his beardless chin. Ellie's eyebrows sewed together. *Does Dad have a dimple?* She couldn't recall. *Do I have-* he ran her thumb over her chin. *Nope.*

"Who knows when the first magical beings arrived in North America?"

A kid in a tie-dye shirt raised his hand, looking way too eager. "Vikings?" he guessed.

Mr. Becker pointed at him like he'd won a prize. "Yes… and no. The Vikings did draw from the Void, but the Indigenous peoples already had magic long before that—just a different kind."

Another hand shot up.

Mr. Becker winced dramatically. "Lemme guess—you're gonna ask where their magic comes from, right?"

"Yeah."

"So sorry, it's ancient magic, complex. If you want to hear more, you will need to attend the Mysteries, Magic, and More class in a couple of weeks. Today we are focusing on witches and wizards who draw from the Void."

A collective hushed "awe" filled the room.

"I know, I know. Break all your hearts." Dramatically, he leaned on tie-dye's desk, took in a deep, dramatic breath through his nostrils. "Will you ever forgive me, uh… Scott?"

There was an awkward silence. "My name's Andrew."

Mr. Becker tossed his marker behind him, like he was throwing in the towel. Like a pitiful puppy, he returned to the front of the classroom. "Will you ever forgive me… Andrew?"

"Yeah, just never let it happen again." Andrew played along.

"Tyrant," Mr. Becker shook his head. "Alright, yes, "So, the Vikings were the first," Mr. Becker continued. "They discovered and created short-term settlements in Newfoundland and Greenland around 1,000 AD. I know many of you immediately think of 'The United States' when you hear North America, Andrew," he added his student's name pointedly. That gained him a few more laughs. "But let's not forget our neighbors to the north and south; Canada and Mexico."

"Mr. Becker," a voice spoke from two seats ahead of Ellie, a young man with neat, short-curly brown hair who timidly lifted his hand.

"Yes, Mister… I'm guessing Fairburg?" Mr. Becker smiled, his eyes kind, his hands behind his back. Ellie had seen her grandpa stand just like that on more than one occasion.

The young man shifted in his seat. "How'd you know?"

"Because, Jeremy, your older brother, Travis, warned me you'd be coming." The smirk never left his lips. "What's your question?"

"Did you bring in the helmet today?" Jeremy sounded hopeful.

"Sorry to disappoint, that is reserved for my Norse Mythology and History class. That won't be offered until…" Mr. Becker rolled his dark eyes up towards the ceiling and pointed to an invisible calendar before him. "Four weeks from now? Either way, you want to see the helmet? Come to that class. It's a good time. Any other questions?"

Not a sound or motion was made.

"Okay, back to… where were we?"

"The beginning." Ellie called out.

"Thank you, Miss?" He tilted his head towards Ellie.

"Becker." Her heart fluttered in her chest.

For a brief moment, the teacher dropped his act and looked at her with parted lips. He gently tilted his head to the side as he assessed her. "Are you…that new girl? From Connecticut?"

"Yes." Ellie felt her stomach twirl with excitement.

"Welcome to Cape Cod." He gestured to the room around them, swallowed hard, then continued on by resuming his teacher's voice. "Back to the beginning! Yes, following the Vikings, that would be European colonization."

The butterflies in her stomach died.

*Well, what were you expecting? He'd just forget about everybody in the room and go through your family history with you? Stop being such an idiot.*

Mr. Becker went on to re-cap the first settlement of Jamestown, Virginia. Just like in Mr. Keyes class, she began to scribble in her notebook. *Waste of time, I could have taught this myself.* One juicy little morsel of new knowledge did float to the surface. The actual first steps in Massachusetts were in Provincetown. As she sketched out the basset hound with a helmet, she recited the next part of the lecture. *And in*

*1622, Wagner heroically led the German witches and wizards down to France where they gained passage and settled in Oren, Maine.*

"Some witches and wizards, mostly those heavily involved in trading with Italy and Spain, made their way onto the Mayflower and hid out amongst the Pilgrims for years until they ran off on their own."

*Mayflower?*

Mr. Becker continued, "Many think that the Purists are the original magical settlers in America, but they are wrong."

*Purists?* Ellie wasn't unfamiliar with that term, she had heard it somewhere before, but she couldn't put a finger on it.

Mayflower, Purists

"Roanoke, I'm sure you've heard of it. You all probably have. Let's see some hands."

Ellie was the only person who didn't raise one. Heat flushed her cheeks and she sunk into her chair.

Roanoke

"Fantastic, yes! 'The Lost Colony', as the non-magical folks know it. Said to have been abandoned, without a trace in the 1580s. Like everybody just-" He snapped his fingers. "Disappeared. All that they left was one word carved into a tree: CROATOAN." He wrote this on the board with the world's squeakiest marker. "Who knows what it means?"

Sporadic hands raised. "Yes, Miss?"

"Collins." Sadie held her head high.

"Collins?" Mr. Becker asked with a tilted head, like he was making sure he heard her correctly.

"Yes."

"Cheater, cheater, pumpkin eater." He went back to the board and wrote beneath the "C", "OLLINS."

"What's the 'R' stand for then, Smarty Pants?" He playfully challenged but stayed facing toward the board, ready to write.

"Rowlyn," she continued with the air of arrogance and perfection. "Oust, Anneston, Thorpp, Okes, Asper, and Norton. All eight founding families."

Mr. Becker struggled to keep up. By the end it was jumble squiggles. He dramatically huffed like he was out of breath and held onto the back of his chair for support. "All… eight. Well done, Miss Collins."

Sadie settled into her chair, like a show dog who just received a biscuit.

"Sorry to be a party pooper, but the mystery was solved." Becker tapped his marker against the board. "The original eight separated from the rest of the colony in the 1580s and moved further inland away from the Indigenous population and founded Alligator." He paused. "Not alligators that go chomp, but Alligator the town. Don't worry, Jeremy, I saw the look of confusion and thought I'd clear that up for you."

The class chuckled.

"Thanks, Mr. B," Jeremy played along.

A raised eyebrow and shake of his head was all the disapproval the class needed for that nickname.

"This specific early group of settlers was dedicated to peaceful living and much of their belief system coincided with modern day Pacifists. The group eventually disbanded in the early 1900s and joined what we call the 'Modern Movement'."

He jotted "Modern Movement" down on the whiteboard.

*Modern Movement?*

"The second settlement, the more pronounced, disruptive settlement, came in 1622, which brings us back to the Purists." He wrote their name , underlining the word on the board.

"Does anybody know why it's considered the most disruptive settlement?"

"It's a cult," Jeremy added. The class burst into laughter. Ellie was the only one not to get the joke. Mr. Becker took a seat on the edge of his desk, his marker turned tip over bottom.

"Cult is not a term to use loosely," he said thoughtfully. "It has negative connotations and can actually be used to mislabel religions, or put them down for not following a similar belief system to your own." He stopped fiddling with the marker. "Used in the context to bring another religion down is a form of discrimination. Discrimination is a form of hatred. I tell you this, because discrimination, hatred, hate, there is no place for that in my classroom. Does everybody understand?"

The room was still for a moment before a collective hum of "yes" filled the air.

"Great, I am glad that we are on the same page. But, Jeremy, the actual term 'cult' *could* be applied in this context." Mr. Becker returned back to the board and his three circles he never completed. "Crap... I blame you all, you distracted me." There were a couple of polite chuckles from the class as he quickly wrote: Cult

"A cult typically has one person, or thing, that is excessively admired. One of the best modern...ish examples is Charles Manson." Mr. Becker drew a stick figure person. "Forgive me, I know there are more modern-day examples, but for me this was modern. I was alive in the 70s like many of your parents and this was all anybody talked about."

He thoughtfully labeled his stick figure. Chuck M.

"Or, it is a small group of people whose beliefs, or practices, are seen by others as being bad, er, I mean strange or sinister because bad is a relative term."

This definition was accompanied by five more stick figures with angry eyes.

"The Purists did have excessive admiration for their original founder." He drew a check beside his stick figure, Charles Manson. "And their practices..."

Mr. Becker drew a circle in the air with his marker in an eerily similar way to how Elijah drew a circle in the air with his fork. "Well, there is an account of the founder tying a clairvoyant to a tree, covering her with honey, and letting the bears take her."

The class fell silent as he checked it off. "So, yes, you could say it is a cult. All religions have their dark days, like the crusades, but not so much-" Mr. Becker gestured to the blackboard. "You did it again, I am off topic. Want more, come to *Magic, Fear, and the Weird* where we go through all of this. Long story short, there is a break amongst the Purists about 30 years after they were founded. One side classifies the other side as a cult. Its classification as such is debated amongst the rest of the magical community. Come to my lecture two Wednesdays from now in the evening, or we will never finish this class on time."

*Magic, Fear, and The Weird*, Ellie circled a few times in her notebook.

He erased Charles Manson from the board along with all but a single head with angry eyes.

"As I was saying before." Mr. Becker placed his hands on the board beside the overlapping circles. "Purists are the only religious-based movement for witches and wizards to stick around today. The reason it is classified as a religion is because,"

The marker squeaked again against the board as he wrote inside the first circle:

*Culture*

"Culturally, they rank individuals by their abilities, which is similar to social class systems seen in the Middle Ages and the caste system in modern day India."

*Belief System* he wrote in the second circle. "Their beliefs surrounding the Void,"

*Extrinsic Values* "and their rejection of the modern world."

He turned back to face the class and continued. "The Purists belief system has adapted and changed over time but has not died out. While their population may not have changed drastically, they can be found throughout New England, and even further south. Which isn't surprising, right? People move." Mr. Becker raised a palm nonchalantly towards the ceiling. "I am sure all of you will leave Cape Cod; some may stay, some may return, but you will mostly all move on at some point or another… don't worry, your parents will forgive you."

The collective, polite chuckle resonated once again.

"Alright, enough about them, let's move on to our very own: Salem. Now, I know you all know about the Witch Trials. It was a horrible time filled with lots of loss, fear mongering, and inaccurate accusations. Between 1692 and 1693, two hundred people were accused of witchcraft, and just under a quarter of them were executed or died as a result of the witch trials. Thankfully, of those, what, 50?"

He looked over his shoulder and locked eyes with Andrew. After a moment he added, "Don't shrug, help me out here."

After a resonating chuckle from the peanut gallery, he shook his head and continued. "Of that 25 percent," he emphasized the number loudly. "One was actually a person with magical abilities. See, the biggest threats to witches and wizards at this time were not the Puritans, or Purists, it was their own kind. That's when a very clever wizard, Anthony Hinkle, created the Channel Needle. Show of hands-who knows what a Channel Needle is?"

Swallowing hard, Ellie gingerly raised her hand.

"Miss Becker?" He raised his eyebrows and nodded.

"It, um, it's a small piece of wood, about the size of a grain of rice used to block the flow, our ability to channel the Void."

"Very good," he took a small step forward. "Why use one?"

"Stop kids from showing off their powers and getting everybody caught." She glanced from her desk up to him. "And to punish murderers?"

"Corporal punishment," he nodded enthusiastically and brought his voice to the rest of the room. "And to stop children from showing off, Jeremy."

"What?" Jeremy gasped. "Me?"

"I'm just messing with you," Mr. Becker waved it off and went back to the board. "The only death of an actual, bona fide witch or wizard, was an orphan child under the care of Matthew and Ophelia Wingham. Charles was seen levitating above a bale of hay in the barn. Fearing he was in cahoots with the devil, his father turned him in. Charles was hung because of religious zealotry."

*Charles Wincham*

Ellie tried to keep her attention focused on Mr. Becker as he continued his lecture about the early settlers. The nagging tingle at the base of her neck forced her to rub her hand over the top of where her needle once was. *But it isn't the witch trials*, Ellie tried to reason with herself. *I just can't wrap my head around why someone would do that today.*

"And that is the end of our lesson." Mr. Becker placed the dry-erase marker onto the metallic tray at the bottom of the whiteboard. A soft tune played over some device hidden near the ceiling. "Ahh. Perfect timing."

The room filled with the usual shuffle—backpacks zipping, chairs scraping, and feet hurrying toward the door. Ellie slung her bag over one shoulder, waiting for an opening, but by the time she made it to the aisle, Mr. Becker was already gone.

*Figures.*

She rode home on autopilot, her mind stuck on everything she didn't get to ask. The Brown house was empty when she pulled in. No cars. No voices. No Gracey. Ellie circled the house anyway, checking every window, every door. Nothing.

With a sigh, she slid the glass door shut behind her. "Sorry, Sadie," she muttered under her breath. "I tried."

# 14
## *Teen Troubles*

Y ou only bought ham?" Gracey shrieked from the kitchen.

Jean stayed calm, holding a jar of pickles in her hand. "Last week you liked ham."

"No, I didn't! Ham is disgusting. Pigs are walking dumpsters. Don't you know anything?" Gracey's voice hit another octave as she stormed outside, her footsteps crunching across the stone driveway.

Jean leaned out the door. "Where do you think you're going?"

"Out!" Gracey shot back.

"You're grounded! Get up to your room."

"Ground this!" Gracey smacked her rump and kept walking.

Jean shook her head in defeat and ducked back inside.

Ellie awkwardly sank into her apartment. *Sorry, Sadie. Talking to Gracey's going to have to wait. I don't want my head bitten off.*

"Before you say anything, Louie..." She looked up to the ceiling. "I'm afraid of her. She's scary."

The book on the table, *Magic and Genetics*, lay open to the same page she'd been rereading for the past half hour. Ellie let out a frustrated groan and slammed it shut.

Her notes from the history class caught her eye. She pulled them closer—doodles of Chuck M. and those three overlapping circles. *Culture. Belief System. Extrinsic Values.*

"It's so weird." She traced the words *Roanoke* and *Mayflower* in the margin. "Why didn't Mom ever tell me any of this?"

She started a new list in the margin:

*Cults*

*Roanoke*

*Purists*

*Mayflower*

But no matter how much she wrote, her thoughts circled back to the one thing that mattered—Louie. That little spark waiting by her puddle in the Void, trying to get strong enough to come back.

Ellie leaned back, staring at the ceiling again. "Any insight here?" she asked quietly. Silence answered her, as usual.

***

The next morning felt off.

Ellie noticed it the second she walked into the Sugar Shack there were only two lattes sat on the table, and Mary was alone.

"Where's Ned?" Ellie asked.

"He's not feeling great," Mary said with a tired smile. "Good thing he froze some scones ahead of time."

Ellie grabbed the tray of frozen pastries. "He gonna be okay?"

"Oh, yes, dear. Treatments just wear him out some days more than others."

The summer sun had barely crested the horizon, but they fell into their usual rhythm—humming along to the radio, rolling dough, and filling trays.

Then, the back door creaked open.

"Morning, Grandma," Nick called as he stepped inside, dressed like he'd just come from soccer practice, with clean sneakers, a dark-gray athletic tee, and loose basketball shorts. He gave Ellie a nod. "Morning."

*Come for his once-a-year visit?* Ellie nodded stiffly in return.

"Nicky!" Mary dropped what she was doing and hurried to hug him. "Look at you! Are you getting enough sleep? You look awful, honey. Want some Second Wind? I think I have a bottle—"

"I'm fine, Grandma," he said, grabbing an apron.

"Are you hungry? What are you here for? I'm sorry, I'm just so happy to see you. Have you met Ellie?" Mary followed him to the center table.

"Really, I'm fine. I ate before I came over." He light-heartedly dismissed her concerns before he joined Ellie at the middle table. "Yeah, we met at the soccer pick-up."

"Nice to see you again," Ellie offered a quick smile and returned to her work.

Mechanically, she placed the final bit of dough on the tray. She went to load it on the proofing rack when he stepped in, forcing it out of her arms. "I got it, I got it."

Ellie stepped back, her eyes on fire as he walked toward the oven.

"That's for proofing," she informed him tersely.

"My bad." He backed up toward the proofing rack and loaded the tray onto it.

Ellie scoffed, rolled her eyes, and returned her attention to the table. To her dread, he took up the spot beside her. Without a word, he cut off an awkward chunk from the massive mound and began to form it with clumsy hands.

"We have to make sure they are close to the same size," Ellie informed him without her eyes leaving her own dough ball.

"I've been doing this since you were in diapers," he countered.

Ellie raised her eyebrows and glanced at his rough pillow of dough in need of a second proof. With a harsh poke, she added, "You're over."

Nick stood back a moment and eyeballed the two. "Well, how do we know yours isn't too small?"

"While you have been doing this since I was in diapers, I've been doing this full-time for weeks. I know what I'm looking at."

"You're not much of a morning person, are you?" The smirk on his face made Ellie's teeth grind.

"I'm fine in the mornings. I just have a lot of work to do and no time to babysit." She set her ball on the new, paper-lined tray and continued.

"Babysit?" He took a step back and eyeballed her. "Alright, alright…"

The way his tongue danced in his cheek, Ellie had to look away or she'd punch it.

"How 'bout this. You and me, dough off, right here, right now. I prove I have a spot at this table."

She placed a third, perfect dough ball on the tray. "What're the terms of a 'dough-off'?"

He rubbed his hands together and shifted his weight from side to side as he decided. "Three balls of dough each. One point for first done, one point for quality, and one point for accuracy in weight."

"Done," Ellie said confidently with pursed lips.

"If I win, I can help here at the table."

"And when you lose?"

"If I lose." Nick glanced around the room as he weighed his options. "I am on dishes."

The dishwasher was brimming with large sheet pans, mixing bowls caked in frosting, and chocolate hardened on to measuring cups. "Deal."

After a firm handshake, Ellie instructed him to grab the scale. He danced around Ellie and returned with the large, flat scale and placed it between them. Ellie wrote *900 g* in the flour dust before them.

"No outside help," Ellie added to the rules. "No do-overs."

"Price Is Right rules," Nick bargained.

Ellie shrugged.

"Closest without going over, wins."

"Works for me."

"Oh, and if you go over, you have to share a secret about yourself, something nobody else knows."

"Sure, but enough chit-chat. Let's get back to work."

Nick dove in and shoved his hand into the dough.

"Dude," Ellie scolded. "Wash your hands."

"Sorry." Awkwardly, he retreated to the sink, washed his hands, and returned to the station.

Bench knives in hand, the two stood at the ready.

"Three," Nick began the countdown. "Two… one."

They both cut off their chunks of dough. Ellie's was a neat, well-trained slice. Nick's was rough and jagged. The table shook beneath the intensity of their kneading and shaping.

Nick finished first. He was sloppy, but fast.

"One point for speed," Ellie admitted. Then, she picked up his dough ball. It split at the seams. "But you didn't close it properly. Mine's better quality."

"Alright, I'll give it to you." He conceded. "You still owe me a secret for fastest, though."

"Slow your roll, we have time." She turned to weigh the dough then stopped herself with a cheesy smile and rolled her dough ball back and forth. "Slow your roll, get it? *Roll.*"

Nick raised his eyebrows judgmentally and mouthed the word *wow*. "That was bad."

"If you can't appreciate puns, you need to get out of the bakery." She picked up her dough ball.

"Was that another pun?" he asked as he rolled his ball toward him.

"Was wha-oh! Knead, need. Ha!" Ellie chuckled. "You know, your grandma likes my puns."

"She's just being nice," he challenged.

A small piece of Ellie flinched away from his comment. *At least Louie likes my puns.*

"Okay, I'll go first." She placed hers on the scale: 898 grams. Nick's weighed 1,003.

"No way, redo, redo." Nick tried to backtrack.

"Nope. Get on dishes, now. You put me behind schedule. I have lots of rolls to make after this." She went back to cutting off hunks of dough and forming the balls before loading them onto the proofing racks.

"Admit it, you don't want me on dishes. You like my company. You want me here with you," Nick said.

"What I want is to get out of here on time so I can hit up Turn of the Page before I have to meet my friend at the beach." Ellie continued to work.

"Turn of the Page? Is that, like, a bookstore or something?"

Ellie kept her attention on her work. "Yes, just plain old books and art supplies."

"Oh, right, right, I think I heard of that place. Is it up in homo-ville?"

"Excuse me?" Ellie dropped the dough ball and took a step back.

"Oh, you're new, right. All those rainbows in Provincetown are because…"

"I know what they mean. Luna explained it to me," she said sharply. "I'm not confused. I'm disgusted by your words."

"What words? Homo-ville?" A smirk formed at the corner of his lips.

"Knock it off," Ellie warned him sharply.

"Look, I have no problem with gay people. They can do what they want behind closed doors. Just don't do it in front of me."

"Do what exactly?" Ellie confronted.

"You know…" He gestured into the air.

"What do you think they're going to do in front of you?" she pushed.

Nick chuckled and took a step back. "Look, I don't want to get into this."

Deep in her stomach, fury boiled. "No, you don't want to be challenged or held accountable for saying hateful things."

"What's going on back here?" Mary asked, coming through the back door.

"Nothing, Gram," Nick responded. "We're fine."

Mary stood in the doorway, skeptically eyeballing the two. "It didn't sound alright."

"Sorry, we'll keep it down," he assured her.

After a brief glance, Mary returned to the front.

"Ellie," Nick began.

"I have to get back to work." Ellie turned her attention to the dwindling dough ball.

"I should have the table cleared off by now." She muttered bitterly as she pulled up the large plastic bag. The rows of round dough bubbles awaited her assessment. As she gathered up the long plastic bag in her hands, a hand came down in front of her and stopped her.

Ellie sighed and looked up to Nick who stood off to the side. His eyes pleaded with her.

"Ellie, I would really like it if you could just forget all about this and we moved forward from here."

The tension in her shoulders melted away as a sense of ease overtook her.

"It was really a stupid thing for me to say, and I am just trying to…" He sighed and shook his head. "I just… Can we start over?"

Ellie looked away from him and back to the bag. The irritation in her stomach fizzled out. "This bread is ready for a second knead."

Despite the conditions of her win, she needed his help to catch up. Within half an hour, they were back on track, and Nick left to do the dishes.

"Alright, alright, alright," Nick called out from the dishwasher over the music. "You can stop pressuring me. I'll tell you my secret."

Ellie stopped rolling her ball of dough and tilted her head to the side. "Oh, right." She stepped back from the table with her hands on her hips and tried her best to engage. "Let me have it."

"Cottage cheese weirds me out," he admitted.

It was such a ridiculous omission Ellie had to make sure she heard him right. "Cottage cheese?"

"Yup." Nick looked up. "Weirds me out. I mean, why's it wet?"

Ellie turned back to her work and called back. "I am going to call bull crap on that." She heard the high-pressure hose spray against metal. "If it's true, I bet your mom knows."

"Dang, you're right." He continued. "I'll think of something."

"Moms always know." Ellie's own words ran back through her head, making her jaw clench. Kimberly was still mentally at the top of the list for Needle suspects. "Do better than that."

"Alright." Nick continued washing dishes. "How about- I'm terrified of horses."

Ellie snorted. "Horses?"

"Really, I'm not joking! Those teeth. They are flat and creepy like human teeth."

Ellie chuckled, which apparently fueled his confidence to continue.

"They are massive creatures, powerful." He demonstrated by stretching his hand above his head. "Okay? One wrong move and they can kick you. You'd be down. Done."

The more excited Nick became, the louder his voice got and the more he spoke with his hands. "You aren't coming out of a blow like that the same. And everybody is always like, 'Oh, well, if you know how to be around a horse it will be okay.' Well, guess what? I don't know how to be around a horse! So they are just confirming my suspicions."

His antics were fun to watch out of the corner of her eye. With a wide smile across her face, Ellie challenged, "You sound really passionate about this. You sure nobody else knows it?"

"Yep. Been too embarrassed to say anything."

"Well, yeah, you should be," she teased.

The rest of the hour went by quickly. Nick distracted her with as much conversation as he could squeeze out before he had to leave for his summer job. He tried to get a secret from her that nobody else knew, but every time she tried to come up with something, Louie knew it.

"Will you be coming back tomorrow?" Mary asked as she followed him toward the back door. "We could really stand to have the lawn mowed, and that piece of siding on the back is still loose."

"I'll let Dad know about that, but yeah." Ellie felt his eyes on her, and she stiffened. "I'll be in tomorrow."

"Thank you, thank you, sweety," Mary added as she followed him out the door.

"Bye, Ellie," he yelled.

"See ya," she called back.

"Such a sweet boy," Mary said as she strolled back in, all starry-eyed.

"You teach him how to bake?" Ellie asked as she unloaded the next tray.

"Oh, Ned and I both did." She beamed with pride. "You know that boy baked his first batch of cookies at five years old."

"Prodigy," Ellie said with a smirk as she continued her work.

"You laugh, but I'd say so."

*Of course you would.*

Mary always spoke highly of Nick. In Mary's eyes, Ellie was certain that boy could do no wrong. *Just another Megan.* Mary continued to talk about his promising skills at such a young age as she leaned against the tabletop and wiped off excess flour into the trash can. "Did I ever tell you that he lived with Ned and me for the first few years of his life?"

"No, you didn't."

"His father and mother, well, you see, Nick was their first child. They were so young, they just weren't ready yet."

"Oh?" Ellie finished unloading the hot bread and began to reload the ovens with the second batch. "Were they teenagers?"

"Well, no, not exactly. But if you aren't ready, you aren't ready." Mary shrugged but didn't meet Ellie's eyes.

"How old were they?"

"Twenty-three." Mary quickly added. "Well, he was twenty-three. They just needed time to find themselves and really solidify their relationship. They were fighting all the time, and a little boy doesn't need to grow up in such turmoil."

"You aren't wrong," Ellie called back as she shut the oven doors and set the timer. *Then again, my aunt was only fifteen when she gave birth to the Void's gift to all humanity.*

"Don't you think?" Mary yelled.

"What's that?"

"I said, 'It's a shame that Nick is single.'" *Jeeze, don't spread that icing thin.*

"He'll find the right person for himself." Ellie had more important things to worry about than Nick Duboise's lack of a love life. She had a soulmate stuck in the Void, after all.

By the end of the day, Ellie had heard about Nick's incredible shot-put win in the fourth grade on field day. She also knew that his favorite meal was chicken alfredo and that in the seventh grade, his hamster was eaten by the neighbor's cat, who hopped in through his open bedroom window—which Mary asked him to shut a dozen times.

By the time the kitchen was clean, Ellie couldn't stand to hear one more fact about Nick. *I would rather read more of Magic and Genetics.* With a flick of her wrist, the dirty apron found its way into the washer, which Mary would run at the end of the day. Ellie pulled the hair tie from her hair, shook her sweaty, damp, curls out, and prepared to step into the sunshine. The air out the back door smelled fresh and alive. Turn of the Page would have their back porch open, all the benefits of sitting by the sea with none of the sand. She'd be able to relax and read.

"Your check," Mary called to Ellie as she scampered out the door. "Ellie, your check! You forgot it yesterday!"

***

Later that afternoon, Ellie stood on a chair in her apartment, with a brush in her hand, staring at the can of beige paint labeled Moonlit Beach.

"It's just beige," Ellie scrutinized. "Could have had something interesting like canary-yellow or lilac, but no."

While she complained, she pulled open the drop cloth and got to work. Remembering Jean's awkward reminder, "This is a rental property. So, as much as I'd love canary-yellow, we must keep it simple, for renters."

"Not like I was planning on retiring here or anything, but," she sighed and shook her head. As much as she loved her time with her aunt and uncle, she couldn't bum off them her entire life.

"We have traveling to do anyway, right buddy?" she called up toward the ceiling. "We could always get an RV or something like that?"

For the next hour, she made plans with the absent Louie or sang along to the music on the television. The list of places they dreamed of visiting played over again in her head. Ellie was lost in thought about Yellowstone and didn't hear Peter knock.

"Hey, kiddo," he called out over the music.

"Hey." She called back from the chair she stood on.

"What are you doing up there?" He must have had the same idea since he was dressed in a paint-splattered T-shirt and jeans. Peter fussed until she got down. "You and Jean," he shook his head. "I'll get the out-of-reach ones, alright?"

"Fine," Ellie conceded. Peter turned down the music on the television with the remote Ellie had propped on the back of the couch. "What time is it? It can't be 3:30 already."

"Nah, I snuck out a little early. I was hoping to get this living room done for you." He gestured to the paintbrush. "Mind if I join you?"

Ellie dramatically gestured towards the wall and bowed for him. "Your canvas is ready."

Peter chortled. He went around after Ellie and painted the cracks made by the molding around the windows, doors, and counters. "Jean said you might be T.A.ing for Adam and Alice in a couple of weeks."

"Yeah, I read up on a couple of their classes yesterday morning. Honestly, it seems easy enough." She continued painting with the large roller.

"Easy?" he scoffed. "You say that because you're good at it."

Ellie's cheeks tingled, but she couldn't hide her smile. "Guilty."

"Not the easiest thing," Peter admitted. "Did your aunt ever tell you about the time I ate elderberries? Thought they were okay."

"Oh," she groaned. "Those are okay—"

"—only when cooked," they said in unison.

"Gave me the runs," Peter added.

"Didn't pay much attention during foraging lessons?" Ellie teased.

"Pfft, they don't teach foraging in public school," Peter reminded her. "My parents also never had a need for it."

"Did your parents use a co-op, too?"

Peter stopped painting and turned to look at Ellie with questioning eyes. "You know I'm not a wizard, right?"

Ellie stopped dead in her tracks and searched through her memory. "No. No? No. Really? I just… I always—"

"Honestly, I didn't even know magic was real 'til your aunt saved me at Robbins Pond." Peter wiped something from the wall before he went back and touched it up with his paintbrush. "I mean, I obviously knew curses were a thing, but never expected witches, or potions, or anything like that."

"She saved you?" Ellie knew very little about the infamous tale of the *tainted* boy who stole her aunt away.

"Hit my head, if you can believe it." He continued painting. "Gave me one of those fancy potions, and before I knew it, I was better."

Ellie continued to watch her uncle as he painted. She awaited a little more detail, something, anything. When he didn't continue, her eyebrows, shoulders, and excitement dropped. Flatly, she commented, "You have a gift for telling stories."

"Forgive me for not having a better recollection of those events. I was unconscious."

"Well, you should have taken notes—" Ellie started to tease him, but the feeling of her phone vibrating in her pocket distracted her. She put down her roller and grabbed it.

Jean danced across the screen.

"The hero of the hour," Ellie answered. "What can I do for you?"

"What are you—ugh, no. Did you pick up Gracey?" Jean's voice was tight and direct.

"Nope, been here painting with Peter." Ellie glanced over to her uncle and mouthed "Jean".

"Put me on speaker, please," Jean said urgently.

"Alright." Ellie awkwardly held out the phone and pressed the speaker button with her unpainted pinky. "You're on."

"Hey, is everything alright?" Peter stepped away from the wall and closer to the phone.

"Gracey's missing. I dropped her off at her lessons this morning," Jean continued. "After I left, she bolted. They said they didn't see her all day."

Peter dropped his paintbrush right onto the floor. "You're kidding me."

He put his paint-flecked hands on his head and ran them through his thick hair. With the full moon growing closer, Peter had some trouble keeping it together with Gracey's bad attitude over the last few days. The muscles along his jaw tightened and Ellie caught a glimpse of sharpening teeth.

"No. I don't know where she could be. I asked her little friend Sadie, and she hasn't seen her all day."

"What are we going to do with this kid?" Sharply, he asked, "Ellie, can you clean up? I'm going to call the police and then start looking."

Jean whimpered on the other side of the phone.

"I'll call Luna. She can check Provincetown, and I'll head toward Orleans."

"Good thinking." Peter pointed at Ellie. "I'll drive around here. Honey, you come home with the boys. Okay? Be home in case she shows up."

"Okay," Jean said. "Okay, I can do that. Should I call Tristan? Maybe he can bring the dogs."

"Maybe…" Peter shook his head, then hurried out of the apartment, grumbling something about teenagers.

"We will find her, Aunt Jean. Okay?" Ellie said.

"I know, I know. Just… Tristan was never like this," Jean muttered, and Ellie heard the car's engine turn over in the background. "We will be home in about ten minutes."

"Alright. Drive safe."

Hours later, Ellie got the text she'd been waiting for. `She's home.`

When Ellie arrived, she heard shouting through the open kitchen window. The forest green Ford with golden writing occupied her normal spot in the driveway.

"You had us all worried," Peter yelled.

"I'm fine," Gracey returned, matching his intensity.

"You can't just run off like that! We lost a Familiar just over a month ago! There are dangerous things out there…"

"Like you?" Ellie flinched at Gracey's implication.

"Hey," Tristan's voice barked.

Even though the screen door was up and anyone walking by could hear this conversation, she felt guilty for eavesdropping. There was a quieter exchange as Jean joined in. Something hard smashed against the floor inside, and Tristan's dogs barked.

"Peter!" Jean shouted.

"I tripped!" Peter shouted back.

Ellie had only ever seen her uncle look that intimidating once before—on the beach the night Louie left. His shoulders were tight, pulled up close to his ears as he whipped the magnetic screen door open and strode outside.

"Just leave me alone!" Gracey shouted.

Ellie hung back by the garage to give him the privacy he needed. His shiny, sharp, white teeth glistened in the twilight. By the time she got inside her apartment, the sound of a tree cracking and falling echoed through her kitchen window.

"Whatever that kid has stuck in her bonnet, she needs to figure it out," Ellie muttered for Louie to hear.

***

The next morning, Nick was back at the Sugar Shack.

"I heard about your cousin going missing. How are you handling everything?" Nick pried.

*I'm going to break Ned's police scanner.*

"I just live in their garage." Ellie tried to change the subject. "Any plans this weekend?"

"Oh yeah, my buddy's coming over from Boston.

*Ugh.*

"We're going to have a barbecue tomorrow night. We got burgers, beer, and probably some games. It'll be a good time. You should come."

"I'm more of an afternoon-plans girl. You know, waking up at three in the morning doesn't exactly leave much space for nightlife."

"Well, you could come earlier if you'd like. Not like many people would be around or much going on, but you and I could just chill?"

"Thanks, but no thanks. If the weather holds up, I'll be out on the beach with Luna catching up on the fungi of the Cape. Besides, I'm a minor. I don't drink."

"You don't have to…"

"Are you taking on that T.A. position?" Mary asked excitedly from across the table.

"I'm leaning toward it," Ellie replied as she loaded buns into the box for The Hut Putt.

"T.A.?" Nick asked.

Mary filled Nick in on her potential T.A. position.

# 15
## *Run*

Elijah Becker sat in his old Chevy, parked outside the farmhouse on Azalea Way, his forehead resting against the steering wheel as he quietly wept.

His daughter was gone. Ellie-Lynne, his baby girl, had walked out of their lives. She would never again fill this house with her laughter or cook her lasagna on a Friday night. To this old, off-white relic, she had become a ghost.

"She's going to hate me," he whispered into the silence. "What do I do?"

He stared at the bushes along the fence line as if they might give him an answer. Nothing came.

He had no one left to turn to—just his brother, Christopher, and his mother. And they'd tell him to stay. To shut his mouth and keep playing along, or risk excommunication.

Elijah swallowed hard as he weighed the consequences of his actions. Here, he had his loving wife, his angel. He had the acres of land under the Becker name. The cost of leaving, to be at Ellie's side, was tremendous. *And she might never want to see me again.* If he left now, he would doom Kimberly and the rest of the Keller-Wagners in the immediate area to be homeless. *Such a stupid deal to make. We should have just left them all in Massachusetts.*

A fresh wave of frustration surged through him. He slammed his fist against the wheel, letting the tears fall again. Years of lies and secrets were unraveling fast, and he was going to be standing dead center when it all came crashing down.

*Please... please don't let them hate me.*

He forced himself to look at the house—every board and brick tied to memories. Kimberly, years ago, standing on the porch in the snow, smiling through tears with a hand on her belly. His angel. His heart.

"You used to say you'd follow me anywhere," he whispered to the memory of her on those steps. "Run off into the sunset, remember?"

Elijah closed his eyes, swallowing hard.

*I hope you meant it.*

He wiped his face, checked his reflection in the rearview mirror, and climbed out of the car. The gravel crunched under his shoes as he made his way to the door. Everything felt heavier tonight—the air, the house, the weight in his chest.

"Eli!" Kimberly called out as she rushed from the kitchen, just like she always did when he came home. She smiled, but it didn't reach her eyes anymore. Not since Ellie left.

He pulled her into his arms and held her tight—longer than usual. He breathed her in. The soft scent of her hair. The way her hands settled on his back. The way she fit so perfectly against him.

"How was work?" she asked, slipping her hand into his as they headed toward the kitchen.

The words *Run away with me* caught in his throat. He swallowed them down.

Instead, she filled the quiet. "Did you hear about the hikers in Canada? Another group gone missing."

He nodded, barely listening, just watching her lips move.

"They say it looks like a bear attack—big claw marks, trash scattered everywhere. But there aren't even grizzlies in that area." She shook her head, already deep in analysis. "Some think it was poachers. It's all speculation."

Elijah stood beside her through the remainder of dinner preparation, the fuss of cleanup, and her retreat to her study. Tonight, he added a few more chocolates to her plate and filled the wine glass a little higher. That look of sweet surprise on her face—he wanted that to be the last thing burned into his mind before bed.

Later, when she finished her research and her cheeks were flushed from the wine, he finally spoke to her. "Kimmy."

She turned toward him, slipping out of the dress she'd worn all day. "Yes?"

"Remember when we were young? Before Ellie was born…"

At the sound of Ellie's name, she stiffened.

"Back then, I'd ask you if you'd run away with me…"

He saw it in her face—in her stiff posture. The answer he already knew. But he said it anyway.

"I'm ready to run."

# 16
## Tea

Ellie sat upstairs at Turn of the Page. The cozy, mustard-colored armchairs were a serious upgrade from the old beanbag chairs at the Naturalist Society. If she shifted just right, she could hang her legs over one arm and lean her head against the back, taking up the whole chair like she owned the place. Despite the steady trickle of tourists below, Ellie had pretty much claimed the space for herself.

She flipped through the final pages of the tale of the girl and the clock, sipping on a paper cup of tea. Steam curled lazily in the light of the rain-soaked window. The sky was a blanket of gray. Back in Connecticut, she and Louie curled up on the couch, her reading aloud while he flopped on her lap, all fat feet and floppy ears.

*I really miss you, buddy.*

She pictured him now, except not as the basset hound. This time, she imagined him in his human form, with those big, warm arms wrapping around her as she read. He'd rest his chin on her shoulder, probably chuckle softly in her ear.

"Should I leave you and the window alone for a moment?"

Ellie jumped at Luna's voice and sat up fast, her heart in her ears. "Oh, shut up."

Luna's whimsical laugh filled the room. "I can go look for another book—"

Ellie stuck out her tongue and adjusted her position.

"How are you liking the book?"

"Feisty female lead? I'm here for it."

Luna grinned. "There's a second one."

Ellie's jaw dropped. "No!"

"Oh, yes. I'll get it to you later." Luna flipped open a sketchpad and studied Ellie. "Go back to how you were sitting before."

"What?" Ellie laughed nervously.

"You looked so peaceful. I want to capture it."

Bashfully, Ellie sank back into her lounged position.

"Perfect." Luna started sketching. "By the way, cute bag."

"You were right. Terri has a gift." She gestured to the new leather bag at her feet, a recent upgrade from her grocery sacks and hiking pack.

"You can look away. I'm just trying to catch the essence." Luna's pencil scratched softly against the page. Ellie tried to refocus on her book, but Luna interrupted again. "You took Matt's class, right?"

"Who?"

"Mr. Becker. The history one."

"Oh. Yeah. I was planning on taking the second part this week. Maybe Magic, Fear, and the Weird next month."

"Well, don't hold your breath. He quit."

Ellie sat up straight. "What?"

"He and his husband took off. Left town. Didn't even leave a note." Luna kept sketching like it wasn't news that just gut-punched Ellie.

Ellie's stomach dropped. "When?"

"Wednesday night, I think. He left a voicemail at the Society saying he was done."

"That sucks." Ellie slumped into the chair again. "I really wanted to ask him about Roanoke... and the Purists."

Luna's tone shifted. "What did you want to know?"

Ellie sighed. "I don't know... how they became a cult, where they settled, how they're still around." She rubbed her fingers over her temple. "Honestly, I'm kind of burnt out on textbooks."

Luna chuckled. "Yeah, Magic and Genetics isn't exactly light reading."

"No one's cup of tea," Ellie groaned.

Luna glanced up. "Well, I'm no expert, but I've heard the Purists are kind of like the mafia. Money laundering. Fake businesses."

Ellie frowned. "That's real? I thought that was just a movie thing."

"Oh, it's real. People hide behind fake businesses all the time. Like a laundromat with no customers that magically reports profits. It takes some fancy accounting."

Ellie shook her head with a laugh. "My dad would never let that slide."

"Your dad's an accountant?"

"Yeah. I used to tease him about how boring it sounded." Ellie smiled to herself.

Luna nodded, still sketching. "You ever heard of Charles Manson?"

"Isn't he a cult guy?"

Luna nodded again. "Total psycho. Used his followers to do his dirty work. It's different from something like the mafia—more brainwashing, less money-laundering."

Ellie made a face. "Gross."

"There are tons of cults like that. Most don't last long. Some are just manipulation disguised as religion. It's pretty terrifying, really."

"Oh." Ellie crinkled her nose in disgust. "That's, um…"

"Terrifying?" Luna joked.

The rain lashed harder against the windows, washing the streets in shimmering waves. Ellie stared outside, suddenly feeling a little small in the world. "Do you think they'll find someone else to teach the class?"

"I doubt it," Luna said flatly. "That class is probably dead in the water."

Ellie sighed, sinking back into the chair again. "Great."

"If you really want to know more," Luna added, "check WebFilmz. It's an app—kind of like a giant movie library."

Ellie perked up. "Oh, the thing the boys use on movie nights."

Luna nodded. "Yup. Tons of documentaries on there."

"The last time I watched the boys, they insisted on a movie about children trained in martial arts, but it inspired absolute mayhem. When Brody karate-chopped his scrambled eggs off a paper plate, Jean banned that movie."

Luna laughed. "You babysit them a lot?"

"Once a week, usually. Depends on Peter's work schedule."

Luna paused her sketching. "Have I told you lately you'd make a great teacher's assistant?"

Ellie groaned. "You sound like Jean."

Luna ignored that. "I've seen you with the boys. You're patient. You'd be perfect."

Ellie laughed. "I don't feel patient. Especially not when Nick's hovering over my shoulder at work."

"That's a different kind of patience," Luna mumbled. Then her eyes lit up. "Oh, remember that Familiar couple—Katie and Jackson?"

"The cheekbone guy? Yeah. What about them?"

"They're having a baby."

Ellie bolted upright. Her knee knocking the table. "Wait—how?"

Luna smirked. "Same way anyone else does."

"No, I mean—he's a Familiar."

Luna flipped the page in her sketchbook. "Apparently, they have to give up their connection to the Void to stay human full-time."

Ellie's jaw dropped. "So... they lose their connection? Forever?"

Luna nodded.

Ellie settled back again, stunned. "That's... kind of beautiful, actually."

Luna teased, "Is it?"

Ellie stuck out her tongue.

Luna flipped to a new page. "I'm just saying... Louie's real cute..."

Ellie grabbed her book like she was ready to chuck it. "Don't make me throw your own book at you."

"You wouldn't dare. You love me too much."

Ellie rolled her eyes, but smiled all the same. After a while, the rain let up, and they gathered their things. Ellie returned home to her half-painted apartment in Truro. The living room hadn't been touched since Gracey ran away. She put on some old clothes, rolled up her sleeves, and turned on some music.

Painting didn't require magic, research, or even much brainpower. Just steady movements and the soft thump of a paint roller against the wall. It was almost meditative.

*I really wanted to take that class*, she thought, frustrated.

Not that it mattered. Her only other teacher, her mother, the queen of research, was over a hundred miles away. *It's not like she'd help me out, anyway.*

Ellie dipped her roller again and sighed.

"Price you pay, I guess."

# 17
## *Surge*

By Tuesday, Ellie was seated in the back row of Adam's class, *Wild Flowers of the Cape*. The twenty-seat room was dim, with the blinds drawn and a screen pulled down in front of the whiteboard. An old projector, donated by Keswick, flickered images of native flora.

Purslane, a thick-leaved succulent with red stems, crept low to the ground. Ellie knew this plant. She had never been able to tear it free with her fingernails. She always needed shears—or Louie's teeth. Not that she could trust him not to eat it.

"It's a delicious vegetable," Adam explained. "You can pull it off the stem like thyme. Eat it raw or boil it. It's rich in omega-3s, which-"

"Reduce inflammation and blood clotting," Ellie murmured automatically.

"Reduce inflammation?" called out Charlie Collins, a younger copy of her sister Sadie, minus the smugness.

Ellie flinched. *Crap.* She still hadn't talked to Gracey.

Charlie couldn't be more than ten, but she was already channeling the Void. According to Adam and Alice, Charlie received her connection to the Void earlier than most, so her parents implanted her with a Channel Needle. Ellie's jaw clenched at the idea.

*"Poor thing's too young for such a gift," Alice had whispered, even though there was no one in the parking lot. "Can't even control her emotions yet."*

*"Her mother said they tried to get her to try kale. Trying to get a kid to eat a gross vegetable?"*

*"I like kale," Alice added defensively.*

*"You're full of crap," Adam had said with raised eyebrows. "And just like that," he had snapped his fingers. "Sent her plate 'cross the room. Just missed her sister's head."*

Ellie looked at the hideous off-white tile floor in the classroom and swallowed hard. *I mean, I can get that.*

"Great job, Charlie," Adam praised.

They went through a few more slides of plants Ellie was intimately familiar with before they turned the lights back on.

"Thank you all for coming. Please remember this Saturday is our annual nature hike along Chatham Lighthouse and down into Morris Island, okay? Each of you has a flier and permission slip from your parents. They are welcome to attend, but if they cannot, we will have chaperones. Arrive by 9:00 a.m. Lunch will not be provided, so bring your own," Adam said. "Does everybody understand?"

"Yes, Mister Adam," the class said in unison.

The students spilled out into a noisy stream. Ellie stayed behind to help raise the blinds.

"So… this T.A. thing," she said casually.

"You're in?" Adam beamed.

"Yeah."

He pumped a triumphant fist. He was in his mid-thirties, if Ellie had to guess, with short, curly hair and a square jaw. His nose was broad, and he had massive shoulders that could support a ship. "We really appreciate the help."

His wife, Alice, and fellow teacher, was a sweet, tall, dark-skinned woman with her hair pulled back into dreadlocks and secured with a bandana. She wore dresses similar to Luna's. Alice shot Ellie a warm smile. "You'll do great."

"I've never done anything like it," Ellie warned.

"Just keep the kids from eating poison and wandering off," Alice said. "If they ask about a plant, ID it if you're confident. Simple."

Ellie stepped back, mock serious. "So, if a kid wants to eat something—I just let 'em?"

Alice lobbed a dry eraser at her.

Ellie grinned and caught it. "Right, don't let them eat it. Got it." She tossed it back.

On her way upstairs, she dropped *Magic & Genetics* on the circulation desk. As she made her way toward the stacks, Ellie opened her flip phone and started scrolling through her book list.

"*Emotions and the Elements*," she murmured, running her fingers along the book spines as she walked the aisle.

A quiet laugh drifted from the other side of the shelves.

Ellie froze mid-step, leaning slightly toward the sound. To look casual, she grabbed the nearest book—*Elemental Magic and Aging: Managing Your Connection with the Void through Menopause.*

She turned it over and skimmed the blurb: *Hormonal shifts are a regular part of every woman's life. From pre-menstruation, pregnancy, and menopause, women's bodies endure…*

And that's when she heard Henry, the librarian. He spoke in a hushed voice. "He didn't just quit—they left town."

Ellie's breath caught. *Does he mean Mr. Becker?*

"Amir was blowing up my phone that night. Apparently, Matt was freaking out that his family found him," Henry said.

Ellie's pulse spiked.

"I thought he was estranged from his family?" the other voice asked. "Are they really that homophobic?"

"He is estranged from them," Henry said quickly. "But it's not that. You know Matt grew up in a cult, right?"

Her heart lurched.

"No way," the stranger whispered.

Henry shushed him. "Yeah. Becker's a big name there. He was supposed to marry some Hurst girl, but he bailed—Amir said they'd kill them if they got caught. Called it something like 'Gilded'? 'Guided'?"

The book dropped from Ellie's hands. She ran.

With her helmet fogging from her breath, she sped through traffic. Horns blared and their shapes blurred past her. Gravel sprayed as she skidded to a stop in the Browns' driveway. Ellie yanked open the sliding glass door.

Jean stood at the counter, washing mushrooms.

"Hey—"

"Why did you run away from home?" Ellie demanded.

Jean blinked, startled. "To be with Peter—and not marry the Canadian boy…"

"Tristan didn't have an arranged marriage." Ellie's nostril twitched.

"Right," Jean nodded slowly. "Marriage isn't for everybody."

"And you don't do Becoming Ceremonies," Ellie added breathlessly.

"Correct…"

"Why?"

Jean set down the mushrooms and dried her hands slowly. "You're asking the wrong question," she said softly. "You should be asking, 'What is a Becoming Ceremony?'"

Ellie sucked hard on her teeth, "What is a Becoming Ceremony?"

"It's an auction, Ellie." Jean's haunted expression didn't change. "A time for young witches and wizards to show off their abilities so their parents can barter their hands in marriage."

Ellie's stomach contorted into a knot.

Jean's face drained of color as she admitted, "It's a Purists' tradition."

Ellie dropped onto the bench, her breath shallow. Jean continued, but the ringing in Ellie's ears drowned out her words.

She thought about the strangers at her ceremony and how Megan was obsessed with the envelopes. In her mind, she saw it all—the old-fashioned dress, her parents pushing marriage, her dad's argument about not wanting to 'sacrifice' his daughter.

Ellie's scalp burned as her mind raced.

*Mee-Maw was unhappy with her marriage to Paw-Paw. He was beneath her.*

Tingling climbed down Ellie's back.

*Their siblings ran away from home.*

The house trembled.

*And all the talk about Oren, a distant land that demanded more and more.*

"Hang on, Ellie. You don't have to…" A loud snap filled the air, and Jean withdrew her hand from Ellie's shoulder. "Ow."

The brick in Ellie's stomach churned. A heat burned from within her and worked its way out to her body.

Snap!

Electricity filled the air around Ellie.

Crack! Snap.

Ellie's body thrummed with power.

Snap. Snap.

The lights blew out with a thunderous crack.

"Ellie!" Jean shouted and took a step away from Ellie.

When Ellie lifted her head, tears streamed down her face. White-blue light shimmered around her. Her hair stood on end.

Michael stepped into the kitchen. "Mom? Why are the lights out?"

"Stay right there!" Jean warned, shielding him.

"Woah," he marveled, staring at Ellie from the doorway.

"Ellie, you've got to calm down. Please don't let that power loose in here," Jean pleaded as she took a step toward her son.

Ellie bolted out the back door and into the cover of the woods. Branches snapped, and bushes sparked. Her arms trembled. "Get off me," she yelled, flinging a branch away with a wave of her arm. A bolt of energy shot from her hand. "Whoa!"

She tried again, this time with more deliberate flicks of her wrist. The concentration of electricity focused and shot from her fingertips toward the ground and scattered to the nearest object.

"Damn it," she yelled and slammed both of her hands down, like she was spiking a basketball into the forest floor. Electricity exploded into the ground, flinging her backward. She landed hard against a rotted log. The forest reeked of ozone. A vast, branching burn stretched from her outstretched hands across the mossy floor.

"What's happening?" she whispered.

It took a moment for the air to settle and discharge from the blast. Defeated, Ellie lay back on the ground and looked at the canopy of leaves and pine needles above her.

"I'm in a cult," she finally said. "Did you know Louie?"

The only reply was her ragged breathing.

"They knew," she said bitterly. "They knew and they still—" Dirt and sweat streaked her cheeks as she wept. "That's why they didn't come out here. That's why Mama didn't want me to leave."

"Ellie!" Jean's voice echoed through the trees.

Ellie raised one shaking hand. "I'm over here."

Jean arrived and stared at the scorched clearing. "Whoa. I heard the explosion, but this is…" She stepped back and marveled at the intricate design created by the lightning. "It's beautiful."

Ellie didn't look at her. "Why didn't you tell me?"

Jean knelt beside her. "What was I supposed to say? 'Hi, I'm your long-lost aunt. Did you know we were in a cult?" She shook her head. "It's not something I'm proud of, honey."

"No kidding," Ellie muttered.

"If it matters at all, I could tell immediately—you weren't one of them. You weren't here to drag me to Oren or to hurt my family. You were innocent and kind."

Ellie gave a mirthless laugh. "Naïve is more like it."

"Hey. Be nice. That's my niece you're talking about," Jean said gently.

"I feel like I've been lied to my whole life."

"Because you have."

Ellie's nostrils twitched.

"Come back to the house. I'll make some tea, and we can talk about it," Jean offered. "Give me the chance to make things right?"

Ellie closed her eyes slowly and rolled her eyes up to look at her aunt.

"Come on. It's better than lying here," Jean added.

Ellie sat up.

Jean picked a few leaves out of her hair. "You did a hell of a number on the ground. Oh, and my electricity is out, so thanks for that."

"Didn't mean to," Ellie grumbled.

"Thankfully, we have a generator." Jean helped Ellie up to her feet.

Back inside, Jean let the kids order pizza while she and Ellie settled into the living room. With a blanket over Ellie's lap, Jean told her everything. About Mee-Maw's forced marriage. About the prestige of the Wagner, Becker, and Hurst names. About Guides—and how the stories were all true.

"That's why we ran, Ellie. Even after Tristan was born—we never stopped. We've spent our entire lives looking over our shoulders."

Ellie frowned. "So, why'd you choose to stay here? It's still so close."

Jean shrugged. "I think we've been forgotten. Besides, it's the only place Peter ever felt safe—a place where he didn't have to hide who he is."

"Speaking of Peter, where is he?"

"Gracey's been pushing his buttons so much he's risked shifting. With the full moon coming, he can't risk it. He could involuntarily shift."

"I thought werewolves could only infect someone on the full moon?"

"Yeah, but a swipe from a werewolf still sends you to the ER—and years of therapy."

Ellie smiled faintly. "Fair."

Jean raised an eyebrow. "You look wiped."

"Void hangover."

Jean stood and pulled a blanket over her. "Yep. I've seen that look a hundred times."

"What look?"

"The 'I'm about to pass out' look." Jean kissed her forehead. "Sweet dreams, kiddo."

# 18
## *T.A.*

As Ellie washed dishes at work, her mind reeled over her new revelation—her family was part of a cult.

Ticking off a mental list, it all seemed so obvious now: w*eird delivery drivers from Oren, Mee-Maw's strange friends, how Mom and Dad hid the televisions when Mr. Anderson came around.*

Then, she remembered what Jean had told her about Guides—that they were sent to retrieve those who didn't follow the rules. She gasped and covered her mouth.

*Mr. Becker must have thought I was a Guide. Henry said Matt's family found him. Was I the family that found him? Did he leave because of me?*

The stories of Guides snatching families from their beds and stealing naughty children away in the night. Recalling the boogeyman-like tales made her shoulders tighten once again.

"Are you excited to T.A. tomorrow?" Mary called from the prep table as she labeled the buns for pickup.

"Yeah," Ellie replied, but her voice faltered. She hadn't even thought about it since her talk with Alice and Adam.

"My kids always loved it," Mary went on. "Are you any good at plant identification?"

"Yeah," Ellie answered more confidently.

*Oh, Void help me. I'm going to be in front of people.* Her stomach flipped. *Do they all know? Will the kids' parents think I'll try to convert them or something?*

"You don't seem like yourself today, sweety. Is everything alright?" Mary's voice was just over her shoulder now.

Ellie's head sank. She knew Mary was a gossip; if she gave the old woman new information, the entire town would know.

*On the other hand, if the entire Cape knows, she already knows.*

"I just, um…" She swallowed hard. "I just found out I'm a Purist."

"Oh." Mary lifted her eyebrows, but the lack of shock in her voice told Ellie everything.

"You already knew?"

"Well, yeah, you're Jean's niece," Mary answered softly. "It all comes together quite quickly."

Ellie winced. "Does everybody know?"

Mary nodded. "Yeah."

"Void, help me." She sank down toward the floor.

"We never judged you for it." Mary tried her best to sound comforting.

"Hey," Mary said softly. "It's plain as day you're not like them. You're not preaching about pleasing the Void. Instead, you're here, *embracing* the modern world, not condemning it."

Ellie lifted her head slowly.

"Or sacrificing children," Mary added.

"What?" Ellie's voice squeaked.

"I mean, they may not do it these days," Mary said. "But in school, that's what we learn."

"Oh, Void help me. How can anybody trust me with their kids?" Ellie stared at the ground. "Should I quit? Tell them I'm sick?"

"No, no." Mary's knees popped as she bent down to be at her side and rubbed Ellie's back. That's when the tears escaped Ellie's eyes. "You go in there with your head held high. You aren't like them. You are kind, smart, caring, and a fantastic baker."

Ellie chuckled through her shaking breath.

"You don't have to do anything you don't want to do, but I'll be blunt with you. People love to make up their own stories and draw their own conclusions. The more you hide, the more they'll talk."

Ellie swallowed hard.

"So, give them something to talk about." Mary squeezed Ellie's shoulder. "Be the girl who beams like the sunshine. Be this badass—"

Ellie chuckled.

"The badass who escaped and remained kind. Make them talk about how strong you are. Make them marvel at you like I do."

Ellie lifted her head to meet Mary's eyes.

"There she is." Mary kissed Ellie on the forehead and brushed the loose strands of hair away from her cheeks. "I always wanted to have a daughter..." she softly chuckled and shook her head. "Up, up. We have lots of work to do and little time to do it in."

With that, Mary turned up the radio and began singing loudly, encouraging Ellie to join in. They stayed busy until quitting time.

"I'll be back in the morning, okay?" Ellie told Mary as she tossed her apron into the wash.

"Are you sure? You'll go hiking smelling like bread."

"There are worse things to smell like," Ellie called as she walked out the door. "See ya."

***

The Monomoy National Wildlife Refuge welcomed visitors with a wide parking lot and a pale-yellow building trimmed in white, its front lined with oversized windows. A ramp curved up the side toward the entrance, where Adam and Alice stood, looking like they'd stepped straight out of a hiking gear catalog. On the lawn, children played while parents gathered nearby, chatting with the two instructors.

*Be the girl who beams like sunshine,* Ellie told herself as she parked her bike.

"Ellie!" a voice called.

She flinched. *Oh no. Not him, too.*

Nick strolled over. "Need any help?"

*Oh man, I can't be occupied with him too.*

"Hey." Ellie forced a polite smile. "I'm good, thanks."

He nodded toward the motorcycle. "That's yours?"

"Yeah. My dad built it." She stashed her helmet and jacket in the sidecar and grabbed her backpack.

"I've seen it at the Shack a hundred times. Didn't realize it was yours." He fell in beside her as she started toward the building. "So, what brings *you here?*"

"I'm volunteering as a T.A." She tugged her bag higher on her shoulder. "What about you?"

"Same. I heard they needed an extra set of hands." He nudged his cap back. "I'm mostly here for crowd control. I'm not exactly a plant expert."

Ellie quirked a brow over her shoulder. "I figured."

He laughed. "Alright, alright. I'm here for the glory of wrangling tiny velociraptors."

"What?"

"You know, like in *Mesozoic Playground?*"

Ellie blinked.

"No way. You've never seen it?" He grabbed her shoulder, spinning her to face him. "It's a classic!"

Ellie ducked out of his grip. "We didn't really watch movies. Mostly whatever we could get on channels three and five."

Nick whistled low. "We gotta fix that. My place, after this. I'm serious."

Ellie backed toward the fence. "I've got to babysit after this."

"Bring the kids. Michael and Brody will love that movie."

Ellie started to respond, but the shrill voice of Mrs. Collins cut through the air. "If she gets worked up again, we're leaving this time-"

Alice waved them over. "Here come our two T.A.s!" Her eyes practically begged Ellie for backup.

Ellie grabbed the stack of papers from Alice. "Want me to start handing these out?"

Before Alice could answer, Sadie appeared, dragging her little sister behind her. "Coach Nick!"

Nick grinned. "Hey, Collins. You joining us?"

"No, she's got plans with Amy and-" Charlie started in with a taunting voice.

"I can hang around if you need me," Sadie offered.

"She can stay." Mrs. Collins shoulders dropped away from her ears. "That'd make me feel so much better."

Ellie exchanged a look with Alice, who nodded in surrender. "Perfect," Alice announced. "Sadie, do you have a lunch?"

"I ate a big breakfast, I'll be fine," Sadie replied. Her mother began to fuss over her kids, and Alice leaned in to the group. "We've got thirty kids, four adults. We're thinking seven kids each for you two. Adam and I'll take eight."

"Sounds good," Ellie replied.

Nick nodded, sliding his sunglasses on. "Let's do this.

Adam continued the briefing by adding, "Since all the kids here are under sixteen, we kept all fungi off the list."

*I've been identifying fungi since I was Brody's age*, Ellie thought, crossing her arms. *Maybe that's a Purist thing*. The thought dried her mouth.

"Kids tend to get a little adventurous, so keep an eye out for poison ivy," Adam said. "Alice and I have ointment in the first-aid kits, but prevention's better than treatment."

Alice stepped in. "We'll meet back here at noon for lunch. After that, we'll head down to the beach. If the tides are right, we might spot some tide pool critters. Remember, there will be non-magical folks around, so no powers or potions unless absolutely necessary."

Ellie nodded. "Got it."

"Any questions?" Alice asked.

"Nope. And—don't let the kids eat anything," Ellie added, glancing at Nick.

Adam smiled. "Right. No taste-testing."

Ellie shook her head, and Adam turned to the crowd. "Alright, kids, listen up!" He clapped his hands.

Some of the kids turned. Some didn't.

Alice let out a sharp whistle that made Ellie flinch. Every kid snapped to attention.

"Welcome to the annual Summer Hike and Scavenger Hunt!" Alice announced. "We're so excited to have you all here."

"Yes, thank you," Adam added. "We hope this sparks a love for plants, wildlife, and all the natural treasures around us. A few housekeeping points with you before we get a move on-"

"I think it's really cool you're doing this," Nick muttered, leaning back slightly to stand closer to her.

"Thanks." She tried to stay focused on Adam's speech.

"As Adam said, we're not collecting fungi or mosses," Alice continued.

Nick leaned closer again. "Can't lie, I never pictured myself doing something like this."

"There's poison ivy, so stay on the trail," Alice went on.

Nick's voice dropped. "I was thinking maybe… after this… we could have lunch?"

"And finally, don't eat anything you find!" Alice finished.

Ellie flinched when Nick poked her shoulder.

"What?" she snapped under her breath. "I'm trying to listen."

Nick held up his hands and backed off. Ellie sucked her teeth and forced herself to tune back in.

Adam clapped again. "Alright, let's head to the trail. Nick, Ellie— you two bring up the rear."

Ellie gave a thumbs-up and stepped aside to let the kids file past. Nick did the same, falling in beside her as the last few kids went by.

Sadie lingered at the back with her sister, walking just ahead of them.

Nick leaned in again and touched Ellie's arm. "Hang back a sec?"

Ellie let the group get ahead before glancing up at him.

"You don't really like me, do you?" Nick asked, cutting straight to it.

"What? No—what are you talking about?"

"You don't want to hang out. You always seem… distracted."

"I've got a lot going on," Ellie replied tightly. "Maybe you haven't heard?"

*I lost my Familiar. I'm in a cult.*

Nick's voice softened. "I've heard. That's why I thought… maybe you'd appreciate some company."

*He pities me.* The realization hit her like cold water.

Ellie started to respond but froze when he gently brushed her hand, forcing her to meet his eyes. His face looked so open. Vulnerable.

"I just wish you'd give me a chance," he said quietly.

The word *wish* hung in the air for her. Maybe it was the adrenaline from her realization, but it felt like the world slowed down for a second and his words fell into her like neat little bricks. Before she could think of a single thing to say, Nick turned, jogging to catch up with the kids. "You ready for a scavenger hunt?" he called, grinning wide as he exaggerated his bounce to get the kids excited.

"Yeah!" Sadie shouted, lifting Charlie's hand in the air.

Charlie groaned and pulled away.

"That's the spirit, Collins!" Nick pointed playfully at her. Sadie beamed.

Ellie sighed, trailing after them, her head low as they approached the trailhead. The group gathered at a wooden information station near the ocean view.

"Okay, let's organize by last name," Alice announced, scanning her clipboard.

The kids groaned in protest.

"First up, Anna Bauch," Alice read.

A tan-skinned girl with a ponytail stepped forward and joined Alice's group, grinning.

"Eric Buchannan," Adam called next. The boy in the ball cap hurried over to stand with him. "Dante Canterberry," Adam continued.

Nick raised a hand, and the boy rushed over, slapping him a double high-five.

"Charlie Collins," Alice called.

Ellie forced herself to smile and wave. Charlie trudged over without looking at her. Sadie, after a reluctant pause, joined them as well.

By the end, Ellie had seven kids—four girls and three boys. Alice passed out colored sheets—maps and scavenger hunt lists, including a diagram of a lily to label, animal sketches, and a bonus harbor seal.

Ellie flipped the page. Plants covered the back on a long list.

*Ambitious*, she thought with a smirk.

"Everyone has their sheets?" Alice called out.

"Yes," Ellie called back.

"Yes, ma'am," Nick returned.

"Great, okay, so each group needs to come up with a team name and a chant. If your group leader calls for a chant, everyone has to find their buddy. Once they do, they have to chant. Understood?"

"Yes," the kids agreed collectively.

"Great."

To anyone walking by, it would look like a gathering of complete chaos as kids offered different calls, claps, and chants. Ellie's group decided on two knee slaps, two claps, followed by a "Woop-woop!"

"Every team has plants, mammals, and avian species listed. Each team's pages are unique, but you'll have some essential plants in common, so it won't do you much good to try and copy from one another," Alice warned. "There is no prize, just bragging rights, for being the first to finish. Now let's hear those team calls."

"Team Nick," Adam started.

"I'm sorry, Adam," Nick began, "we are actually Team Big Blue." He gestured backward toward the surf behind them.

"Okay, Team Big Blue," Adam corrected himself. "What do you have?"

"Huddle up," Nick called out in his well-practiced coach call. The kids gathered around him and put their hands in the center. They started their call low and ascended. "Team Big Blue!"

"He's so cool," Sadie muttered to Ellie as she admired him.

*Ugh,* Ellie thought, but she didn't respond.

Everybody politely clapped.

"Ellie?"

Ellie put on her big smile for the kids. "Clap in three… two… one."

In unison, the group slapped their thighs twice, clapped their hands twice, then threw a hand up in the air as they shouted, "Whoop-whoop!"

"Got some 'whoops' going on. Nice." Adam smiled approvingly. "My dear, would you like to go next?"

"We'd be delighted." Alice pinned the clipboard between her knees. "Let's hear that clap."

Her group let out two slow claps, then three quick ones.

"Alright, alright, simple and clean. I like that," Adam added favorably.

"And you?" Alice took the remaining papers from her husband.

"Ready?" he called out to his group.

"Yeah," they returned. As a group, they stomped their right feet twice. Then, they clapped twice and shouted, "Yeah!" to finish it off.

"Does my heart good." Alice stuffed the excess paper inside her backpack. "Alright, let's get this scavenger hunt officially started!"

The kids cheered and scattered excitedly down the trail.

"Stick together!" Alice called after them one last time.

The next hour and a half blurred by in a mix of excitement—and the chaos of herding cats.

"Ellie, what's this?"

"And this?"

"Oooh, what's this?"

Ellie knelt beside one of the kids, pointing at a gnarly, rust-brown, bubbling growth on a birch tree. "That's Chaga. It's a type of mushroom used in salves and teas," she explained.

Of course, that unlocked a floodgate.

"So, everything on trees is a mushroom?"

Ellie sighed. "Nope. See that one?" She pointed to another. "That's black knot disease. It only grows on certain trees, not birch." The guesses only went downhill from there. "That's a bird's nest." Until finally, "Just a plastic bag."

Physically, the hike wasn't bad—mostly flat, with wooden planks and stairs on the steeper parts. But the constant stream of questions wore her down fast. Eventually, she started pushing the kids to make their own guesses. And when someone actually showed real curiosity— not just a desire to check off boxes—Ellie would take the time to show them details: the texture of a leaf, the scent, or the ways people used that plant.

"Don't chase the frogs," she repeated for what felt like the tenth time.

The groups stayed mostly together. More than once, Nick crossed paths with her. Ellie found herself tossing him apologetic glances. By the third time she met up with him, Nick finally cracked a grin, easing the tight knot in her gut.

Periodically, Alice would whistle like a pro and call for a headcount. "Can I get a whoop-whoop?"

The kids answered loud and clear, rallying together before running off again in search of their next discovery.

Sadie, of course, had long abandoned Charlie to hover around Nick's group. Meanwhile, Charlie had teamed up with Ethan from Adam's group, the two of them sticking closely together as they combed the edges of the trail.

The path looped around toward the ocean, climbing a small rise. From the top, the kids could see the water stretching out toward the horizon.

"Hey, check it out!" Sadie pointed. "There's a seal!"

The kids scrambled to the edge of the trail, craning their necks and asking in overlapping chatter, "Where? I don't see it! Where?"

Sadie pointed again toward the bobbing dark shape, its round, slick head glistening in the waves. While the rest of the group crowded forward, Ellie scanned the kids quickly. *One. Two. Three. Where's Charlie?*

She checked again.

*I don't see Ethan, either.*

Ellie's stomach dropped. She scanned the woods behind them, but the two kids were gone. She hurried over to Nick, keeping her voice low. "Hey, Nick?"

He turned with a smile. "Yeah?"

"Charlie and Ethan… they're missing."

Nick's smile vanished.

"Can you hold the group here while I go look for them?"

He started to step toward her. "Yeah, but are you sure you don't want me to—"

"No, it's fine. Honestly, you're probably better at keeping them from scattering than I am." She nodded toward the group of kids still chattering about the seal.

Nick nodded grimly, stepping up to regroup the others while Ellie turned back toward the trees.

The spot where they'd stopped earlier wasn't hard to find—trampled footprints, broken sticks, and flattened grass marked where the group had gathered. Ellie slipped off the trail, weaving through the dense tangle of trees. Sunlight barely filtered through the leafy canopy above. Birch, pine, and oak crowded in on all sides, their trunks rising like pillars beneath a ceiling of green.

Dead leaves rustled under her boots as she pushed deeper into the woods. Candy wrappers and bits of paper littered the ground like breadcrumbs. She'd barely gone a hundred yards when the earth trembled faintly beneath her feet.

*What the…?*

Ahead, branches snapped, and trees groaned. Ellie ducked behind a wide oak trunk and peeked around it. There they were.

Charlie sat on top of an enormous tree root, bouncing gleefully as Ethan, with his hand pressed firmly to the base, used his magic to lift and lower it like a ride at the fair.

Ellie hurried toward them, raising her hands in plain view. "Whoa, hey. No. That's not safe."

Ethan flinched and dropped the root, looking sheepish. He had the exact same guilty face Brody and Michael wore when they got caught.

"We talked about this," Ellie reminded them gently. "No magic outside, remember? We have to follow the rules."

Charlie slid off the root, scowling. "We were just having fun."

"Fun's great," Ellie agreed, motioning toward the trail. "But not like this. Come on. Let's head back."

"I don't want to go back." Charlie stomped her foot. "We're fine out here. No one even saw us."

"You can still hang out together. You just can't—"

"You're not my mom! You can't tell me what to do!" Charlie's voice shot up an octave.

Ellie kept her voice steady. "Charlie, I'm not trying to—"

"Shut up!" Charlie screamed. "Shut up, shut up, shut up!"

Ellie braced herself as the surrounding air began to vibrate. Dust, twigs, and leaves started rising off the ground. Charlie's hair floated around her face.

*She's supposed to have a Channel Needle…* Ellie's pulse quickened. She shifted, subtly stepping between Charlie and Ethan.

"Come here, Ethan," Ellie said quietly, stretching out a hand.

"No!" Charlie screeched, stomping again. "Stay here!"

Ellie raised her voice, still calm but firm. "He doesn't have to stay if he doesn't want to."

And that's when it happened. Something invisible slammed into Ellie's side, knocking her sideways. She crashed into a rotten log with a loud crack. Groaning, Ellie scrambled to sit up—just in time to hear more footsteps crashing toward them.

"What's going on?" Alice's voice called from behind.

"We heard screaming!" Adam wasn't far behind.

"Leave us alone!" Charlie shrieked again, her voice shaking the air.

Ellie scrambled to her feet, her heart racing. Leaves, dust, and sticks still swirled around Charlie like she was at the eye of a storm.

And then…a single note rang out. Soft. Pure.

Alice had her hand to her heart, humming softly. "Charlie…" she sang gently. "It's time to sleep…"

Like a switch had flipped, the storm around Charlie began to settle. Her fists unclenched, her hair fell back to her shoulders, and her face slackened, as if she were waking from a trance.

Ellie exhaled in relief—but that's when she heard it. The low hum. The kind that meant bees. The first sting hit her left calf, sharp and searing. She yelped, staggering back.

"Bees," she shouted.

A cloud boiled out of the rotten log behind her, thick as smoke. Ellie bolted, sprinting through the trees. Another sting bit into her upper arm. Then another on the back of her hand.

Her pulse thundered in her ears as she pushed toward the light ahead—the trail, the open space.

*Just get to the trail. Get out of their territory.*

A fourth sting seared into her ankle.

"Ellie?" Nick's voice rang out from somewhere up ahead. "What's wrong?"

"Get back," she screamed, her voice ragged. "Bees!"

She veered hard left, scrambling off the path to keep the swarm away from the kids. Another sting slammed into her shoulder. Then another.

*Void help me.* Her breaths came in short, panicked bursts. *Where's my bee bully?*

Another sting. Her foot snagged on a root, and she hit the ground hard, shoulder-first, skidding in the damp earth. "Ah!" She gasped, clawing at the ground as the stinging built to a fever pitch. "Louie!" she choked out, her voice breaking. "Please, Louie!"

Twigs cracked, and she realized it was someone running. Heavy footsteps were closing in. Then, she heard a voice, deep and firm, cut through the chaos:

"Stop. Leave."

The command rippled through the air like a pulse, and the buzzing stopped.

Ellie squeezed her eyes shut, gasping for breath, her whole body trembling.

Just then, hands touched her shoulder, turning her carefully onto her back. She flinched, expecting another sting—but instead, she met familiar green eyes.

*Nick.*

"Are you okay?" he asked, his voice breathless as he crouched beside her.

Ellie's throat tightened. "No," she whispered, her voice cracking. "I'm allergic."

19

## A Lighter Side

They couldn't risk treating Ellie with salves out in plain sight. While Adam carried the sleeping tyrant, Charlie, back to the Center, Nick awkwardly carried Ellie. Each bounce brought intense pain radiating through her. Her back felt like a hot dog left alone too long in the microwave, threatening to split at each end. With gritted teeth, she tried to smile so the kids wouldn't worry. Thankfully, the direct path to the parking lot wasn't far.

When they finally got into there, Alice told Nick, "Put her in the back of the Jeep. I've got some salve in my pack."

Alice lowered the back seats, and Nick gently guided Ellie into the car. Adam placed Charlie in the front seat.

"How's your breathing?" Alice asked.

"Fine, it's just hives," Ellie whimpered. "But it's never hurt like this."

"Yeah, you had an entire swarm on you." Nick forcefully grabbed Ellie's cheeks and made her look him in the eyes. He studied her face.

"What are you doing?" Ellie mumbled.

"Making sure your face isn't looking fat."

"Thanks," Ellie spat.

"No." He rolled his eyes and let go of her face to take the salve from Alice. "Bees release venom. You're sensitive to it…"

He hooked a glob of the salve with his finger, grabbed her chin with his hand, and squeezed her cheeks. Ellie started to pull back in protest when he shoved his finger into her mouth. The salve was *not* Focus. It was thick and oddly chunky, like tahini. Like a dog trying to get a taste out of her mouth, she scraped it off on the roof of her mouth and swallowed it whole.

"One bee sting gives you hives, but a dozen make your eyes puffy," Nick said as he untied her boot. She sucked hard between her teeth and pulled her ankle away from him. "I know you're in pain, but the faster we treat it, the better."

"I can do it." Ellie stubbornly tried to pull her leg up to untie her boot, but the sting on the backside of her calf stopped her.

"Ellie," Nick snapped. She looked up at him and met his eyes. "I'd really appreciate it if you'd stop being stubborn and let me help you."

Her jaw unclenched. Ellie lowered her head and sheepishly nodded. Nick pulled off her hiking boot.

"Where'd they get you?" Alice asked as she came back around the back of the Jeep.

"All over," Ellie replied through gritted teeth. With no children around to put on a show for, she let every wince show and every groan out.

"Helpful," Nick teased.

"Sorry, my back is an itchy fire." She reached up with her right hand and made a clawing gesture.

"Don't worry," Alice said. "This stuff will have you right in a snap." She tapped the open container Nick was working out of.

Adam's voice came from the front end of the vehicle. "I'm sorry to interrupt, but I could really use a hand out here."

"What's wrong?" Alice asked.

"Lunches are all mixed up, and we have to call Charlie's mother."

Alice put up a hand and let out a sigh before zipping up her backpack and slinging it over her shoulder. "I-I've got it. Ellie, Nick, is it okay if I leave you two?"

There was an awkward silence.

"I'm fine with it if she's fine," Nick said.

"Honestly, I don't care who does it," Ellie muttered and turned her attention to the back of her left hand. The mound of flesh was like an egg, with a small black wedge protruding from it. "Oh ew!"

"What?" Nick jumped to attention.

"The stinger's still in it." With gentle fingers, he took her hand and pulled it close to him.

"You sure you've got this?" Alice asked.

With great focus, Nick slid his fingernail over it and pulled out the barb. "No worries here, Alice. I have some experience with this from coaching." He placed the stinger out of Ellie's sight on the floor, grabbed the salve, and tentatively applied a thick layer.

Ellie's cheeks felt hot, and she swallowed the excess saliva. Her stomach churned as Nick tended to the wound on her calf and then the one on the back of her arm.

"The rest are on your back?" he asked.

"Yeah."

"Lower or upper?"

"All over," she admitted.

Nick looked at her, then down at the floor. He seemed uncomfortable as he calculated his next move. "Adam or Alice, can you turn on the air conditioning? I have to shut the back door."

After a few moments of fiddling, the Jeep roared to life, with music playing softly over the radio, and the air conditioning filling the car. Nick turned away and instructed Ellie to take off her shirt.

"Excuse me?" Ellie raised an eyebrow.

"How else do you expect me to treat them? By feel?" Nick pulled his hat down over his eyes. "Look, I'm completely blindfolded. You have privacy. Get comfortable because however you lay down is how you'll be staying for about fifteen minutes."

Ellie swallowed hard again, but not because of her turning stomach. She glanced out the car window where children sat eating lunch. *Thank the Void it's tinted.* She could see Alice on the phone, her cheeks flushed as she spoke.

"You sure they can't see in?" Ellie asked.

"I promise."

Ellie tried to pull off the T-shirt without fuss, but the fabric rubbed against her irritated skin. She bunched the material up around her good hand and used it as a pillow to rest her cheek on. Once she was comfortably lying on her stomach and certain she maintained her modesty, Ellie told him he could turn around.

He sucked air between his teeth.

"That's reassuring," she grumbled.

"Sorry, you just… they got you good." Nick settled in at her side. "I have to remove a few more stingers."

Ellie groaned and bit down on her shirt.

"You ready?"

"Mhm."

Her skin was so inflamed that even the quick brush of his fingernail made her toes curl.

"Sorry, sorry. One more." This time, Ellie closed her eyes tight. Prepared, she barely whimpered when he touched her. "Worst part's over."

There was a moment of silence as he grabbed the thick, chunky paste.

"Coming in," he warned her before he applied the first glob. The cooling effect from the aloe spread over the burning skin and offered her relief. In the privacy of the van, Nick asked, "By the way, who's Louie?"

"What?" Ellie lifted her head from the shirt, the cotton fabric still clenched between her teeth.

"Louie," he repeated. "You were crying out for him when you were getting stung. Is that your Familiar?"

"Yeah." She felt him move onto the next welt.

"You sure he's alive?" Nick's fingers tenderly moved from the epicenter out to the rest of the rash.

"Excuse me?" Ellie winced under his touch.

"What I mean is… I'm not him, and I couldn't resist coming to your side." The throbbing in the back of her hand began to fade as the salve's power seeped in.

"He's sick," Ellie said, not liking the implication. "Our Seer is nursing him back to health."

A surprised chuckle left his lips.

"What?"

"Just, never thought of a Seer as having a bedside manner, or any form of manner at all." The cooling sensation spread across her upper back as he worked. "I guess, um, my point is, while you're waiting for him to come back… well, I'll keep an eye on you."

Ellie's lips parted to protest Nick's offer, to reassure him she'd be okay on her own, but his earlier words, '*Give me a chance,*' ran through her mind, and she felt the hairs on the back of her arms stand up. The sensation took the words, the desire, right out of her mouth.

"Alright, I'll come back to you in about… fifteen minutes?" Nick pulled away from her. "Then you'll be all set."

"Thanks," she uttered.

With a knock on the large window, the back door opened. Nick slid out the back and left Ellie to her thoughts in the air-conditioned Jeep. A familiar song from the bakery played over the radio. She closed her eyes and got lost in it.

***

Tales of Nick's bravery and heroism found their way to the Sugar Shack. When Ellie went to work on Sunday, Mary sang his praise before, during, and even after his small stint of work. Of course, he ate up every moment of it with very little modesty.

"I have an idea," Mary said excitedly. "Tomorrow, Ellie, how about we go a little off script?"

"What do you mean?" Ellie asked as she loaded the large metal mixing bowl into the dishwasher.

"What if you made the special?"

"Me?" She never had much say in what was being baked at the Sugar Shack. The specials seemed to be on a bi-weekly rotating basis.

"Yeah, why don't you make something that you enjoy making? I can take on the regular bakes."

Ellie smirked. She knew exactly what she would make.

# 20
# Pink Lemonade

*The Sugar Shack.* It was just how Ellie had described over the phone: a miniature house with yellow siding and white trim. There were overflowing flowers, a comically large chair on the left-hand side of the small porch, and a handwritten special board. Elijah recognized the handwriting. A tender smile tugged at his lips.

*Ellie's Pink Lemonade Macaroons - 2 for $3*

Elijah had not slept in over twenty-four hours. After Kimberly's outburst, her pleading for him to stay, followed by another outburst, a thrown lamp, and a heartbreaking scream, Elijah was clothesless, exhausted, and low on gas. It took all his strength to pull himself from the driver's seat, shut off the engine, and face the second fiercest woman he knew: Ellie-Lynne Betty Becker.

The purple and lime-green Honda he spent many hours repairing sat in the parking lot with the cover over it. The small Connecticut license plate adorned the back.

Elijah walked as one condemned up the front steps of the Sugar Shack and onto the front porch. To his right, a hanging basket sat with a generous bunch of sage poking out the side. He could hear his darling Kimberly in his memory. *"A witch is nothing without a good clump of sage."* His mustache quivered as he opened the screen door and stepped inside.

The little room had a cozy, empty lounge chair in the corner with a well-worn groove in it. There were not many seats for patrons. Toward the back of the room was the cash register, accompanied by a display case filled with scones, muffins, and the little yellow Macaroons filled with pink frosting.

*She did such a good job.* Pride filled his chest, but it didn't reach his eyes when he smiled.

"Welcome." Elijah knew that this plump lady, with a friendly, wide smile and big glasses, was the woman his daughter had told him about for the last month. "We have fresh, local coffee. Will you be dining in with us or taking it to go?"

Elijah Becker was never one to be at a loss for words, but today, he found himself struggling to find them.

"I, um, oh… pardon me, I forget myself." Elijah brought his hand to his forehead and closed his eyes. He took a deep breath to fill his lungs. "You must be Mary." Elijah recovered, lifted his head, and extended his hand. "I'm Elijah Becker; I believe you employ my daughter."

It took Mary a moment. Her hand accepted his, but when she realized who he was, her mouth dropped open excitedly. "Oh! You're her dad. Oh, how lovely. She will be so happy to see you. She talks about you all the time."

As wonderful as that news was, it made his heart hurt.

Mary continued on in her excitement and directed Elijah down the hallway to the employee entrance beyond the bathroom. He could hear the woman on the other side of the door speak excitedly to Ellie. Elijah peeked through the window in the employee door to see his daughter at the metal tables in the center of the room. It was neat and tidy back there.

Ellie sat on a stool with her legs crossed, thoughtfully decorating a small cake. Her skin was tanned, her hair was pulled back into a loose bun, and she wore comfortable-looking clothes.

*She's doing fine on her own.* A pained smile crossed Elijah's lips.

"Come in, dear," Mary called out.

Pulled from his thoughts, Elijah pushed on the door. The hinges squeaked open, and those beautiful blue eyes found him. The widest smile, that only rivaled the smile she had on her face when she first embraced Louie at her Becoming Ceremony, pulled at her lips.

Ellie hopped from her stool and ran over to Elijah. "Dad! What are you doing here?" He held her tight. "I'm so happy to see you. Wait… is Mom okay?" Ellie tried to pull back, but Elijah held her close.

"Mom's fine."

"Oh, good." Ellie chuckled and squeezed him tightly again. "What are you doing here?"

"I needed to see you." Elijah finally eased his vice-grip embrace and pulled back far enough to take in the details of her face. "I've missed you so much."

A loud sniffle caught their attention. Ellie and Elijah turned their heads to see Mary bawling into a napkin. "Oh, I'm so sorry. It's just so sweet." She excused herself and walked out of the room.

"Sorry, she can be a bit like…"

"Aunt Kelly," they said in unison.

"When do you get off work so we can talk more privately?"

"Not until—"

"Now! She can get off now," Mary called from the other room.

Ellie glanced unimpressed toward the dining-room door. "An hour early today." Ellie laughed. "Finish up the cakes for me?"

"Yes, yes, just go," Mary called back.

"Let me just punch out, then you can follow me to *my* apartment." Ellie's face beamed with pride at that statement.

"Of course, sweetheart."

*** 

Ellie's first visitor couldn't have come at a better time. The walls were painted, and Jean had finished the carpeting. In the rearview mirror of her motorcycle, she could see the Chevy rumbling along behind her as she pulled into the driveway. With a finger, she directed him to park out of the way of Jean and Peter's normal parking spaces.

"We're going upstairs," Ellie called to her dad as she pulled off her helmet and stepped off the bike. Elijah politely followed her

165

instructions and walked with her to the stairs. She gave him a tour the moment she opened the first door.

"My laundry room." She gestured like a game show assistant to the appliances. "And my dining room-living room combo."

"It's very open," Elijah said flatly.

*He's being weird again.*

"Make yourself comfortable. Can I get you anything to drink? Some tea?" Ellie skipped around the false wall.

"Scotch?" His joke caught Ellie off guard. She never heard him even mention a drink outside of dinner wine.

"Fresh out," she said awkwardly.

"Sorry, stupid joke." Elijah said as he sauntered around the back of the living room. Ellie took a moment to really take him in. His shirt wasn't fully tucked in, and his pants were wrinkled. Even his hair was frayed. The most appalling issue of all, though, was that his mustache wasn't perfectly tidy.

Ellie took off her shoes and sat back in her dining room chair. He *looks like a mess.*

"So, Dad, what did you want to talk about?"

Elijah let out a shaky breath before he turned to face his daughter. The light of the sunshine outside poured through the window, and dust danced in its wake. "Where to start?"

His eyes searched the surrounding room, but never landed on Ellie. Elijah ran his hand over his mouth and brushed his mustache with his thumb.

"About a year or so before I got my mark, my brother Matthew ran away from home."

Ellie gently nodded.

"Well, I overheard my parents talking one night about what this meant for the family… You see, your uncle Matt has the ability to track animals. With the Becker name, that ability made him a very desirable match in Oren. Ellie, do you know where the Beckers stand in the magical world?"

"I'm aware," she said coldly.

Elijah swallowed hard. "Oh, good. I… um… I'm glad your class work is paying off." He licked his lips and continued. "Your grandma Edna and grandpa Ralph paired Matt up with this lovely young woman. She had the ability to heal without potions. It would have been a dream match for the Becker name. Everybody would have attended the wedding. The Beckers would have become even more prominent. It was all perfect." Elijah broke from his rant to glance up at Ellie. "Are you following me?"

"Continue," Ellie said.

"Okay. The issue for Matt, aside from the fact that he didn't want the life they had laid out for him, was that Matt's gay. There was no way he could go through with this marriage." Elijah quickly added, "And there's no reason he ever should have been put in that position."

Ellie sucked on her teeth.

"Anyway, he packed his bags one night and snuck out the back window. I learned from their conversation that your grandma and grandpa were willing to put their son's happiness on the back burner for prestige." Elijah drew a line with the side of his hand. "No parent should ever do that."

He let that point hang in the air before he continued.

"But more importantly, if you had a gift that was powerful, something that could provide food or protection for the community, everybody knew about it. You were this… this hot-ticket item."

Elijah's hands lifted in the air with as much enthusiasm as his tired body would allow.

"Everybody wanted to be at your side. You were like the celebrities in *THEM Timely*. Suitors, or their representatives, would line up at the door for a chance to make an arrangement. If they were young, their parents would show up. Or if they were older or … well, hell, even my age." Elijah gestured to himself. "Could you imagine?" The abhorrence in his eyes glimmered as his voice rose. "A man my age with some child? It's disgusting."

"Quite," she said pointedly.

"Sorry, my mind is everywhere." Elijah placed his hands on his face and took a deep breath. "If you had a desirable name and a desirable power, you were under everybody's notice. Not just in the family, but in Maine as well. You'd have people flocking to your Becoming Ceremony to witness your ability and place bids on you, as if you were some sort of object…" Elijah's voice cracked when he said, "Not my daughter!"

He tried to cover his mouth and restrain himself. It was then his exhale brought tears to his face.

"You know what happens when you are wanted like that?"

Ellie slowly shook her head.

"Your life doesn't become your life. When everybody knows about you, you don't have anonymity. When everybody wants you—and will pay—that's right, *pay* to have you, then you become a commodity. You're like a rare car or a handbag—not a human."

Elijah stopped for a breath.

"Ellie, at eleven years old, I learned the best thing that can happen for you, me, for all of us, is that you are born without a desirable family name or with a completely useless ability."

Elijah looked at his daughter with pleading eyes. The light from the window only partially touched his body now.

"Then you could have freedom. I only had the option of pairing with your mother because I downplayed my own abilities. That's why I *had* to do it. I… uh… I put the Needle in your neck."

Ellie's nostrils quivered.

Elijah let out a big, shaky exhale. "I did it. I did it to protect you."

"Protect me?" Ellie's words left her mouth like a roar. "Are you really trying to justify how you… You violated me?"

Elijah flinched. "Please don't say it like that."

"What word? How? How would you describe it, *Dad*? Should I even call you that? Who are you to me? This isn't what a father does!"

"Parents protect their children," Elijah reminded her softly.

"Tell me! Talk to me! Don't leave me to figure it out by my friend prying it out of my neck with a steak knife," Ellie spat.

Elijah said nothing.

"I could've…" Ellie's nostrils flared again, and the lights in the house flickered as she felt her head grow warm. "I could've *done* something." She spoke deliberately now. "You weren't on that beach.

You didn't see it! You didn't watch someone you love tackle that monster to the ground."

With a single downward swing of her fist onto the wooden table, the entire house shook with the intensity of the power surge.

"You didn't watch your soulmate nearly die." Her voice cracked, and a bulb in the kitchen shattered.

The look of absolute terror on Elijah's face made Ellie's anger come to a sudden halt. Her rage summoned the memory of Louie, the human man and the basset hound, as if their ghosts stood in her living room by Elijah's side.

*How would he look at me now? Would he be as terrified as Dad?*

Ellie's tense muscles shuddered as she exhaled. Tears of fury welled up in her eyes. She couldn't prove him right, that she *needed* the Needle to be controlled like that Collins girl.

"Let me guess. You're going to tell me now that we're Purists? Members of a cult? I figured that one out." She shook her head and collapsed back into the chair. Ellie pinched the bridge of her nose. "I-I don't know if you can make this right. If there's any coming back from this."

"Please don't say that," Elijah pleaded.

"How could you? What could you possibly do?"

"There's so much more I want to tell you, sweetheart… by coming here… to your side… your mother is all alone."

"What? Why?" Ellie spat back. "You can't go back?"

Slowly, Elijah nodded his head. "Neither of us can."

Ellie licked her lips. "She made her choice." Unable to hold still, Ellie released her nose and stood from her seat. She muttered, "Can't go back? Why would I even want to go back?"

"Can we please talk about this?" Elijah tried to follow her as she paced.

"Why would I even want to go back?" She directed the question at him this time. "Make it easier for the Guides to find me, right?"

"That's why I told you to avoid anyone from Oren," Elijah reminded her. "I fixed up the bike so you could leave. I saved up money so you could get far away and settle down. I suppressed your powers so you could slip away unnoticed."

"Oh, so I should just thank you for all of this?" Ellie extended her arms out. "All of the lies?"

"No, you don't have to thank me." Elijah dropped his head in defeat. He held it there for a moment while he thought.

"Thank you for your permission," Ellie added as she continued her lap around the apartment.

"I know you're mad. That's perfectly understandable—"

"Great. That's what I need, understanding." Ellie rolled her eyes.

"I hope that one day you can forgive me for lying, but understand it was the best I thought I could do at the time." Elijah's voice grew small. The air stood still in the small apartment.

"I think you should go."

Elijah gently nodded. "Yes, of course, as you wish." He walked toward the door like a puppy caught chewing on an expensive shoe.

"Wait," she commanded.

He stopped in his tracks.

She walked down to the linen closet, reached into the far back shelf, and retrieved the small Tupperware container. She placed the container in his hand. "I don't want this in my house."

The needle rolled across the plastic bottom.

# 21
# *Coal*

Elijah's admission rattled around in Ellie's mind as she stood in her living room. When the sound of the Chevy's heavy tires slowly faded away, she curled up in layers of blankets on her small, second-hand bed. Holding the shell close to her cheek, she closed her eyes, and collapsed into herself.

She didn't find her way out of her apartment until late Tuesday afternoon. The desire to be at the library, to be around people, to cook, it all felt like too much. She wanted to just close herself off and wait for Louie to come back home.

The food in the fridge had gone bad. The vegetables wrinkled and grew spots. Out of desperation, in her finest baggy shorts and a T-shirt, she descended the stairs and opened the magnetic screen door to the Brown's house. To her surprise, at the kitchen table, she saw the welcoming face of her uncle Peter.

"Afternoon." He greeted her with a warm smile and typed away on his laptop. "To what do we owe the pleasure?"

"I was hoping to raid your fridge," she admitted, suddenly aware of her own state. She hadn't showered since work the morning before.

"Still leftover barbecue in there, if you'd like. Going to throw it out tonight." He looked refreshed and at ease. "We missed you the last few nights."

"I had an unexpected guest," Ellie grumbled as she opened the fridge door. The large Tupperware container that they used to submerge her shell a few weeks earlier housed a massive amount of barbeque pulled pork. Ellie pulled it out along with the smaller containers with collard greens and mashed potatoes.

"Oh? That boy who keeps following you around?" He leaned towards his screen as he inspected some detail.

Ellie dropped the containers from a few inches above the countertop. Peter jumped and looked up at her. She had high eyebrows and a small smirk on her lips.

"Your aunt tells me things," he admitted. "Was I not supposed to know?"

"Gossip," Ellie teased and grabbed a plate from the cupboards behind her. "First, there's nothing going on between us." She grabbed a fork from the drawer below. "Second, the visitor was my dad."

"No shit?" Peter looked much more interested and leaned back in his chair. "Oh, sorry, I shouldn't..."

"Shit, shit, shit." Ellie grinned mischievously. "I'm an adult, remember?"

"I know, I know." He shut his laptop and knelt on the counter, his posture mimicking Jean's from the day she told Ellie about the classes. "So, he left? Where is he now? What did he want?"

"I don't know where he is," Ellie said, stabbing the pork. When she pulled it out of the container, Peter grabbed a hunk and ate it. "Hey!"

He smiled wide as he chewed.

She couldn't be mad at his chipmunk-like cheeks when he smiled like that. "Next one comes at a price," she warned him, brandishing her barbecue sauce-tainted fork.

Peter narrowed his eyes, as if challenging her. After a playful back and forth, Ellie managed to scoop pork out onto her plate.

"He, um, he came..." Ellie smacked her fork down into the pile of meat on her plate. "To relieve his guilt? I don't know."

"What do you mean?"

"Well, as you probably know... I'm aware that I am... well... *was* a Purist."

Peter nodded his head.

"Anyway, in addition to that, he told me *he* was the one who placed the Channel Needle in my neck."

Peter's expression softened. "*He* did? Elijah?"

"Yep." Ellie nodded slowly, then angrily scooped collard greens onto her plate.

"Did he... Why?"

"To protect me? He said that having a weak power would give me more freedom, more anonymity, and fewer people would put bids on me during the Becoming Ceremony."

"Ah." Peter nodded along. "That." Her normally cheerful uncle looked down at the countertop as he thought. "How are you feeling about all of that?"

"Terrible," Ellie admitted. "Mad."

"Why mad?"

"It's just the lying." Ellie's overly enthusiastic hand ended up flat in her mashed potatoes. She left it there, looked at it, and sighed. "Damn it."

Peter handed her a paper towel.

Ellie accepted it and cleaned her hand as she spoke. "It just feels like everything has been a lie."

"How?"

"The prophecy, trying to keep me home, the needle, the suitors, and even—even my history class..." Ellie stopped and adjusted her weight onto her back foot. "Did you know that Wagner didn't lead the first group of witches and wizards to America? That apparently it was Roanoke, like twenty years earlier?"

Peter awkwardly looked around and shrugged.

"Right, not a wizard..." She would have to save that bit for Jean. "Well, trust me, it wasn't him."

Peter waited a moment before he responded. "Maybe I am wrong, and you can clear some things up for me."

"Okay." Ellie shoved her plate into the microwave and began heating up her food.

"Keeping you home." Peter created a box with his hands. "That was your mother, right? I thought your dad made you the bike to leave on?"

"He did."

"Okay. So, I do have that right." Peter adjusted his weight before he continued. "Your father maintained communication with you, gave you your cell phone—even though he wasn't supposed to talk to you, right?"

"I guess." Ellie sucked the remaining barbeque sauce off her fork.

"And, he put the needle thing in your neck to make you…" The expression of discomfort on his face was enough for Ellie. "Make you less appealing, we will say."

Ellie grimaced but nodded.

"Right." Peter stood thoughtfully and put his hands together, his index fingers pointing up. "Ellie, I won't tell you how to feel. You are entitled to feel angry, hurt, betrayed, and sad. That's your choice. As someone who spends a lot of time in anger, I want to share a Buddhist proverb with you that has helped me to try and choose my battles."

"Okay." Ellie leaned back against the countertop as the microwave hummed behind her.

"Holding on to anger is like grasping a hot coal with the intent of throwing it at someone else. Only you get burned."

Ellie sucked on her already clean fork. "You're saying I need to get over it?"

"No." Peter shook his head. "You handle this however feels right for you. Just don't hold on to it. Luna would tell me to feel my emotions, process them, and let them go when I was done with them."

Ellie took a deep breath in through her nose and let out a slow sigh. Her lip turned up at the corner. "I got Luna-ed, and she isn't even here."

"That woman has a gift beyond gifts."

Ellie pulled her hot plate out of the microwave a second before it dinged and set it on the counter. She pulled her fingers away quickly as she did and sucked air in through her teeth. "Frig- It's hot."

"Careful, careful, careful." Peter came to her side with paper towels in hand. "No need to get burned." Using the paper towels like oven mitts, he placed her plate on the kitchen island. Then he pointedly cleared the microwave screen.

"Thanks." She stepped back toward the kitchen island.

"I have one last thing to say on this subject." Peter gestured toward Ellie and raised his eyebrows, as if he was asking for her permission.

She nodded.

"I am an old werewolf, so take this… well, however you like. You are my niece."

"Fact." She smirked.

"If someone tried to harm you, to take you from us against your will, whatever it is—a part of me would come out that I am not very proud of." Peter couldn't maintain eye contact with Ellie after he said that. "I'm not trying to scare you, but what I mean is, *you* are my family. I would protect my family at all costs… even if that meant you couldn't look at me the same way anymore…"

Ellie's facial muscles softened.

"At least you'd still be around to look at me again someday…" The way he spoke, it was like a distant memory haunted him, or a nightmare came to the surface he never wanted to acknowledge while the sun was up.

Ellie couldn't help herself. Fork and all, she wrapped her arms around her uncle and pulled him into the tightest hug she could manage. He hugged her back.

When Ellie pulled away, Peter wiped a tear away from under one of his eyes. "Jean said you caused a power surge?"

"Oh, I messed up the transformer." Ellie recapped the story for her uncle. "…and it just fried the ground."

"That's so cool," Peter exclaimed. "Can you generate it yourself, or…"

"I guess not. I have to pull from things around me." She gestured to the power socket on the other side of the room.

"Be crazy to see you in Boston or New York, with all that power around. Man!" He shook his head. "That's really cool."

She chuckled bashfully and finally began eating her food, which had since cooled down. Peter tossed around ideas for battery packs she could carry on her and pull from if she was in an emergency or something.

*What a nerd.* She smiled as he continued on with his plans. *He and dad would be like mad scientists in the garage.*

Her heart sank in her stomach, and her appetite threatened to run away as she thought of her father once again. Peter's words of wisdom weren't lost on her, but she wasn't ready to let it go yet.

Peter went back to his at-home workstation at the end of the table and began drafting something on his computer while muttering about batteries. The clock showed it was just before 3:00 p.m. when Gracey hurried through the front door and ran up the stairs.

"Leftovers in the fridge," Peter called to her.

"Not hungry," Gracey shouted back, and her bedroom door slammed behind her.

Ellie had finished up the food on her plate, cleaned her mess, and wiped her hands off on the sides of her pants as she looked through the living room to the ominous stairs. *Guess it's now or never.*

"Try not to work too hard," she gave her uncle a pat on the shoulder before walking into the living room.

No flight of stairs ever seemed so dooming. Each step felt like she was walking closer and closer to a firing squad.

Ellie walked down the hallway to the door decorated with painted flowers and a sign that read *Gracey.* Gently, Ellie knocked on the door.

"Not now, Dad," Gracey snapped.

"It's Ellie."

Surprisingly, she heard movement from inside, and the door unlocked. Gracey opened the door a crack. The once well put-together teen now looked disheveled with unkempt hair, and her beautiful brown eyes were furious.

"What?" Gracey snapped, but not as harshly as she did at her parents.

Ellie couldn't help but think of her uncle's words about the coal. Gracey had been constantly angry for weeks and pushed everybody away. Ellie hadn't seen her with her friends, witnessed a smile, or even heard a snarky remark.

"You have a minute?"

Gracey just sighed and leaned against her door frame. "They send you to lecture me, too?"

"No." Ellie shook her head. "One of your friends did, actually. She said you've been pushing everyone away."

"And?" Gracey raised her eyebrows, her tone annoyed.

*Don't do it, don't give in.* Ellie couldn't take the bait. It was like speaking with her mother or grandmother. She had to stay levelheaded. "I know you're not okay…"

"You don't know anything about me."

"You're right," Ellie said, her eyes widening as she shrugged. "What I am saying is, I want to."

Gracey closed her eyes for a long moment before she opened them. Even the weary action was seeping with attitude.

"I'm new here, too, just learning my abilities, alone, without anyone who understands my life…" Ellie could swear Gracey's shoulders softened. "I may not understand what you're going through, but I'm here if you want to talk."

"What good does talking do?" Gracey didn't meet Ellie's eyes. "Just means everyone has something they can use against you."

"If people wanna find a way to hurt you, they're going to hurt you. Words or not." Ellie shrugged. "The world sucks and people make up their own stories when they're bored. But maybe it won't suck so much when you know your cousin is there to listen— or let you crash on her couch."

Gracey briefly glanced up at Ellie and bit her bottom lip. "Thanks."

"Any time," she said.

With that, Ellie turned and took her leave, heading back to her apartment.

## 22
### Pirate's Cove

Friday afternoon, Ellie stayed late at the bakery, prepping for the New Moon Celebration they'd cater the next day.

*Just five extra minutes today could be a lifesaver tomorrow,* she kept reminding herself.

Even with Nick's help that morning, she found herself rushing to label the last of the boxes for the morning pickups.

Tired, she said her goodbyes to Mary, tossed her soiled apron into the wash, and stepped outside. The air smelled like rain. Beads of water shimmered on the bright green leaves out back, making the woods sparkle.

"Didn't get me this time," she muttered with a grin as she pulled the water cover off the bike, shaking it out before tucking it into the sidecar.

The engine roared to life, and she took off toward Truro to run through her post-work routine. Tourist traffic was brutal. The lovely folks from Boston had arrived, clogging the peninsula with luxury cars and loaded minivans in one painfully slow caravan.

Ellie leaned back on the seat, her arms crossed, as the line inched forward. She entertained a couple of kids through the back window of a minivan, then caught sight of the tackiest landmark on the Cape—the Pirate's Cove liquor store. A life-sized pirate statue, complete with a hook hand, guarded the door like a bad joke.

She blinked in surprise. Parked out front was a familiar Chevy with Connecticut plates. She'd memorized that plate as a kid. With a sinking feeling, Ellie steered out of traffic and into the cracked parking lot.

The inside was even worse—parrots, treasure chests, pink flamingos, and a sad inflatable palm tree surrounded by bottles of rum.

She looked beyond the plastic tree, and there he was—her dad. He looked disheveled, wearing a sweat-stained undershirt, swim trunks, and flip-flops. In his hand, he held a long blue tube with antlers printed on it—premium scotch.

"Need help finding anything, Miss?" the bearded man behind the counter asked.

"No," she said softly, never taking her eyes off her dad. "I found what I was looking for."

With her helmet in hand, she walked toward him. He didn't notice her until she stood right beside him. The sweet, sharp smell of alcohol clung to him like sweat.

"What are you doing?" she whispered.

"El… Ellie?" Elijah straightened, puffing his chest and pulling his shoulders back like he could sober up by sheer will. "What are *you* doing here?"

"I asked first." Her voice tightened. "And looking like *that?*"

"I—" He hung his head and lifted the tube.

"Premium scotch," she muttered, snatching it from his hand.

*Only you get burned.* Peter's warning echoed in her mind as she fought back the frustration boiling in her chest. She took another long look at her father and felt pity rising in her throat.

"Where are you staying?" she asked quietly.

"Cabin." The word barely made it out of his mouth.

"Alright, come on." She grabbed his forearm and pulled him out of line.

Elijah followed like a scolded child, setting the scotch on the counter on his way out.

"His car's the Chevy out front," she told the clerk. "We'll come back for it tomorrow."

She tucked him into the sidecar like delicate cargo and drove him back to her apartment.

A shower, clean clothes, and a cup of coffee later, Elijah looked more like himself. His hair was brushed. He didn't stink. But he still couldn't meet her eyes as she plated chicken tenders, fries, and broccoli.

"Looks delicious," he tried. "Must've taken you all day."

"Slaved over a hot stove," Ellie dipped a fry into ketchup.

The silence was awful. Beckers weren't built for quiet dinners. But what could she say? He already looked like he was punishing himself harder than she ever could.

"Spoken to Mom recently?" she asked, finally breaking the ice.

"She won't take my calls." His voice stayed low.

Ellie nodded, tapping her foot under the table. "You tried Mee-Maw?"

Elijah snorted. "No. No, I haven't."

"Guess that was dumb."

"No dumb questions," he reminded her softly, picking at a fry.

The silence crept back in.

After dinner, she put on a movie just to fill the air. When it ended, she grabbed his clothes from the dryer and dropped them on the coffee table.

"I've got work tomorrow," she told him, clearing her throat. "It's the New Moon Celebration. We're catering, so I'll be pulling overtime." She paused. "You, uh… want to come?"

Elijah lifted his head, and his red-rimmed eyes flickered between hope and disbelief. "You *want* me to go?"

"Yeah. You could meet Jean and Peter." She nodded toward the house next door. "Meet my friends. See what the big deal's all about." She hesitated. "Have you checked out the library yet?"

Elijah shook his head.

"So, what? You've been drinking alone in that cabin for a week and a half? Drunk dialing Mom?"

Elijah flinched, covering his face with a shaky hand. His shoulders started to tremble.

Ellie sighed and sat beside him, leaning her head on his shoulder. "She's crazy about you," she whispered. "She'll come around."

The words broke him. He turned, pulling her into a crushing embrace as the tears came hard and fast. "I'm sorry. I'm so sorry, El. I'm sorry, I'm sorry, I'm sorry."

He cried until he passed out on her couch. She covered him with a blanket and tucked a pillow under his head. Standing in the doorway, she crossed her arms and whispered into the quiet. "What are we going to do with him, Louie?"

Louie didn't answer. But she hadn't expected him to.

Ellie kissed the shell on her necklace and climbed into bed.

***

The bakery was just as chaotic as last month's celebration—maybe worse. The only thing Ellie *didn't* have to worry about this time was finding flowers, as the florist had dropped them off directly, saving her the scramble.

But all the prep work she'd done the day before barely made a dent in the madness. Tourists flooded in and out, keeping Mary too busy to take charge. Nick helped until nine, and Ned stuck around as long as he could.

By the time they finally closed, Ellie and Mary were sweaty, exhausted, and both still dusted in frosting from a shared cake disaster. Together, they loaded up the van for the event.

"I'm gonna shower, get changed, grab my dad, and meet you there," Ellie told Mary as they packed the last box.

"Wait—" Mary stopped her. "Your *dad's* still here? He's coming?"

"Yes." Ellie left it at that and slipped out the door.

Back at her apartment, Ellie rushed to get ready. She wrapped her bouquet in damp paper towels and plastic, then brushed out her hair while pacing the hallway.

Elijah emerged from the garage, his hands and shirt smeared with grease, but his expression was lighter. "Hey, sweetheart. Didn't hear you pull in."

"Sorry. Just grabbing a quick shower before we have to load up at the house," Ellie explained as she finished brushing her hair. She changed into jeans and a flowy, off-shoulder blue top with tiny sparkles stitched into the fabric.

Elijah gave her a look. "You've been working since four this morning—how could you—" He cut himself off, raising his hands in surrender. "You're an adult. Not my place."

"Thank you." Ellie smirked, throwing her hair into a loose bun. "And Mary's Second Wind potion is magic."

"Second Wind? Impressive." Elijah actually sounded excited. "Yeah, Peter's got some great ideas for your battery packs."

*Knew it.* Ellie shook her head with a smile. "Of course he does. You coming to the ceremony?"

"Wouldn't miss it. I'll be there with bells on." He grinned—though it didn't quite reach his eyes. "Not literally with bells on... just an expression."

"I get it." Ellie chuckled. "Don't overdo it. Nobody's that formal."

"I can be casual." Elijah tried on a few awkward stances before returning to his normal posture.

With a glance at the clock, Ellie grabbed her leather jacket. The flowy shirt puffed out awkwardly under it. "I've gotta go. Mary needs me there by four."

"Drive safe." Elijah's smile faded as she walked out.

***

It was a relief to attend a New Moon Ceremony *without* being the center of attention. Tonight, her dad was the guest of honor. Tristan came up from Sandwich and brought his Australian Shepherd, Calie, with him. Mitsy and Calie became quick friends, running up and down the beach together, cuddling by the fire, and playing fetch with the boys.

Elijah fit right in. He drifted from one casual conversation to the next before settling at Ellie's side, deep in brainstorming again with Peter. For the first time in weeks, Ellie actually *relaxed*.

She sat back, watching the fire shift from blue to orange to yellow. Embers popped and danced toward the cloudy sky. Somewhere among the stars, she knew Louie was watching. She gave a small, timid wave.

"What are you waving at?" a familiar voice asked, breaking the moment. Nick, as usual, wore his never-changing ball cap.

Ellie sighed. "Just saying hi to Louie." She sat up straighter, the bouquet resting between her and her dad.

Nick looked up at the stars and gave a respectful nod. "Sup, man." He gestured to the empty seat beside her. "Mind if I join you?"

"That's Luna's seat, so you might get kicked out when she gets back." Ellie leaned over and nudged Elijah. "Dad."

Elijah excused himself from Peter's conversation and stood as Nick approached.

"This is my friend Nick, from work. Mary's grandson."

"Work friend?" Nick chuckled nervously, but extended his hand.

Ellie watched as her dad squared his shoulders, sizing Nick up before clasping his hand. "Pleasure."

Nick added a second hand on top. "I would really like it if this was a start to a solid friendship."

Elijah froze, then awkwardly withdrew. "Yeah... me too." He sat back down, returning to Peter. "As I was saying, I don't think that'll hold a strong enough charge."

Ellie turned back to Nick, who leaned in and whispered, "I don't think your dad likes me very much."

"You're the first guy friend he's met." Ellie winced. "Give him time."

Nick nodded, loosening his shoulders. "Protective. I can dig that." For a while, they chatted about the ceremony, but Nick eventually leaned in again. "I was wondering... you free this week?"

Ellie glanced toward her dad. She'd promised to keep him company for the foreseeable future.

Nick leaned closer. "I know you work crazy hours, but I thought maybe we could grab some of Grandma's Second Wind and check out the meteor shower. There's a great stargazing spot on Marconi

Beach—super close to the bakery. I've got an old telescope we could set up. What do you think?"

Ellie blinked. She hadn't even *thought* about the meteor shower. The last time she'd gone stargazing was with Louie, lying in a field the night before he fought the Corrupted Familiar. They lay beside one another as she retold him ancient stories of constellations as the wind danced along the tips of the grass. A smile crossed her lips.

"Is that a yes?" Nick asked.

"Yeah, that'd be really cool."

"Awesome! I'll meet you there at ten?"

"Sounds good."

"Right, I'll see you at the bakery." Nick stood just as Luna returned, carrying a tired Mitsy.

"Boy's so giddy he's practically skipping," Luna teased as she settled back in.

"He's just excited to finally hang out." Ellie shrugged.

"*Hang out?* Girl, that's not hanging out. That's a *date*."

"A date?" Ellie blinked.

"Oh yeah."

Mitsy squirmed until Ellie took her. Ellie stroked the little dog's patchy fur. "We never actually called it a date."

"You can call a cow a table, but at the end of the day, it's still a cow," Luna shot back.

Ellie groaned. "Void, help me. I don't *want* it to be a date."

"Then cancel."

"That'd hurt his feelings."

Luna threw up her hands.

Before Ellie could respond, Peter and the others chimed in, teasing her relentlessly. Even the little cousins joined in.

Later, at the Calling Circle, Ellie guided Elijah to the Seer. He gave her the bouquet and offered his thanks for watching over the family.

Ellie squeezed in a quiet whisper. "Tell Louie I miss him."

***

Back at the apartment, Elijah flopped onto the couch with a thoughtful look. "Such an interesting creature. That's Betty Fischer, right?"

Ellie nodded, presetting the coffee pot.

"I think your mom has a journal of hers in that library," Elijah mused, tugging at the cushions on the couch.

"Actually, *I* have it," Ellie said, rounding the corner. "What are you doing to the couch?"

"Peter said it's a pull-out." Elijah grabbed the handle and unfolded the frame. "That's why it's so heavy."

Ellie watched as he struggled for a second, then casually lifted the entire couch with one hand to adjust it.

"Well, that's something," she muttered, stacking the cushions.

"Told you I suppressed my powers." Elijah grinned. "That was a piece of cake."

Ellie checked the pillows and blankets. "Go, Dad, go."

As he made the bed, Elijah glanced up. "I want you to know—I appreciate you pulling me out of that scotch-soaked cabin." He kept making the bed as he talked. "I want to respect your space… so I've been looking for apartments. Jean found a place in Wellfleet. I put a deposit down."

"You didn't have to—"

"I *wanted* to." He looked up. "And when your mom comes around, we'll need somewhere for our things."

"You really think she will?"

"Absolutely. She just needs time… and to get away from her mother."

A flicker of hope sparked in Ellie's chest. "Think she'll come around to me?"

Elijah's voice softened. "She misses you so much."

Ellie gave a small, pained smile. "What about the house? The library?"

"That'll go to your Uncle Chris." Elijah sighed. "I'm not sure what'll happen with the rest of the family on Azalea Way."

"They won't run?"

"No. They're set in their ways."

"Mom too? Is *that* why she's so… difficult?" Ellie chose her words carefully.

Elijah pressed his lips together. "I'm not sure. She goes through phases. I think… she just wants her mother's approval."

Ellie scoffed. "Mee-Maw only likes herself."

Elijah didn't argue—just smirked knowingly. "You're right about that."

# 23
# *Redemption*

lease, Mr. Anderson, *mein Häuptling…* I know if you just speak with him, Elijah will come back." Kimberly clung to his forearm, desperation trembling in her voice.

Anderson sighed. "Kimberly, we both know this is more than abandonment." He shook his head. "I only wish you'd been honest with me from the beginning. Maybe I could have helped before it came to *this*."

Kimberly glanced around the house. Men in bright orange windbreakers, each with a buzzed haircut and a burned symbol on the back of their left hands, moved through the space like ants, hauling away boxes of books, furniture, and clothes.

A man in a forest green windbreaker approached, standing at rigid attention. "Sir," he said. His buzzed mohawk didn't so much as shift as he held up a small frame—a family photo of Kimberly, Elijah, and Ellie. In Ellie's arms, she cradled a fat Basset hound.

"The Familiar is dead?" Mr. Anderson asked without looking at the photo.

Kimberly swallowed and nodded.

Anderson glanced at the man in green. "Send *der Führer*. They should have the chance to earn redemption through service… just as Kimberly shall."

# 24
## *Marconi*

**M**arconi Beach felt like the middle of nowhere. Ellie pulled into the sandy lot near a faded gray food stand and a changing station with bathrooms, just like every other beach on the Cape. She parked beside Nick's beat-up red truck, the smell of old fryer grease and fish hanging heavy in the air.

A single plastic candle-shaped light was taped to the stairwell railing, flickering as it led down toward the beach. From up above, Ellie spotted the soft glow of candles outlining a blanket on the sand.

*Oh no. It **is** a date.*

Sighing, she grabbed her leather jacket and headed down the winding stairs. Anticipating the chill, she'd worn her baggy lilac sweater and jeans. A cool breeze rolled up from the water, carrying the salt and hum of the tide. Waves rumbled against the shore like a steady heartbeat.

"Hey, you made it," Nick called, hurrying toward her, his grin glowing in the flickering light.

Ellie's shoulders loosened slightly. *Give me a chance.* His words echoed in her mind.

"Wouldn't miss it," she replied politely.

"Can I take your jacket?" he offered, holding out his hand.

"Sure." She handed it over.

"Come on." He nodded toward the blanket.

As they walked, he offered his arm. Ellie hesitated… then hooked her elbow through his.

"We couldn't find the telescope—guess Grandma sold it at a yard sale." He stopped at the edge of the blanket, motioning for her to sit first. "But I brought binoculars. Not the same, I know."

"Yeah, probably not," Ellie muttered, eyeing the over-prepared picnic setup—blankets, pillows, and a basket tucked to the side.

*He really went all out.*

Nick leaned into the shadows and pulled out a long-necked bottle with a golden label that caught the light. "Can I interest you in a drink?" he asked with a grin.

Ellie's polite smile wavered. "No, thanks."

"You don't have to be shy," he teased, cracking open the bottle with a *pop.*

"I'm not being shy. That's wine, right?"

"Yeah, pinot grigio." He took a swig and offered it to her.

"I'm nineteen."

"I won't tell anyone." He winked. "Our little secret."

Ellie stiffened. Her stomach churned. That phrase. It dragged an old, ugly memory to the surface—the smell of Mee-Maw's horrible chocolate cake—and words she could never forget.

She forced the memory back.

"Hey," Nick reached out, hooking his finger beneath her chin to tilt her face toward him.

*Stop touching my face.*

His green eyes shimmered in the candlelight. "I just wish you'd give it a try before you decide you don't like it."

The world around her felt like it slowed down, and his words walked slowly through her mind. *Oh, I have to stop. I'm losing him, too.* His eyes broke away from her, and he began to take the bottle back.

"Hand it over." Ellie leaned across the blanket and snatched it from him before he could pull the bottle away. She squeezed her eyes shut and took a big gulp—only to gag and spit it out immediately. "Oh, that's gross."

Nick laughed. "Wimp." She wiped her mouth, but Nick just nodded toward the bottle again. "That doesn't count. You have to *actually* swallow it."

Ellie shot him a look, but he just grinned wider. Sighing in defeat, she took another sip—forcing herself to swallow this time. The warmth crawled down her throat like battery acid. She hugged her knees again, trying to ignore the burning.

"Come on, lay back. Get comfortable. Take off your boots," Nick coaxed, leaning back on his hands.

"I'm fine like this."

*This isn't anything like when Louie and I go stargazing.*

"You're getting sand everywhere."

"Alright, alright." Ellie scooted to the edge of the blanket, kicked off her boots, and lay back stiffly.

Nick sighed. "Why are you being so difficult?"

"I'm not. I'm comfortable." She laced her fingers over her stomach and stared at the sky, silently begging Louie. *Great time to crash through some cake now, buddy.*

But there was no fireball tonight. Just countless stars, blinking silently above her.

Nick shifted, stretching out beside her. Ellie crossed her ankles tighter.

"See anything yet?" he asked, taking another swig.

"Plenty."

"Like what?"

She pointed to a kite-shaped pattern overhead. "Aquila."

"A-what-a?"

"It's a constellation."

Nick chuckled. "So you're one of *those* girls."

Ellie turned her head, raising an eyebrow. "*Those* girls?"

"Yeah, you know—into stories and star personalities and all that."

She bristled. "And if I am?"

He smirked, holding up the bottle. "Not a problem. Just… interesting."

*Any time now, bud.* Ellie looked away.

"I promise it gets better the more you drink."

She clenched her teeth, grabbed the bottle, and pretended to take a big gulp—barely letting it touch her tongue.

"There you go," he teased, taking it, had another sip, then put the cap back on.

"I'm not getting the hang of it," Ellie muttered. "I just don't like it."

"I think you decided not to like it before you tried."

Ellie blew a sharp breath through her nose. Suddenly, something jabbed her side. She yelped, twisting away. "What the—"

Nick burst out laughing. "You're *so* tense! Relax!" He flopped onto his back. "Good booze, good music, good company—what else could you want?"

Ellie's chest tightened. "Is this… a date, Nick?" she asked quietly.

"Well, yeah."

Ellie's heart sank. She stared at the sky. "I've never been on a date before," she whispered.

"For real?" Nick shifted toward her, blocking her view of the stars.

Ellie laughed nervously, covering her face with both hands.

"Nope. You don't get to hide after dropping that bomb," he teased, leaning his weight over her.

Ellie squealed and squirmed, but he held her there, tickling her side until she laughed uncontrollably. When she finally pushed herself halfway up, they were nose to nose. Nick leaned in and pressed his lips to hers. Soft. Gentle.

He pulled back just enough to search her eyes. "First kiss?"

Blushing, Ellie nodded.

"Well." He sat back on her thighs, grinning. "I won't push my luck." He flopped back onto the blanket beside her.

Ellie let out a shaky breath, grateful for the space.

*That's it?* she thought. *Why was I so worked up?*

Nick's finger brushed her hand. "Not a lot of guys in Connecticut?"

"Homeschooled after I got my mark," she explained.

"No playground kisses?"

Ellie smirked at the memory. "Nah, I beat boys up."

"No way!" Nick laughed. "You?"

Ellie nodded, trying not to laugh.

"Details, *please*."

"There was this boy picking on my best friend, Mindy. I launched myself off the swing and decked him."

Nick brayed with laughter.

"He ran off crying. After that… yeah, I wasn't popular with the boys."

Nick finally caught his breath. "You just need someone who can handle your attitude."

Ellie rolled her eyes.

"Exactly—who needs boring mutual respect when you can have emotional distance and sass?"

"I'm not emotionally distant," she shot back.

"Says the girl sitting like she's bracing for impact."

Ellie exhaled, trying to loosen her posture. Just then, she spotted something. "Oh—there's one!" she pointed.

A meteor streaked across the sky.

"There's another." Nick pointed out another, closer to the horizon.

Over the next hour, they watched hundreds of meteors light up the night sky.

"You know those are all Familiars, right?" Ellie whispered.

Nick snorted. "Those are meteors, Ellie."

"Same thing. Different words."

Nick leaned in, kissing the corner of her mouth. "If they were the same thing, why different words?"

Ellie smiled at the sensation. "They're called synonyms."

As she spoke, he kissed the corner of her lips.

"Syno-blah-blah." As he teased her, he firmly kissed her lips, and this time, his lips lingered longer.

It was after midnight when they packed up. Back in the parking lot, Ellie reached for her keys.

"You sure you're safe to drive? I mean, you did have *two* sips of wine," Nick teased.

"*Three*," Ellie corrected, holding up her fingers.

"The first one didn't count."

"It so counts."

She turned toward her bike, but he blocked her with his arm. "Does not," he continued. It was like this aura around him imposed on her, and though they weren't touching, she could still feel him. A rough finger came up along her cheek and gently brushed the hair behind her ear. In a soft tone, Nick added, "Don't worry, by the end of the summer, I'll have you doing shots."

Ellie's stomach dropped. *There it is.*

She rolled her eyes. "Such a romantic—"

Nick cut her off, kissing her hard enough to pin her back against the window. Her small "hmph" of protest went unnoticed as he tried to deepen the kiss.

She turned her head away. "I should get home."

"I'll follow you. Make sure you get home safe."

At a loss for words, all she could manage was, "Okay."

Nick followed her back to Truro. Ellie couldn't put her finger on it, but the situation didn't feel right. The kiss, the date—it didn't feel wrong, but it didn't feel right either. The sensation that she couldn't shake off gnawed at her the entire drive back. As she pulled into the driveway, she killed the engine and let the bike quietly roll in the driveway up to her normal parking space. The truck rolled in behind her, and to her surprise, Nick got out.

*What is he doing? I'm home. I'm safe.*

"I should walk you to your door," he said, adjusting his hat.

*Ah, right.*

"You don't have to." Ellie fumbled for her keys.

"Gotta be a gentleman." He rested a hand on her lower back, nudging her toward the stairs.

They rounded the corner, and there, sitting under the porch light, was Gracey.

"Ellie?" Gracey's voice was small.

Ellie turned to Nick. "I'll see you tomorrow."

"Coach Nick?"

He waved awkwardly.

Gracey stood and started down the stairs.

"Go," Ellie whispered to Nick, waving him off.

He sighed loudly and retreated to his truck.

On the steps, Gracey tried to brush past Ellie.

"Wait—" Ellie caught her arm.

"Don't let me get in your way." Gracey wiped at her eyes.

"Get in my way?" Ellie scoffed. "Never mind. Come on."

Gracey finally followed her inside.

"You two, like… dating now?" Gracey asked, arms crossed.

"Dude, I don't even know." Ellie dropped onto the couch to take off her boots. "I basically got ambushed by a date, so you've got about as much info as I do."

"That's lame." Gracey cracked a smile.

Ellie smiled back, grateful to see it. "You good? Or just need a place to crash?"

Gracey bit her fingernail.

*Not good.*

"Are you hurt?"

"No, nothing like that." Gracey sat at the table. "I just… What happened when you first got your mark?"

Ellie exhaled. "You *really* want to know?"

Gracey nodded.

"Two kids called me a weirdo for believing in Skinwalkers. I slipped on slush, fell on my back, and started my period… in front of the entire school."

Gracey brayed.

Ellie deadpanned, "Thanks."

Gracey calmed down. "No, I meant… your ability."

Ellie nodded, remembering. "There was a storm over the orchard. I could feel the static. Something just told me to stay…" She looked at her fingertips. "That's when it started."

Gracey slowly nodded.

"That's what's been going on with you?"

Gracey sat down hard, staring at her hands. "I used to be… pretty. The prettiest girl in my class."

*So humble.*

"And now… I'm a monster."

Ellie's stomach sank. "I thought the werewolf gene wasn't genetic."

"Well, *something* passed down," Gracey whispered. "I'm trying to control it, but… it happens even when I'm asleep. I wake up with claws and fur and teeth… I'm hideous."

"Gracey…" Ellie reached for her hand, but Gracey pulled away.

"Don't tell me I'm beautiful. You haven't seen it."

Ellie nodded. "Okay, no pretty words. But let me tell you—puberty sucks for *everyone.*"

Gracey didn't look convinced.

"And I can't imagine going through it *plus* a physical transformation."

Gracey's shoulders softened.

"That really sucks."

Gracey nodded, her lip quivering.

Ellie leaned forward. "I saw your dad on the beach, mid-transformation, the night Louie left."

"Me too," Gracey whispered.

"He was *amazing,*" Ellie said. "Fastest thing I've ever seen. Strongest, too. No one would dare mess with him. And you've got *that* in you? That's so cool."

Gracey blinked, surprised. "You think so?"

"Oh, yeah."

They stayed up the rest of the night talking. By sunrise, Gracey was curled up on the couch, finally at peace.

# Ghosts



I really enjoyed our time together last night.

Ellie stared at the text on her phone. A bitter taste filled her mouth as she remembered how pushy Nick's kiss had been at the truck.

*Glad one of us did.*

She snapped the phone shut and went back to adding creamer to her coffee.

"That's cold."

"Ah!" Ellie jumped, spilling creamer across the counter.

Gracey doubled over laughing. "You jumped... *so* high."

Ellie shot her a look, but the smile still crept onto her lips. "Don't do that."

"I wasn't trying to!" Gracey giggled, grabbing a glass from the cupboard. "I was just getting water."

"And decided to snoop," Ellie teased.

Gracey smirked, eyeing the flip phone. "Can you blame me? It's *Coach Nick.* All the girls on the team have a crush on him."

"Right…" Ellie wiped up the mess with a hand towel. "I forgot how goo-goo eyed you were at practice pickup."

"I wasn't goo-goo eyed—I was smooth." Gracey struck a pose.

"As chunky peanut butter."

Gracey wrinkled her nose as she gulped her water. "*That* was then. This is *now*. So… you gonna see the tool again?"

Ellie sighed, carrying her coffee to the table. She tossed the phone down beside her. "I didn't really want to see him the first time." She slouched in the chair, rubbing her face. "Honestly, I've got enough going on with Louie… and my dad needs me right now. I don't have it in me to *entertain* someone."

"You're entertaining *me*," Gracey pointed out.

"Entertaining a thirteen-year-old is *not* the same as entertaining a grown man."

Gracey rolled her eyes and ran her fingers through her hair. "Girls mature faster than boys. And I have been told I'm mature for my age… so, like, that makes me at least sixteen."

Ellie swallowed a laugh. "Sure, Gracey." She sighed again. "Still… I don't think I'm ready for *any* of that."

"You need to tell him that," Gracey warned, sitting down next to Ellie. "Otherwise, you're ghosting. And ghosting's *super* mean."

*Ghosting.*

Ellie stared into her coffee, swirling the creamer around. Just months ago, she used to dream about having a boyfriend—romantic dates, a perfect first kiss… And now that it was actually in front of her, she just wanted to turn away.

"I don't even know *what* to say," she admitted, leaning over her mug.

"I'm *really* good at breakups," Gracey offered. "I could do it for you."

Ellie gave her a look.

"What? I am," Gracey defended. "I broke up with Calvin. I broke up with Jordan for Sadie. And I broke up with Tia for Sharon."

"I'll handle it." Ellie rubbed her face again. "I just need more coffee first."

"I can start the text if you want." Gracey reached for Ellie's phone.

"Breaking up over text?" Ellie scoffed. "That doesn't count."

"Does too!" Gracey crossed her arms. "It's better than ghosting."

Ellie stared at the phone, tempted. "Call me old school, but I think I should tell him in person."

"But then I'll miss it," Gracey whined.

Ellie smirked. "I'm *so* glad my personal suffering entertains you."

"Well, at least let me show you *how* to text, in case you change your mind," Gracey said.

With a little coaching, she showed Ellie how to use the clunky flip phone to text.

"This is *so* tedious. Why do people prefer this?" Ellie groaned, jabbing the keys repeatedly to type the right letters.

"That's why most people use smartphones, Grandma," Gracey teased.

Ellie flicked her arm in retaliation.

"Ow!" Gracey yelped, then flicked her back.

Ellie decided to end the flicking war, remembering how fast Gracey's temper could flip. Instead, she said, "Okay. I did it. I texted him to meet me."

"Good job," Gracey replied.

Nick's reply came almost instantly.

`Yeah. I'll see you at Fresh Grind in an hour.`

***

Fresh Grind looked exactly how Mary had described it—plain, cramped, and nothing like the Sugar Shack. Wedged between a laundromat and a nail salon, it barely stood out. One window displayed mugs, and the other had a rope ladder sign listing drinks in mismatched wood panels.

*Cappuccino*

*Latte*

*Tea*

*Americano*

The rundown laundromat on one side and the nail salon on the other did nothing for Ellie's cafe bias.

*Please don't be like the Bluffin' Muffin.* She groaned as she stepped up to the cement curb and pulled open the glass door.

The white tile floor was scuffed and dirty. The booths offered no privacy. A long counter stretched along one wall, stacked with bagels, sandwiches, and snacks. A chalkboard hung overhead with messy, hand-drawn cups and menu items.

"Can I help you?" The barista barely looked up. She couldn't have been much older than Ellie. She had a lip piercing that looked fresh and irritated from the barista poking it with her tongue.

"Yeah… just a small—" Ellie leaned over to check the flavors. "Do you have caramel?"

"Yep."

"Caramel latte, then."

"For here or to-go?"

"To-go's fine."

"Four fifty-seven."

Ellie paid, then awkwardly wandered the nearly empty café while she waited. She skimmed the old black-and-white photos on the wall— Cape Cod in the '50s, young couples on the beach, a seal lounging on a bench.

> Walter, Chatham's resident seal, visited the small town
> every October and took over park benches. While not
> the most neighborly resident, Chatham grew to look
> forward to his visits until 1974.

*Why doesn't that surprise me?* Ellie smirked.

"Miss, your latte's ready," the barista called.

Ellie grabbed the cup and took a booth. She brushed away the crumbs from the table and took a sip. A moment later, the door opened, and Nick walked in, pulling his sunglasses up with a grin.

"Hey, sorry I'm late," he said, making his way over. "One cup of black?" he called to the barista, then turned to Ellie with open arms. "Don't I get a hug?" His green eyes sparkled.

"Of course." Ellie chuckled awkwardly and stood up from the booth to politely hug him. He wrapped his arms around her, encompassing her upper and lower back. He pulled her body flush against his. Then he emitted a satisfied hum and snuck a kiss at the corner of her mouth.

*Void, help me. I can't do this,* she thought to herself as they pulled apart. Her heart pounded, but she also felt awkwardly heavy. *This isn't right.* She took a seat back on the bench, and he slid in across from her, taking off his hat and setting it down on the table.

"Couldn't wait to see me again, huh?"

"Yeah," she chuckled half-heartedly and began to nervously pick at the cardboard sleeve.

"One cup of black coffee." The barista set down a normal-sized mug in front of Nick. It was beige-colored, covered in advertisements for businesses up and down the Cape, with a small handle. She gestured to the other end of the table. "Cream and sugar are right there."

"Thanks." Nick turned back to Ellie. "Why'd you get it to-go? I wasn't *that* late."

Ellie swallowed hard. "I just…" She exhaled and leaned back. "I think… we want different things."

Nick winced, leaning forward on his elbows. "Is this because I tried to walk you up to your door last night?"

"No, not—"

"I'm sorry. I know you said it was your first date. I thought you were moving fast, but you gave me those *signals*. I totally misread it. I promise. We'll go at *your* speed."

Ellie blinked. "Wait, wait… signals?"

"Yeah. When we were at the truck. You gave me that look." He bounced his eyebrows suggestively. "You *know* the look."

Ellie sat up, frowning. "I did? I *didn't*—did I?"

Nick chuckled, reaching across the table to grab her hands. He held them gently, almost condescendingly. "Of course you wouldn't know. It was your *first* kiss."

Heat flushed her cheeks, and her jaw tensed.

*He's trying,* she reminded herself. *Just explain.*

"It's not just that. I have a lot going on and—"

"Ellie." He squeezed her hands, pulling them to his lips for a kiss. "*Your* speed. I promise."

Ellie swallowed hard. *Give him a chance.* She forced her shoulders to relax.

"Alright. That aside… the meteor shower was really cool."

"I told you you'd like it." He winked. "Next time, though, we do something I like."

Ellie's stomach churned.

"Beer, pizza, and all three *Mesozoic Playground* movies. You're *so* watching them with me."

Ellie pulled her hands back, crossing her arms.

Nick grabbed sugar and creamer, adding casually, "I told you—I'm going to corrupt you by the end of the summer. Shots, scary movies… *everything.*"

## Rusty

*A creature of darkness…*

Ellie lay awake, clutching Louie's old helmet. Her phone cover lit up, showing the time—just past two in the morning—and a new message waiting to be opened. She sighed, set the phone back on the nightstand, and curled tighter around the helmet.

Work had been the only thing pulling her out of bed the last few days, but even that couldn't stop the nightmares. Nothing could. Not Nick. Not her dad. Not even Luna. The emptiness Louie left behind refused to let go.

Over the week, Ellie's social life demanded so much from her that she was unable to keep up on summer classes, her aggressive reading list, and cult research. It was only a week into dating Nick and she already regretted not following through with the break-up.

The phone vibrated.

She leaned over and saw the text logo dancing again.

"What in the Void?" She groaned and rolled over to look at it. "Better be an emergency."

Hey

You up?

*No, I'm sleeping. Like any normal person at two in the morning.* She snapped the phone shut with more force than necessary and tossed it onto the dresser. *What kind of idiot texts at two a.m.?*

She pulled the helmet back to her chest and mumbled, "I'm gonna corrupt you this summer," mocking Nick's words under her breath. "Who is this guy? He doesn't even know real corruption."

With one last huff, she rolled over and finally drifted back to sleep.

A few hours later, Ellie bolted upright at the sound of cupboard doors slamming.

*Gracey.*

Dragging herself out of bed, her body heavy from a restless night, she shuffled toward the kitchen. Static prickled along her skin with every step. She flicked her wrist to discharge it, sending a tiny spark zipping through the air.

Gracey sat on the counter, filthy and barefoot, eating peanut butter straight from the jar.

"You're like a gremlin," Ellie muttered, rubbing her eyes.

"Good morning to you, too," Gracey shot back, swinging her legs happily. "You look like something I dragged in."

Ellie ignored her and started the coffeemaker. "Nick kept texting me," she finally admitted.

Gracey raised her eyebrows. "I thought you broke up with him last week."

"I tried, but I couldn't do it," Ellie mumbled, scratching her head.

"What do you mean you couldn't do it?" Gracey waved her spoon. "It's easy—'Nick, it's over.' Done."

"Says the girl who breaks up with people over text," Ellie shot back, leaning on the counter. "Can we not do this until I've had coffee?"

Gracey nodded, still smirking.

Ellie pulled down a mug, creamer, and a carton of eggs. Mid-reach, she paused, eyeing Gracey's bare legs and torn shorts. "Where've you been?"

"I'll tell you after your coffee." A mischievous smirk pulled at her lips.

Ellie flicked the kid's kneecap before she fumbled through her morning routine. It wasn't long before they sat at the table, eggs before both of them, the coffeepot on a hot pad, and Ellie on her third cup.

Gracey finally asked, quieter this time, "You still have nightmares about it?"

Ellie nodded slowly.

"You know they're just dreams, right?"

Ellie exhaled, staring into her cup. "It's… you know that feeling? Like… right when fear starts to hit you? That flutter in your stomach. It's like the moment just as you're becoming afraid. That small surge of adrenaline that feels like, I don't know, light as a butterfly but as present as a baseball bat to your face."

Gracey's playful expression faded.

"The nightmares leave me with that feeling. Long after I wake up." Ellie poked at her scrambled eggs.

Gracey swallowed. "I don't think I've ever had a dream like that."

"I hope you never do."

They sat in silence for a while before Gracey perked up again. "So… tell me what Nick wanted."

"I swear you're like a dog with a bone." Ellie chuckled. "I think he just wanted to chat. Said something like, 'Hey, what's up?'"

"Did he say 'what's up' or 'you up'?" Gracey leaned in.

Ellie squinted. "Does it matter?"

"Oh, it matters."

Ellie finally caved, got up, and grabbed her phone. She handed it over. Gracey clicked around, then burst out laughing.

"That's a booty call!"

"A what?"

"A booty call! When a guy texts you in the middle of the night asking if you're awake? That's totally a booty call!"

Ellie's eyebrows pulled together with confusion. She glanced back at the message, then to her cousin, who kept teasing that she got 'booty-called'. Thankfully, the front door creaked open, cutting off the onslaught.

"Hey Dad, what are you doing here?" Ellie called.

"Morning, girls." Elijah smiled as he stepped inside. "Babysitting duty for Brody and Michael. Thought I'd catch you before you left for—" he paused. "Work?"

Ellie smirked. "Day off, Dad."

"Even better." He tucked a strand of hair behind his ear. "Want to join me?"

"I'm good," Gracey said quickly, tearing her toast into pieces. *I see right through you, Becker.* "Yeah, I'll keep you company."

After breakfast, Gracey headed home. Ellie and Elijah spent the afternoon with the boys, starting with a jigsaw puzzle.

"Brody's too young for that," Ellie whispered, swapping it for a game instead.

"Yay! 'Burgs and Boats!'" Brody cheered.

Ellie set up the mechanical board on the table. Colorful boats, hand cranks, a timer, and a stack of cards.

"Go Fish rules," she explained to her dad. "Two pairs score points. First with three pairs down triggers the timer. Whoever gets their boat across with the most points wins."

"Hmm, fascinating" Elijah muttered and thoughtfully stroked his mustache. "I wonder if this is inspired by that Titanic craze at all?"

"Titanic?" Ellie blinked.

"Mom loves that movie," Michael chimed in between sips of his juice box.

"It's more than a movie," Elijah corrected gently. "The Titanic was real. A ship bigger than any before it… and it sank." He went on to explain the disaster in graphic detail.

Michael's eyes widened. "How many people died?"

Brody pushed the little glacier on the game board with a frown. "I don't wanna play this game anymore."

Ellie sighed. "You're rusty, Dad." As she packed up the game, her phone buzzed again.

    `Sorry, friends took my phone last night.`

# Jellyfish

Somehow, between work, Gracey, her dad, worrying about Louie, trying to keep up with reading, and the occasional sunbathing session with Luna, August arrived. The air was still warm and smelled like summer, but every breeze whispered that Fall was coming. In just a few weeks, the kids would be back in school, and—according to Mary—tourism on the Cape would dry up. Businesses would close for the season, and life would slow to a crawl.

"The local economy thrives on tourism," Elijah confirmed as they walked a pine needle-covered trail.

Michael and Brody ran ahead, chasing each other through the trees.

"Really?" Ellie asked.

"Yeah. Boston's the hub, but smaller cities—Portland, Dover—they depend on it, too."

Through the trees, sunlight danced on the water. The boys slid down the slope to the beach in a game of tag.

"What does *Oren* depend on?" Ellie asked, ripping off the band-aid.

Elijah sighed and picked up a pinecone from the path. "Slave labor... and vegetable sales to local supermarkets."

Ellie raised an eyebrow. "I thought they rejected the outside world?"

He handed her the pinecone, its empty sheaths fanned open. "They make people *think* they reject it. Meanwhile, they gather up shipments from small farms—like ours—then repackage and ship them out through the front gates."

Ellie turned the pinecone.

"Pure profit, little overhead, and the worship of the blindly loyal." Elijah tossed the pinecone back into the thinning trees.

The memory of hauling baskets of tomatoes to Mee-Maw's shipping crates. A sour taste filled her mouth. "Is that why Mee-Maw wouldn't let me eat the blueberries when she was around?"

Elijah smirked. "Maybe. Or maybe she's just a joy sucker."

The boys raced back to the trail, breathless and grinning. Brody shoved his little hands into his pockets and pulled out a handful of shells. "Ellie, can you hold these?"

Ellie knelt, smiling. "Sure thing, buddy." She slipped them into her backpack.

"Stay in our eyeline, boys," Elijah called. "If you can't see me, I can't see you."

Ellie smiled softly, hearing the echo of words she'd heard her whole childhood.

Elijah gestured toward the boys, who were climbing on a fallen tree. "See what they have?"

"Unending energy?" Ellie guessed.

"No," Elijah chuckled. "Well, yes, but no. They're free. They don't have to follow a strict dress code or work in fields. They have their entire lives ahead of them. Lives filled with possibilities, the world to explore, and the best part is, they get to be kids." He sighed. "That's what I wanted for *you*."

They turned toward a set of paint-chipped stairs leading to the beach.

"Boys, come back! We're heading down," Elijah shouted.

Ellie nudged him with her elbow. "I think you did alright."

"Thanks." He gave a half-hearted chuckle. "Your mother deserves a lot of the credit. We had to keep up appearances, but she tried."

"You really miss her, don't you?"

Elijah's smile faded to something softer, heavier. "She's the love of my life. My soulmate."

Ellie nodded. "They'll be back with us before we know it."

Elijah glanced at her. "Oh, that's right. Familiars are soulmates." His tone shifted, thoughtful. "Are you going to stop seeing that boy before Louie comes back?"

Ellie sighed. "I'm *not* seeing him. We went on *one* awkward date that I have no interest in repeating."

Elijah's expression lifted slightly.

"Besides," Ellie added defensively, "I haven't decided if Louie's supposed to be… *that* for me. He's my best friend. Maybe that's all he ever needs to be."

Elijah smirked. "Your mother's *my* best friend. That bond got us through some pretty rough times."

"Ellie, Uncle Elijah," Michael called out. "Can you come here?"

"Be right there," Elijah waved to him. Ellie and her father hurried over to the damp sand. Brody sat back on his heels and looked intently at something in the sand.

"What is it?" Michael pointed to a translucent blob with brown, triangular patterns.

"It looks like pie," Brody said, reaching toward it.

"Don't touch it." Ellie gently pulled his hand back.

"I think it's a jellyfish," Elijah said, motioning for them to step away. With a flick of his wrist, he lifted the creature into the air. The tentacles were translucent and stuck together like rice paper.

The boys leaned in, wide-eyed. "They sting, right?" Michael whispered. "I read about them in my *Creatures of the Atlantic* book."

"Yes, the head here is safe, but it is the tentacles that can sting you." Elijah went on to explain their hunting technique. "You know what you do if you get stung?"

Ellie smirked, knowing what was coming.

"You have to pee on it," Elijah whispered.

"Ew!" the boys squealed, and Ellie joined in with exaggerated disgust.

"We'll just put this little fellow back where he belongs." Elijah sent the jellyfish sailing into the water with another flick of his hand.

Back at the bakery, life didn't slow down at all. Wedding cake orders kept pouring in. The weekly bun rush never let up, and Ned's scones sold out daily. Nick had returned to football, so he didn't show up at the bakery during the week anymore, but he didn't like how busy Ellie was.

```
I didn't realize I was in a relationship with
                    your phone.
```

The texts kept coming, and so did the calls she couldn't answer. It seemed like every time she was cooking with her dad, working with Gracey, or deep in potion-making, there he was again, blowing up her phone.

Gracey, on the other hand, was getting better. Two weeks of meditation and a visit from Luna helped her start to control her shifting. She was finally gaining confidence again.

The night of the full moon, Peter was out of town, and Elijah came and went. Gracey sat on the living room floor with her nail polish collection spread out, toe-spacers that looked like medieval torture devices, and a few spices Ellie picked up from the co-op. Lilac nail polish adorned Ellie's separated toes. When there was a knock on the door, she awkwardly waddled on her heels to answer it. In the porchlight was Nick. Her stomach dropped. Ellie slipped through the door and shut it behind her.

"Hey. I've been trying to get in touch with you," Nick said, trying and failing to smile. "How—how you been?"

"Busy," she admitted. "Helping my dad… helping Gracey…"

Nick's gaze dropped to her painted toes. "Right."

"She's come a long way," Ellie added, filling the silence.

Nick rubbed the back of his neck, then looked away toward the side of the house. "Do you even want to be with me?"

The question hit harder than she expected. *I have a soulmate.*

"I—I thought you were giving me a chance," Nick continued. "But you're just writing me off after *one* date?"

Ellie took a step back. "I've barely had time to think about—"

"Oh," he winced. "Oh man, I thought it went better than that. I am that far off your radar that you haven't even thought about it? I thought- you were giving me all these signals." He dropped his arms back. "I'm such a moron."

"I'm sorry. I know I hurt you. I've just had so much going on—"

"Too much to return a phone call?" he snapped. "Maybe you're just one of those girls who likes the attention but never actually does anything with it."

Ellie's jaw dropped. "Excuse me?"

Nick let out a bitter laugh. "No, excuse *me*. I should've seen this coming. You're just another tease."

The word hit like a slap. "Watch it," Ellie snapped, the air around her crackling with static. "I've been trying to be nice to you, but you keep poking and poking…"

Nick flinched but didn't stop. "Maybe I'm mad, okay? I've tried. I've put in the time to get to know you, and—"

"You don't know me," Ellie cut in. "If you did, you'd know my dad needs me right now more than you *ever* have."

Nick lazily threw his arm in her general direction before he turned down the stairs. "It's just excuse after excuse with you. I can't. You know what? Don't even return my call, okay?" He stopped two steps down and looked back at her. His eyes were fiery. "I asked you to give me a chance, and you can't even return my call."

He turned and stormed toward his truck, slamming the door hard enough to rattle the frame.

Ellie stood frozen, heat rising to her cheeks. She touched the doorknob, discharging the static before stepping back inside.

Gracey didn't even look up. "What was *that* about?"

"Boys being buttheads, that's all." Ellie flopped onto the couch and grabbed a bottle of bright pink nail polish.

"Do all boys act like that?"

Ellie sighed. "I don't think so."

*Louie never acted that way.* "People are complicated, right?"

She picked up the color Gracey had chosen. "Green?"

Gracey shrugged. "It looks good on me!"

"Lime green doesn't look good on anyone," Ellie teased.

# 28
## *Calls*

**N**ick's presence at the Sugar Shack dried up completely after that—even on the weekends. He still left late-night voicemails and text messages —bouncing between sweet and apologetic to sloppy and angry.

*I just don't have time for this*, Ellie kept telling herself, fighting the urge to call him back and explain.

Between work, caring for Elijah, and helping Gracey find control with Luna's guidance, Ellie still made time to talk to Louie.

"She was just so wound up," Ellie told the night sky. "But Gracey managed to keep her head. No claws, no fangs… nothing. I really admire her control."

"Yeah, I'm pretty great like that." Gracey popped around the corner, bounding up the stairs two at a time. "Talking to Louie?" she asked.

"Yep. My nightly call," Ellie reminded her.

"Hurry up and get here, Louie," Gracey said, meeting Ellie's eyes with a Jean-style wink.

Ellie smirked. "You sure you don't want to ride with us tomorrow?"

"No, I—uh—I made plans to ride with Sadie."

"Really?" Ellie squealed, pulling Gracey into a hug.

"Get a grip," Gracey groaned, but Ellie felt her hug back around her forearm. "You're worse than my mom."

"I'm just so happy for you," Ellie said, pulling away and standing tall.

"I uh... I wanted to say, thank you for... well, you know." Gracey awkwardly nodded her head toward the apartment, but didn't keep eye contact with Ellie. "I know you have that shell Louie gave you. I see you playing with it." Gracey pulled something from her pocket—an elastic bracelet filled with silver and blue beads, with tiny plastic charms dangling from it. "I know it's kinda lame, but..." she pointed at the charms, "The paw print is for Dad, the fish is for Mom, the cheese is for—"

"Brody," they both said simultaneously.

Gracey kept going, but Ellie didn't wait. She hugged her again—tighter this time, resting her head on top of Gracey's. The teen didn't pull away. She just stood there, soaking it in.

When they finally let go, Gracey cleared her throat. "Tell anyone I let you hug me, and you're dead."

Ellie grinned as she slipped the bracelet onto her wrist. "You got it."

Gracey descended the stairs and, to Ellie's surprise, opened the sliding glass door to the Brown house.

"Any leftovers?" she asked as she stepped inside.

Ellie waited for the door to shut before she whispered to the sky, "We did it!"

That night, as she climbed into bed, Ellie kissed the shell on her necklace and whispered, "I promise, no cotton candy without you."

The next day, Luna's Toyota rolled into the drive just before noon, blasting upbeat hip-hop. Ellie descended the stairs in her sandals and jeans, her loose white top slipping casually off one shoulder. With her sunglasses pushed up into her hair, her bracelet dangled proudly on her wrist.

"Ow-ow!" Luna cheered from the driver's seat.

Ellie twirled dramatically before striking a pose and lowering her sunglasses to her nose.

"You're ready for the stage, darling," Luna called out in a terrible French accent.

With a clumsy curtsy, Ellie climbed into the passenger seat. Mitsy popped her little head up from the back, begging for attention. Ellie reached back to give her a rub before buckling in.

Traffic down the Cape was slow, as expected. They passed the Sugar Shack, now shuttered with a 'Closed' sign in the window. A car with out-of-state plates sat in the driveway.

"I guess everyone's going to the carnival?" Ellie asked.

"Oh yes. One last big bash before the season ends," Luna replied, skipping to the next song on the dashboard. "Your dad coming?"

"Yeah, he and Peter took the Chevy. More room for snacks and blankets. Jean has the boys."

"They could've come with us."

"He's trying to give me space," Ellie explained. "Besides, Peter's his new best friend."

"That's so wonderful." Luna sighed. "Peter's usually pretty guarded."

Ellie almost added, 'Dad's a good person to get close to,' but that old unease crawled up the back of her neck. She shook it off and said, "Stupid question—what's a booty call?"

"What?" Luna chuckled.

"Gracey said that's what Nick's been doing. When I asked for clarification, she just kept repeating that's what it was."

"That's typical. Knows the term but not the meaning." Luna continued, "That's when a guy wants to have relations in the middle of the night. It's a call for that booty."

"Ah," Ellie nodded and sat back in her seat. Irritation boiled up from within her. "So, I tell him he's my first kiss, I want to go very slow. He says that's cool and respects it. Then gets upset, calls me a tease, and tries to booty call me when he's drunk."

"Sounds about right," Luna commented.

"I don't get it. I feel like I've been clear, Luna. Clear as day. I tell him it's my first kiss and he tries to make out with me at his truck. He tells me I gave him all these 'signals'. I gave no signals, I swear."

She sighed.

"I told him that my dad and Gracey needed me, and instead of being sympathetic, he went on a rant about having a 'relationship with my phone.' He had the audacity to accuse me of poking at him, like I'm trying to irritate him. But how can I be doing that if I am supposedly ignoring him?"

Luna shrugged and shook her head as she drove.

"I literally can't be doing one of those things and not the other. I feel like I'm being portrayed as some inconsiderate jerk, when all I've done is try to be honest with him. What am I doing wrong?"

"It's not you," Luna said. "He's just immature and thinking about himself and his needs."

Ellie covered her face. "Are all guys like this?"

"No," Luna said gently. "There are plenty of good ones. Like Louie. Like your dad. Like my Samuel. But yeah… You usually have to kiss a few toads first."

Ellie chuckled quietly, remembering Louie nudging frogs by the pond back home, giggling as they just sat there licking their eyes.

"What's so funny?" Luna asked.

Ellie smiled softly. "Just… Louie. He loves frogs."

They finally rolled into Sandwich over an hour later. The town was alive with tourists and local vendors. Katie and Jackson's property felt like stepping into another world—a private oasis tucked between trees and the shoreline. Their yard was comparable to the orchard back in Connecticut. The Toyota scooted along a private, paved driveway, engulfed by woods. Cars were neatly parked alongside it, much like how they populated Keswick's street during the ceremonies.

"Are we still expected to do a Calling Circle at midnight?" Ellie asked as the car rumbled along.

"No, this is more of a reprieve from the usual sorts of celebration," Luna explained as she parked.

Mitsy barked excitedly as they approached the event entrance—a fenced-off area manned by a familiar face.

"CJ!" Luna waved.

CJ grinned and waved her card off. "I know you by now."

He bent to kiss Mitsy on the head, then turned to Ellie. "Card, please."

Ellie fumbled for her backpack. "Can I just… show you my mark?"

"Even better." CJ nodded as she tilted her head down, parting her hair.

He unlocked the gate which groaned on its hinges. "Enjoy your night, ladies."

As they entered, Ellie noticed a broad-shouldered, tan-skinned man with thick, dark curls waiting near the gate, holding a bouquet of roses.

Luna lit up like Christmas. "Baby," she squealed, rushing into his arms. "What are you doing here? I thought you were still working."

"I wanted to surprise you," he replied, handing her the flowers.

"They're beautiful," Luna cooed. Then, she turned to Ellie. "This is my Samuel. Samuel, this is Ellie."

"It's a pleasure to meet you," Samuel said, extending his hand. His voice warm and kind.

*I could listen to him read me a phone book*, Ellie thought as she shook his hand.

"I've heard so much about you," Ellie said. Just then, Luna shot her an apologetic look, but Ellie waved her off. "Go. Have fun. I'll catch a ride with Dad."

Ellie drifted toward the lights and music, past food stalls, rides, and laughter, soaking it all in.

# 29
## The Carnival

Fried foods and sugary sweets filled the air. Everywhere Ellie turned, people held oversized turkey legs, cotton candy, or fried dough. Kids ran from bounce houses to spinning rides. After making a full lap, Ellie grabbed a corn dog and found her dad by the arcade.

"Looks like it's just the two of us," Elijah informed her. "Gracey is with Sadie. Michael and Peter are determined to beat Yo-Yo Boys in the arcade, and Brody is trying out every ride he's tall enough to be on and Jean is keeping him company."

"Perfect," Ellie said, linking her arm with his. "Want to give it a shot?"

Ellie pointed to a water gun game.

"Nice pun." Elijah rolled up his sleeves. "You're on."

Ellie mounted the chair and put two dollars on the counter.

Elijah took out his water pistol. Once the bell sounded, they hit the little red buttons on top of their guns' handles and the boats took off. With great concentration, Elijah focused his stream on the little bullseye in the center. Ellie glimpsed over to see his boat skyrocketing toward the top. With a mischievous foot extended, she kicked his shin.

"Cheater!"

"What's wrong? Can't hit the mark?" Ellie continued her assault as she leaned awkwardly and tried to hit her bullseye.

"No cheating!" The attendant in the brightly colored vest tried to sound authoritative, but a laugh left his lips.

"I'm not cheating." Ellie retracted her foot. The bell sounded as Elijah's boat beat hers.

"I didn't know we were fighting dirty; that changes the game."

Elijah and Ellie bopped around between games into the late afternoon. When the attendant looked away, Elijah would send the dart, ball, what-have-you into the center of the target. When he'd get too cocky, Ellie would send a little zap to him and ruin his focus.

Ellie was breathless with laughter when they finally crossed paths with Katie and her Familiar, Jackson. "Hello again," Ellie greeted them. "Katie, Jackson, this is my father, Elijah."

"It's a pleasure to meet you," Elijah said, extending a hand.

Jackson shook it firmly. "The pleasure is all ours. This is my fiancée, Katie."

"Thank you both for coming," she said softly.

"Thank you for having us. This is great!" Ellie struggled to keep her plethora of teddy bears under her arms from falling away. "And congratulations. I heard a baby is on the way."

"Thank you." They both chuckled excitedly.

"We are so excited. Is this the first time you've been to the carnival?" Katie asked.

"Yes—the first time for both of us," Elijah answered.

"Well, wonderful, we hope you enjoy it."

With that, they moved along to the next little group and greeted them.

"Beautiful couple," Elijah commented.

"Familiar and his witch," Ellie informed him.

Elijah's head reeled back, and he looked back at the two. "Fascinating."

True to her word, Ellie never tried cotton candy. The Beckers gave their extra tickets to kids playing games, gave away their teddy bears like they were candy, and partook in some more adrenaline-inducing rides. Ellie's favorite had her on her stomach and mimicked paragliding through the air.

As Ellie and her father sat on a bench enjoying the mystery of a funnel cake, Ellie's eyes landed on the athletic figure donning its normal basketball shorts and hat. Nick stood with one hand on the lower back of a beautiful blonde girl, the other hand guiding hers on a basketball shot. The girl's skirt was so short, Ellie looked away and blushed for her.

"I never thought something described as a 'funnel' would be so delicious," Elijah said between bites.

"Yeah, who'da thought." Ellie's curious eyes glanced up once more.

Nick stood behind the girl, his chest to her back, and his hands guided her hands to make a shot with a basketball. They were so close a pencil couldn't fit between them. Ellie muttered to herself, "I guess I shouldn't be surprised."

"What's that, sweetheart?" Elijah asked mid-bite.

"Nothing." Ellie quickly looked away from them to her father. Powdered sugar clung to his mustache.

"What? Do I have something on my face?" Elijah asked, brushing at his chin.

Ellie laughed again, grabbing a napkin. "Yeah. Just a little powdered sugar—everywhere."

Before she could clean him up, Nick's voice cut through the crowd. "Hey, Ellie. Elijah."

Elijah stiffened. "Mr. Becker."

Nick shifted awkwardly. "Sorry—Mr. Becker." He glanced at Ellie. "Can I talk to you for a sec?"

She turned to her dad. "You gonna be fine on your own with the powdered sugar?" Elijah just smirked and shooed her away. "I'll be right back. You save me some of that."

After Ellie followed Nick behind a food stand, she glared at him. "What do you want?" she asked flatly.

Nick sighed. "You're mad."

"No, but I'm not really sure there's anything left to talk about."

"I just wanted to see you—to see how you're doing." He raised a helpless hand. "It's been a bit since we talked."

Ellie crossed her arms. "Oh, you mean the night you didn't let me get a word in edge wise and stormed off? And let's not forget, you called me a tease."

"Yeah, I lost my temper. I'm sorry for that."

Ellie gave him a quick, fake smile.

"For calling you a tease," he clarified. "I shouldn't have done that."

"Great. Thanks for the apology. Now what?" Ellie asked.

"Look, Ellie, I'm trying here."

"No, you're on a date with someone else," Ellie reminded him. "We went on a date. You kissed me a few times, then yelled at me, and now you're here with someone else. That tells me that whatever we were trying is done."

"She doesn't mean anything. I want to work things out with you, but you're not available."

Ellie sighed. "I was honest with you. I told you I needed to be there for Dad and Gracey."

"Well, to me it looks like you're jealous now that someone else wants me. You're so immature."

Ellie's stomach twisted. "Immature?" She reared her head back and put her hand up in the air. "Okay. I'm done." She turned to walk away.

"Are you really going to walk away?"

She turned back around. "Yes. I refuse to fight with you in the middle of a carnival."

She turned to leave again, and Nick grabbed her wrist. "Ellie—"

"Do not touch me." She glared, trying to pull away, but his grip tightened.

With her other hand, she reached toward the sausage cart, drew a surge of static, and zapped him.

"Ow!" Nick jumped back, clutching his hand. "What the hell was that?"

Ellie scoffed. "Right… you still don't even know what my ability is."

"Is everything okay over here?" Elijah's voice boomed as he stepped into the alley between the food carts.

"Everything's fine, Dad," Ellie said confidently and stepped back toward him. "I was on my way back anyway."

Nick glared at her as he massaged his hand.

Ellie met her dad, who put a protective arm over her shoulder. The funnel cake was long gone.

"You sure you're okay?" Elijah whispered to her, kissing the top of her head.

"Yeah, just…" She rolled her eyes. "I don't want to talk about it."

Elijah pulled a small stuffed hound dog with massive eyes out of his shirt pocket and handed it to her. Out of all the plushies they had won that day, he held on to the one that looked most like Louie. "Are you ready to head back?"

"I think so." Side by side, Ellie and Elijah walked back towards the gate. "Unless we pass a face-painting booth."

On the way, they ran into Peter carrying a sleeping Brody. Jean followed with Michael, carrying his mother's teddy bear and a plastic bag filled with water.

"Hi, guys. Are you about to head out?" Elijah asked.

"Yeah, we just have to find Gracey. I'm worried about her. Everything is too loud here, and she isn't answering her phone." Jean ran a hand through Michael's hair.

With a massive smile, Michael held out the plastic bag filled with water. A little orange fish swam around inside.

"Did you win this?" Ellie asked him.

Over her, Elijah spoke to Jean. "I can go find her if you…"

Just then, something crunched behind them. The sound was loud and metallic, like a giant tin can being crushed in a fist.

Screams rang out.

Ellie spun around just in time to see a massive crash—the pirate ship ride tipping sideways, collapsing onto the Ducky Dunk booth with a spray of splintered wood and twisted metal.

Water gushed across the midway, carrying rubber duckies and plastic bags of stunned goldfish. The carnival music, once background noise, now crackled through broken speakers in eerie slow motion.

And then, through the wreckage, they appeared.

Three figures.

At the center stood a man in a high-collared black windbreaker. Broad-shouldered and square-jawed, his crewcut hair was sharp against the overhead lights. His fierce eyes locked onto Ellie and Elijah. In his left hand, a photograph.

Flanking him on either side were two others. A tall, wiry man in forest green stood stiff with his arms at his sides. His dark hair was buzzed short. On the left, a shorter, thick-set man in bright orange glared. He was bald, heavyset, with a crooked nose and bruised face that told a story of too many fights—and too few victories.

The man in black raised the photograph high. His voice boomed, cutting through the chaos with icy precision. "Ellie and Elijah Becker—identified."

# 30
# *Reinstenkodex*

"Ellie, get back." Elijah stepped forward, shielding her with his body.

The air around them thickened, humming with unseen tension. Ellie could feel it—people holding their breaths, the press of the silent crowd behind her like a wall of static.

"What's going on?" she whispered.

Elijah's voice was tight. "That's a Guide, Ellie. Der Führer."

Before she could process it, CJ—the gatekeeper from earlier—stepped out from the crowd, squaring his shoulders like he'd been waiting for this moment all night. "Excuse me, what's going on here?"

His words were polite, but his fists clenched. Metal shimmered over his forearms and knuckles with a threatening grin.

The man in black didn't flinch. "Stand down," he ordered coldly. "We are here on official business."

CJ took another step forward. "Yeah? Well, I'm here on official business to bounce troublemakers."

He cracked his metal fists together with a deafening clang. The crowd shifted behind Ellie, the air bristling with low murmurs. Parents tugged children behind their legs.

Before CJ could close the gap, a twisted metal sign from the Ducky Dunk stand exploded toward him, slamming into his chest and hurling him across the midway like a rag doll. He hit the far fence with a heavy thud and collapsed.

A collective gasp rippled through the onlookers. Someone shouted, "That was a cheap shot," but no one dared step forward.

The Guide's voice boomed through the stunned silence. "Would anyone else like to interfere?"

The crowd fell utterly still.

"Good." The man in black raised a photograph in the air. "Elijah Paul Becker and Ellie-Lynne Betty Becker," he announced with chilling clarity, "under order of Der Rat, you are hereby summoned to return to the Reinsten path—the path to redemption."

"We don't recognize the Council here," Elijah fired back. "We are free people."

"Yeah," Ellie added, her voice steady.

Elijah flinched slightly, shooting her a warning glance.

The man in black continued, smug and unfazed. "Kimberly Becker has already accepted her opportunity to earn her place back in the community and the favor of the Void."

Elijah's jaw tightened. "Where is she?"

"She is serving her penance," the man replied coldly. "And you, Elijah, are offered the same. Return with us as an Abandoner. Serve the Void. Earn your redemption."

Elijah bristled, readying his stance. Ellie could feel his body vibrating with tension.

"If you refuse…" The Guide's voice dropped, deadly calm. "…we are authorized to terminate you both and return your bodies to the Void."

Ellie's throat tightened. "Terminate?"

"Elijah Paul Becker," the man pressed, "do you accept?"

Elijah stayed silent.

The Guide turned his focus to Ellie. "Ellie-Lynne Betty Becker, you stand guilty of seven counts of violating Reinstenkodex by attending public school, one count of desertion, and fourteen counts of failing to respond to suitor requests. Charges were brought by the Wagner household and Der Rat. Do you acknowledge these violations?"

Ellie started to speak, but Elijah cut her off. "Ellie. Don't."

Ellie bit her tongue, swallowing the lump in her throat. "I'm with you, Dad."

Elijah stepped forward. "Who brought these charges?"

"Pamela Keller-Wagner, head matron of the Wagner household."

Ellie's stomach sank. "I can't believe it…"

"Believe it," Elijah muttered bitterly.

The Guide raised his chin. "I will ask one final time. Elijah Paul Becker, do you accept the path of redemption?"

Elijah's voice rang out, strong and unyielding. "We are free people."

The Guide nodded toward his men. "Elijah and Ellie Becker—you have chosen termination."

The man in orange dropped to one knee and slammed his bare fists into the pavement. The ground rumbled, and cracks split the pavement beneath him. Then, stone surged up his arms, encasing them in jagged rock. With a guttural grunt, he pushed off the ground and charged, barreling toward them like a wrecking ball.

Elijah braced himself. "Ellie, stay back."

"Dad, no—"

But before she could react, a feral growl ripped through the air. A massive, fur-covered form lunged from the shadows. Peter, fully shifted, with his teeth bared and his eyes blazing, collided with the man in orange. His jaws clamped down on the man's neck with a sickening crunch. The man screamed, blood spraying across the ground as Peter tore into him.

But the man didn't fall.

With a snarl, he slammed his stone-covered hand over the bleeding wound, digging his heels into the earth to stay upright. And then—he smiled.

The Guide didn't flinch. "You keep filthy company," he sneered.

"Peter!" Ellie gasped.

"Stay calm," Elijah warned. "Keep your channel open. Don't show your full hand. We still don't know what green can do."

"But we have to help him—"

The man in orange gripped Peter by his scruff and hurled him across the midway like a broken toy. Peter hit the ground hard, his claws scraping against the pavement as he snapped back onto all fours, a snarl ripping from his throat.

The man in orange staggered forward, with blood pouring down his arm.

Elijah nodded. "I think Peter's got this."

But then—CRACK! A metal rod ripped loose from the wreckage, twisting unnaturally through the air.

The man in black barely lifted a hand as the rod hurtled toward Peter and slammed into his side with bone-jarring force.

Peter tumbled, landing with a pained whimper.

"Don't touch my dad!" Gracey's voice split the air. She bolted forward, her flip-flops slapping the pavement.

Jean's panicked shout echoed behind her. "Gracey, no!"

Gracey vanished behind the overturned booth. For a heartbeat, Ellie lost sight of her—until she burst out again, mid-stride, her body already contorting as she ran.

Suddenly, Gracey's legs snapped backward, her joints shifting until they bent like a cat's hind legs. Her arms stretched as her muscles thickened, and then she curled her fingers, as claws pushed through her polished fingernails.

Gracey arched her spine, and her shoulders hunched forward. With each stride, her face shifted outward, the bones cracking as her nose and mouth stretched into a panther-like muzzle. By the time she leapt onto the man's back, she was fully transformed—a living nightmare of fur, claws, and fangs.

Ellie's heart pounded as her cousin pounced, landing squarely on the wounded man's back. Claws slashed at his shoulder, ripping through flesh. The man howled, blood pouring freely as he staggered, fighting to stay upright. He swung wildly with his good arm, but Gracey ducked and weaved, dodging every blow like a predator toying with its prey.

Then, Peter lunged again, joining the attack. Together, they took him out at the knees, dragging him to the ground. His screams choked off in a wet, gurgling hiss, silenced beneath the weight of fang and claw.

The Guide didn't even blink. "Leon, your debt to Der Rat is paid. May the Void find use for you."

Peter and Gracey fell back toward Elijah and Ellie, forming a defensive line.

The man in green shifted his stance, glancing toward the Guide. "Do you want me to handle them?" he asked, his voice sharp and ready.

The Guide didn't even look at him. He adjusted the cuffs of his jacket with eerie calm. "No," he said smoothly. "I'll take care of it." The Guide took a step forward. "Come now, Elijah. Do you really want to see your friends slaughtered for you? Or would you rather face us like a man?" He shifted his gaze to Ellie. "You could still surrender. Oren could still use you."

Ellie's nostrils flared.

"He's baiting you," Elijah whispered.

"I can't stand by again," Ellie growled.

Electricity prickled at her fingertips. The air shimmered, the energy thick as molasses. She could feel every lightbulb, every speaker wire, every scrap of metal around her, calling to her. She raised her hand, gathering the charge.

"Don't show them everything yet," Elijah coached. "Make them reveal their cards first. Never take your eyes off the enemy."

Peter growled low in his throat. "Don't let them flank you."

"I won't let them," Gracey added, her voice more growl than words.

The Guide raised his hand, ready to strike again—but the ground rumbled. A low vibration rippled through the air, climbing up Ellie's spine. Static prickled at her skin. The lights overhead flickered, then pulsed brighter.

The Guide's hand froze mid-signal. His head tilted toward the sky, his eyes narrowing. "No…" he muttered. His voice dropped to a venomous whisper. "I thought the Familiar was dead."

Then a shriek tore through the sky. A fireball, burning hotter and brighter than anything Ellie had ever seen, ripped through the clouds, hurtling straight toward them like a comet. The impact sent a shockwave rolling across the midway, knocking Ellie back on her heels.

Flames roared, swallowing the man in green in a blast of molten light. His scream cut short as the fire devoured him, leaving nothing behind but scorched earth and the acrid smell of burned fabric.

Ellie's eyes darted toward the Guide—but the man in black had vanished, leaving only a swirl of smoke and twisted metal in his place.

For a breathless moment, the entire carnival stood frozen. Someone screamed. A child wailed. People scrambled backward, knocking over chairs, booths, and snack carts as they fled toward the parking lot. Shouts and hurried footsteps echoed in every direction, but Ellie couldn't move. All she could do was stare.

When the smoke dissipated, only one figure stood in the wreckage—a man with broad shoulders, messy blond hair, and a familiar grin.

Ellie's breath caught in her throat. *It's him.*

Time slowed, and the chaos, the wreckage, the blood—all of it fell away.

"Louie…"

Her feet moved before she could think. She ran as fast as her legs could carry her, launching herself into his arms. He caught her, spinning her once before clutching her close.

Ellie buried her face in his neck, laughing and sobbing all at once. She kissed him over and over, unable to stop whispering, "It's you… it's really you… it's you…"

Louie held her tighter, his breath warm in her ear. After a long moment, she leaned back just enough to meet his eyes. He smiled—softer than she remembered, but so very Louie.

And in that familiar, gruff voice, he whispered, "Hi."

229

Thank you for reading! I hope you enjoy this picture of Louie as a basset hound! Stay in touch via www.kcfetchwrites.com or find me on social media @kcfetch.writes for updates on extra content and book 3.